The Lost Soul
The Raven Saga Part III

SUZY TURNER

Published by Suzanne Turner Publishing 2012
Copyright Suzy Turner 2012

ISBN 9789899734876

For more information about the author
and her upcoming books, please visit her website

www.suzyturner.com

ACKNOWLEDGEMENTS

Huge thanks to author Bryna Butler for her fabulous proofreading skills, as well as for saving me great embarrassment by pointing out that Velociraptors don't actually have wings! I'm forever grateful, Bryna!

Shalini, Jill and Liz... thank you so much for your constructive comments too. I always value whatever you have to say about the written word.

Heartfelt thanks go to author and book cover designer Emma Michaels for creating such beautiful brand new covers for The Raven Saga. You did a sterling job, Emma!

As always, a massive thanks to my rock, Michael, for the constant support he always provides.

Suzy Turner is a British author who moved to Portugal with her family when she was ten years old. She loves to travel and write books for young adults.
The Raven Saga was inspired by a visit to British Columbia, Canada in 2009.

Other books by Suzy:
Raven
The Lost Soul
The Ghost of Josiah Grimshaw

For more information, visit:
www.suzyturner.com

- Chapter One -

The stench of something rotten filled the air as the man tried to lift his heavy head. Opening his eyes, it took a moment for them to adjust to the strange dull light of a new day. Wincing, he managed to hold his head up just long enough to notice the smell belonged to a rotting corpse to his side. He heaved, but there was nothing left in his stomach. He hadn't eaten in days.

Weak, cold and hungry, he curled into a ball on the mossy ground and sobbed.

When he no longer had the strength to even do that, he stared up at the sky; the orange and yellow hues entwined in a rainbow effect as far as his eyes could see.

The only sounds that could be heard were his rough breathing combined with the gentle whooshing of the silver trees that surrounded the deep ditch within which he found himself.

A hummingbird appeared from nowhere, hovering above him, flying up and down and around his face. The man tried to focus his eyes upon it but his vision had become blurry.

When the bird came to an abrupt halt almost touching his nose, he realised it wasn't a bird at all.

A faint giggle erupted from the creature, making him jump.

"No, this can't be," he whispered, hoarsely.

The little creature with large blue wings nodded back, "Yes, it can," she responded, "I can see you are in dire need of help. I will gather my friends and we will return to get you out of here. You will be safe. Do not worry."

Disappearing out of sight in a flash, the man collapsed once more before he fell into a deep sleep.

- Chapter Two -

"Still nothing," whispered December as she opened her eyes again, after focussing hard for what seemed like the twentieth time that day.

"We've been trying to get through to him for weeks. What's going on? I hope he's okay?" questioned Lilly.

"Yeah, I know. I wish we could do more but we don't even know who *he* is. We don't even know why there was a connection in the first place," sighed December, propping herself up against the pillows on Lilly's bed. Looking out the window at the forests beyond, Lilly wished the spirits would contact her again and give her a clue but she had neither seen nor heard from her mother or sister since they had pointed her in Sammy's direction a year ago.

Turning her attention to the shards of light that twinkled across the bedroom, she followed them as they moved across the room like miniature rainbows. The crystal angels given to her by Oliver gently swayed on either side of the window and made her smile. As if on cue, there was a tap at the door.

"It's just us," came a familiar voice as the door was pushed open to reveal a tall blonde haired boy with hazel eyes and his companion, a slightly smaller but no less attractive boy with shoulder length brown hair.

"Oliver!" squealed Lilly, jumping up into his arms and knocking him back into the wall. Giggling, she kissed him gently before hopping down and taking his hand.

"Hey Chris, good to see you."

"You too, Lilly," said the brown haired boy as he sat down next to December and smiled warmly at her.

Shaking her head, December laughed at her best friend, "You'd never know it was only yesterday that you two saw each other."

Oliver's cheeky smile said it all. He and Lilly had only recently got back together and they had lots of catching up to do.

"Hey... why don't we get out of the house today?" asked December.

"Good idea, what shall we do?" Oliver replied.

"Is it really such a good idea?" Chris said sheepishly, "We still haven't found Jemima."

"Well then, perhaps we should go out and try and find her. It's been a few weeks since her disappearance and there haven't been any vampire attacks that we know of. For all we know, she could be trapped."

"Lilly... you're always so eager to go out and track down danger. Why don't we just go out and try and have some fun?" suggested December.

"She's right, you know," answered Oliver as he playfully punched her on the shoulder.

"If the Elders haven't found her yet, what makes you think we will be able to? Let's just go and chill out. You've spent the past few weeks either looking for Jemima or trying to communicate with your so-called Lost Soul. It's time for F.U.N., babe."

"Okay, okay... it looks like I'm outvoted anyway. Give me a few minutes to get ready," she said, releasing his grip and rushing out to the bathroom.

Ten minutes later, they were all getting ready to head out the front door.

Sammy and Tiffani watched an old re-run of The Lost Boys on TV while Tabitha and Zoltan were deep in conversation in the kitchen. None of them even noticed the group as the door closed behind them.

"Are you sure you don't want to borrow a jacket, Chris? I have a spare one in the truck."

"Erm, Oliver, I think you keep forgetting that vampires don't feel the cold. I'm fine like this, really."

Rolling his eyes, Oliver chuckled as the four of them climbed into his pick-up and they set off towards the town.

#

She had no idea how long she'd been trapped in that dark place. There were no windows. Day and night had blended into one, yet she was sure she had been locked up for days, perhaps even weeks. When she had first awoke in there, she'd felt physically stronger than ever before, yet she was incapable of breaking down the heavy duty steel door that now resembled the car bonnet of a hit and run accident.

No matter how hard she threw herself against the cold steel, it wouldn't budge. She was stuck and her body was weakening from the intense hunger she had felt ever since she came to, and found herself alone, trapped. It was the kind of hunger she couldn't describe because she didn't know what it was that she hungered for. What she did know was that she no longer seemed to need water and the cold didn't affect her the way it used to.

The initial fear had been and gone and was replaced by emotions she had never felt before.

Screaming in frustration, the teenage girl flung herself against the door again and again, but to no avail. She was trapped and there was nobody to help her.

#

Walking through the busy streets of Powell River, December sighed.

"What's the matter?" asked Chris as he playfully grabbed her arm and pulled her to a standstill, making Oliver walk right into the back of him.

"Oops, sorry," he said as he and Lilly stood motionless, following December's gloomy stare across to the other side of the street.

A woman of about sixty was being comforted by her husband as they sobbed together, carefully placing poster after poster around town.

Leaning on the wall to her side, Lilly turned to see yet another copy of the paper pasted to the bare bricks. Jemima stared back at her happily. Above her was the word 'MISSING'.

"I feel so awful for her family. They have absolutely no idea what has happened to her," whispered December as she leaned her head against Chris's shoulder. They all stood watching, as did so many others along the street.

"Come on, let's get out of here. I can't even think about having fun when I know Jemima is out there somewhere. I thought I could, but I can't. Sorry guys," sighed Lilly.

"I'm the one that should be sorry," replied Chris. "Duran made my life hell for so long and then he did the same thing to Jemima. I was with him... I should know where he put her..." he stuttered.

As the four of them climbed back into the pick up truck, Oliver turned to him, "We looked in all the places you knew of and so did the Elders... don't blame yourself for this. Duran obviously had another hiding place he kept from you."

As she slammed the car door, December winced suddenly and began to cradle her head in her hands.

"Are you all right, December? You've gone, like, really pale all of a sudden."

A faint grimace crossed her lips, nodding just as Oliver pulled the truck away from the kerb and they headed back towards Lilly's house.

"This is the second time in two days you've come over all weird like this... maybe you should see a doctor?"

9

suggested Oliver as he glanced at her in the rear view mirror, but she shook her head.

"No, I'll be okay. I just need to lie down."

The friends looked across at each other but nobody said a word as they drove out of town, towards the immense trees that towered over the top of the tarmac road, creating a temporary cover of darkness.

As they emerged into the light and turned off the main road down the dirt track towards the wooden house Lilly called home, December slumped suddenly to her side, whacking her head on the window which had been opened to give her some fresh air.

"Oh God!" yelled Lilly as Oliver turned to see what was happening.

"Is she okay?" he asked as Chris leaned backwards and helped Lilly to sit her upright.

"I don't think so. Her forehead's bleeding and she won't wake up. Oliver turn round and drive to Rose's... fast. Moira's there, she'll know what to do."

Slamming the brakes on and then putting the truck into reverse, Oliver deftly drove backwards until a clearing allowed him to turn the vehicle around. With wheels screeching, they continued at break neck speed until they reached the little cottage that belonged to Lilly's Aunt Rose and her Uncle Walter, and where December's mother Moira was currently staying.

Hopping out of the truck and running as fast as she could to the front door, Lilly banged hard and yelled out to Moira and Rose before she returned to her injured friend.

"Come quick! It's December!"

As Oliver and Chris gently lifted the petite flame-haired girl from the back of the truck, they were soon joined by a beautiful white-haired lady and a pretty young woman who was the image of her daughter, with wild red hair and large eyes.

"December? Angel?" whispered her mother as she was carried safely indoors and placed on the soft sofa in the living room. A number of cats scattered at the commotion.

"What happened?" asked Rose who used a damp cloth to wipe the blood from the girl's forehead.

"I don't know. She just went really pale and then she just slumped over unconscious. She banged her head on the open window."

"She said she had a head-ache yesterday," added Chris quietly.

Moira looked up at her close friends and smiled, "don't worry, I think she'll be fine. I used to get head-aches when I first learned of my magic. It's probably just that. She just needs some rest. Maybe it would be a good idea to put her in bed?" she asked Rose who nodded.

"I'll take her," offered Chris as he leaned forward and lifted her as if she was merely a rag doll.

"Where to?" he asked as Rose and Moira led him to the spare bedroom while Lilly and Oliver settled in the lounge.

When the phone rang, the two of them jumped, making them giggle nervously.

"Hello?" answered Lilly.

"Lilly? It's Sammy... what's going on? We heard Oliver's truck and then all kinds of screeching..."

After Lilly had explained what was going on and Sammy was content there was nothing to really worry about, she turned to her boyfriend and sat on his lap with a long sigh.

- Chapter Three -

"How long has he been unconscious?"

"About five days."

"Whoa... do you think perhaps we should try to wake him?"

"Sheharazalea says not to."

"What does she know?"

"She is the chief's daughter... we'll get into trouble if we go against her wishes."

"That's true... but it doesn't usually stop us, does it?"

He heard faint voices as he drifted out of a long deep sleep.

"Hmph?" he muttered, interrupting the discussion that was going on so close to his face.

He tried to open his eyes but they felt like they had been glued shut. And when he tried to lift his arm, a dull pain prevented him from making any further movement with it.

Lifting his other arm, he managed to rub at his eyes, unsticking them from their days old sleep.

His head throbbed and his whole body ached as if he had been run over by a bus.

"Wh...at's.... going... on....?" he croaked as he tried to locate the sound of the voices.

"We're in BIG trouble now," said a squeaky voice.

"You got THAT right," replied the other.

Peering upwards, he spotted what appeared to be two brightly coloured humming birds flitting backwards and forwards right above his head.

"We'd better get out of here!" yelled one of them, before they zoomed off into the distance.

"What....the...?" he said to himself before he could take in his surroundings.

Placed on a soft bed of what appeared to be silver hay, he gently used his stronger arm to lift himself upwards.

"Where am I?" he croaked to no-one in particular.

Squinting at the bright sunlight, made all the more shiny by the silver that seemed to be just about everywhere, the man shivered, reaching for the soft blanket that had kept him warm the past few days and wrapped it around his semi-naked body.

Shuffling to his feet, his body wasn't strong enough to take his weight and he stumbled, falling to his knees with a thud.

A stifled giggle echoed not too far away before a woman's voice yelled, "Glypholia and Evanessa... get away with you! He is suffering and you do nothing but wake him and giggle at his weaknesses. My father will hear about this. Be away with you and go and make yourselves useful," she scolded before she appeared before him in all her splendour.

His breath caught in his throat. It felt like it had been an awful long time since he had seen such beauty, but then his memories had all but disappeared and he couldn't be sure. The sudden realisation he had no idea where he was, or even who he was, caught him off-guard and his muscles all but gave way altogether, leaving him completely slumped to the ground. Gentle sobs began to leave his lips as the emptiness gripped his chest. His heart, which felt like it had been shut down for so long, began to ache uncontrollably.

"Oh my," said the woman, approaching him calmly. "Let me help you up," she said as he gratefully took her arm and pulled himself up back onto the bed.

"Here, my dear... lay back down. I will return in a moment with some broth to warm you. And perhaps some tea to help your sorrow."

He watched her walk away, her thick, long black hair skimming her bottom, bringing back a very vague memory of another woman. A woman he had absolutely no idea who she was. His sobbing became louder and louder until, eventually, he had neither the strength nor the tears left to continue.

With a heart so heavy, he closed his eyes and waited for the gentle woman's return.

Minutes later, a soft smooth hand gently traced the contours of his face. Opening his eyes, he was greeted by two huge lilac eyes framed by long silver lashes, a small button nose and a pretty little pink mouth. Her presence soothed him as she helped him sit up, placing a soft cushion behind his head.

"Drink this," she said, offering him a coconut shell filled with warm golden liquid.

"You're probably wondering where you are?"

He nodded, wincing.

"We found you at death's door. Another day and you would not have survived. You are very lucky that we have some very inquisitive folk among us. We are told not to wander out of our kingdom but some of us do from time to time. It was one of our wanderers that found you."

"But... where is this? Where am I?" he asked, the drink finally giving him back his voice.

Smiling, the young woman stood up, turned away from him and flicked her hair sideways.

He gasped at what he saw.

She turned suddenly, confused, "Have you not seen my kind before?"

Shaking his head, his eyes grew larger as he admired the two small wings that sprouted from her shoulder blades. Wings that had previously been hidden by her hair. Lilac in colour, they matched her eyes.

"Then forgive me. My name is Sheharazalea, and this," she said, holding out her arms and looking around her proudly "is Argentumalea, home of the Malean faeries, among other kind. My father is Chief of the forests of

14

Moharth." She smiled as she watched his expressions change. "Perhaps you can tell me a little about yourself?" Before saying another word, he took another sip of the golden liquid and placed the coconut shell on his lap. "Sheharazalea?"

A smile touched her lips and she nodded, "That's right."

"I'm....I d... don't remember," he sobbed.

"You don't remember your name?"

Gently shaking his head, the man rubbed at his temples. "I... I can't remember anything."

"I am so sorry, my friend. Do you remember how you got here, to the outskirts of my kingdom?"

He shook his head, "I really don't know. I feel like I've been in a nightmare for a long time. I wish I knew but I don't know... I don't know anything any-more," he sobbed.

"Now, now. You are safe now. We will care for you until you are strong once again and have regained your memories, and perhaps then we can help you find your way home."

"Sheharazalea! Sheharazalea!" shouted a voice in the distance.

"I am here, Father. I am with our guest."

The young faery stood and smiled as in strode a tall striking man, bearing a full white beard and long white hair that had been plaited and hung down his back in between his two larger silver wings. His silver eyes twinkled as he approached.

"I am glad to see you are awake and well, dear friend. It is a pleasure to see. It is not often we have strangers in our midsts and to have almost lost you to the other side. Well, that would have been tragic, tragic. How are you feeling?"

"To be honest, I don't feel so good, but grateful, so grateful to you and your daughter. Thank you, thank you for helping me."

"It is our great pleasure to help you. Now tell me, who are you? What is your name? Where have you come from? Do you think you could find your way home?"
"Father, he has only just awoken from his five day sleep. He is exhausted. He is not ready for your inquisition. Plus... his memories have gone. He remembers nothing."
"Forgive me... it is not often we receive company. I am eager to hear more about you. But my daughter is quite right, as usual. You must rest some more. We will talk when you are feeling a little more... alive. Perhaps then your memories will have returned. It is clear you have been through tempestuous times," he smiled and turned to walk away.
"My father is very keen to learn about other kingdoms, please forgive him," said Sheharazalea shyly.
"There is nothing to forgive. He seems like a very pleasant gentleman, erm, faery... chief."
Sheharazalea smiled at him and placed her soft hand against his face once more. The sorrow that filled his every pore made her feel sad, an emotion she knew only too well. Ever since her younger sister had disappeared, Sheharazalea had felt a deep sense of sorrow herself.

- Chapter Four -

"There's more to these headaches than meets the eye, you know Moira?"

"What on earth do you mean, mother?"

"I'm not sure, it's just something I can feel. I can feel it in my bones."

"Oh mother, for heaven's sake. You don't have any bones! How can a dead woman feel anything in her bones?"

"I'd really rather prefer it if you didn't refer to me as a dead woman. I find it dreadfully disrespectful, you know, darling."

"Well, what should I call you then?"

"I'd rather be called a ghost than a dead woman, if it's all the same to you."

"Fine!"

"If you two have finished, we were talking about my headaches," interrupted December who sat on the sofa in Rose's cottage, propped up by a couple of large fluffy cream pillows.

"I am sorry, my darling, I do get distracted when someone calls me a dead woman," answered December's grandmother, Ruby.

Moira raised her eyebrows and shook her head. The three of them chuckled together as Lilly and Rose walked back into the living room carrying a pot of tea.

"Where are the boys today?" asked Rose.

"They're with Carmelo and Jo. They offered to go help look for Jemima again."

"Oh I do hope they find that poor girl," sighed Ruby, floating from one end of the room to the other.

"How are you feeling, December? Have the headaches eased at all?" asked Lilly who sat on the sofa with her friend.

17

"No, they seem to come and go in waves. One minute I'm fine and the next it's excruciating and I feel almost like I'm floating, you know. Like I'm having an out of body experience. It's so weird."

"Well Mother, I guess you were right. My headaches were never like that. They were quite painful, but I don't ever remember having out of body experience-type feelings. I think we ought to get her checked out."

"I can't very well go to a doctor, Mom... not if it's connected to my being a witch, anyway."

"That's not what your mother was suggesting, my dear," said Ruby, drifting over to December's side.

"Your mother was suggesting we need to head back home, to communicate with the dead."

"Oh... can't we communicate with the dead here, Mom... please? I really don't want to go back to Washington. I want to stay with Lilly," said December, linking her best friend's arm through her own.

The two girls gave Moira a wide-eyed look but her mother had made her mind up.

"Nope, I'm sorry girls, but we can only communicate with these particular spirits in our own basement. To set up another purple room here would simply take too long." Seeing the girls' expressions, she added, "Perhaps Lilly can come with us for a few days instead?"

Lilly's face lit up like a Christmas tree.

"Oh, but what about school and work?"

"It'll only be for a long weekend. I'm sure Ben will be okay with that and as for school, we'll speak to your teachers and assure them you'll catch up when we all get back," said Rose with a cheeky grin.

"Hang on... did you just say 'when we all get back'?"

Moira, Rose and Ruby shared a look and all three grinned at the same time.

"That's right... we weren't going to tell you yet but I guess the secret's out now. Your mother has bought old Mr.

Black's cottage. We're moving to Powell River!" announced Ruby as the two girls squealed and jumped up and down until December winced.

"Oh, sorry, December... I'm just SO EXCITED! We're going to be neighbours! Wait until we tell Chris and Oliver! Wait, we need to go and tell them, like NOW!"

"Woah, woah, slow down, slow down," said Moira, "let's just calm down for a second, okay? We'll go back to Lilly's, get all packed and then we 'll try and get hold of the boys, okay? The most important thing now is to get to the bottom of these headaches. So calm down."

The two girls finally plopped themselves back down on the sofa, neither of them able to wipe the huge grins from their faces, even though December's headache was getting worse.

#

"Do you remember coming to Lund with Duran, Chris?" asked Carmelo as he sat in the front passenger seat alongside his soon-to-be wife, Jo, who had convinced him she should drive the car for once.

Chris, the younger vampire, sat next to Oliver in the back. "Yes," he nodded, "We did spend a little bit of time here hidden in the forest by the water. He had a cave we used to hide in, but he never brought Jemima with him."

Leaning forward and feeling just a little bit awkward at being the only non-vampire in the vehicle, Oliver tugged at the collar of his jacket absent-mindedly, "But I thought you guys looked all over Lund for her?"

"We did, but we just want to be sure we didn't miss her. Duran was a smart guy. He could have out-witted us," replied Jo, taking her foot off the gas and easing the car into a parking space just metres from the famous Historic Lund Hotel.

"He might have outwitted you, as for me? Well..." said Carmelo with a grin. He was one of the strongest vampires in western Canada, especially now Duran was dead. But an uneasiness shrouded his head concerning Jemima's whereabouts. Duran had pretty much told them he had turned the high school cheerleader into a vampire and he'd also suggested she was particularly well hidden. Carmelo was determined to find her before she became a risk to the people of Powell River or... if she was trapped, before she became too weak to survive. It had been known to happen before.

As the wind shook the trees, and the water glistened ahead of them, Oliver took a deep breath as he watched a fisherman climb out of his small boat, tying it up at the small harbour located right in front of the hotel, before he ambled towards them.

"Morning. A good day for fishing?" Oliver asked politely. Smiling oddly as he eyed up the strange looking group, one of the elderly men rubbed his gloved hands together and shook his head, "No, unfortunately not. It might appear calm out there now but there's a storm brewing. It's heading right this way. By this afternoon, we won't know what's hit us," he said before scurrying away towards the car park where he quickly climbed into his little car before driving away with a worried glance in his rear view mirror.

"It always gets me how these fishermen can tell exactly what the weather's going to be doing."

"It's called The Weather Channel," chuckled Jo.

Rolling his eyes at her, Oliver shook his head with a smile.

"I know what you mean. They've been fishing almost all their lives, these guys. They can read the oceans, the sky, the clouds, every last natural motion around them tells them exactly what they need to know. I'd take note of what he just said... we need to get out into the forests and

20

look around before all hell breaks loose," Carmelo added as he turned away from the water's edge.

Following him, the group was careful not to be seen as they dipped secretively away, deep into the dark, damp forests that surrounded the small village of Lund just half an hour's drive from Powell River.

With Chris up ahead, followed by Jo and Carmelo then Oliver at the rear, the group walked at a regular speed in order not to lose him.

"Look, this is stupid. You guys are capable of covering huge distances at speed. You go on ahead without me. I'm just slowing you down. I shouldn't have insisted on coming along. Sorry, guys," said Oliver, realising how much weaker and slower he was than his vampire counterparts.

"I guess you're right. Here, head back to the car," said Jo, tossing him the keys. "Actually, why don't you take the car back home. We'll catch up with you later on foot."

"Good luck!" he yelled as the three of them disappeared right in front of his eyes.

"Have a nice drive home..." he said to himself as he turned back. The ground beneath his feet was slippery and slimy and he struggled to remain on two feet as he grabbed the nearest tree trunk to prevent himself from falling.

As he stood looking around, it suddenly dawned on him how eerie it was now he was alone. He shivered, thinking back to when Duran and his evil vampire crones were still alive. Had they found him alone now, they would have torn him apart, feasting on his blood.

Leaping away from the tree he was practically hugging, Oliver soon forgot about the slipperiness of the ground beneath him and ran as fast as he could back towards the car. Horrible haunting thoughts filled his mind.

As the thick trees began to open up, revealing cloud covered sunlight and the green-tinged blue ocean far off in the distance, he slowed, chuckling to himself at his erratic behaviour. But just as he thought all was clear, he heard movement behind him.

His heartbeat thumped in his chest as he slowly turned to see what was so threatening. Laughter blurted from his lips as he took stock of the two innocent beavers gnawing at a tree just metres away. Looking up at him, almost in disgust at the rude interruption, they turned their backs on him and continued their gnawing as if he wasn't there. Oliver chuckled before walking out into the open, blustery air. Rubbing his hands together energetically, he headed to the warmth of the hotel, where he sat and ordered a hot cup of coffee to warm up before he headed back home, alone.

#

Stretching his arms out to his sides, with huge black wings strutting out from his shoulder blades, Sammy leaned back and accepted the glass of milk Tiffani handed to him before she sat down and sipped at her own warm drink.

"Tell me about your homeland," he said after he downed it and returned the glass to the coffee table by his feet. Sensing her tension and seeing a tear develop in her eye, he quickly added, "but you don't have to if you don't want to. I wouldn't want you to get upset again."

But it was too late. Tiffani's shoulders shuddered, her paper-like wings fluttered and tears sprung from her eyes as she recalled the home she missed so much.

It wasn't just memories of home that led to Tiffani bawling her eyes out, it was the mention of anything remotely sad. She simply could not stop the tears from falling whenever she heard tales of woe.

As he gently placed his hand over hers, Tiffani turned towards him and smiled, the tears receding.

22

"Forgive me, Sammy. I wish I could stop this from happening but I cannot."

"It's okay, it's a part of you. I think it's rather sweet actually."

Blushing, Tiffani carefully wiped away the dampness from her rosy cheeks before taking another sip of her milk.

"Argentumalea," she sighed. "That's my home. It is the kingdom of the Malean faeries, of which I am the chief's daughter. I have an older sister, Sheharazalea. How I miss them," she sobbed for a moment before continuing, "Argentumalea is within the silver forests of Moharth. Our kind is not permitted to venture far out of Moharth."

"Why not?" he asked.

A vague memory flashed within her mind, leading to a frown creasing her forehead, but she shook her head trying to rid the negative thoughts from her mind. The childhood myth was surely that... a myth? She shivered. But she knew there had to be some truth to it; she was no longer in Moharth, after all. She was trapped in a land far from home with no idea how to return.

Sammy watched the pretty faery as all kinds of emotions etched across her face, but he didn't push for more details. She was obviously hurting and he didn't want to be the one who brought even more pain.

Sensing his eyes on her, Tiffani smiled, "I'm sorry, I've been pushing these thoughts from my mind ever since I became lost."

"No, I am the one who's sorry. I shouldn't have asked you. It's clearly still very painful for you. Let's talk about something else."

"No Sammy, you were right to ask. How will I ever return home if I don't start remembering all of these things? The Elders tried to encourage me to talk about it before but I wasn't ready then. Although it is incredibly hard, I must remember. I want to go home. More than anything else in this world, I want to go home."

- Chapter Five -

It had been several days since the faeries of Argentumalea
had rescued him from near death. His recovery was going
well and he was becoming increasingly stronger each day,
yet he was still unable to recall what had happened prior
to his rescue, or anything else for that matter. He didn't
even know his own name.

The only memory etched in his mind was of the
decomposing corpse which lay in the ditch where he had
been found.

Had he been dumped? Presumed dead?

Keen to discover what had happened, he asked Zalea (she
had thought his continued failed attempts at pronouncing
her name quite amusing, but in the end had suggested he
settle on calling her Zalea instead) to try and help him
reconnect with his missing memories.

"I'm afraid I cannot help you with this matter, my dear,
but I do know of someone who should be able to," she
had answered, "but only when you are strong enough to
walk."

That time had arrived. He was now able to support his
own body weight, thanks to the help of the faeries and
the nourishing food and drink they had continued to ply
him with. He was truly thankful, but he was now ready to
get back to investigating who he was and where he had
come from.

Making sure he was warm enough, Zalea and her close
friend, Ameleana, stood at his side helping him into a
long white robe which they tied snuggly around his thin
frame.

"You are still a little weak and the cold air will only make
you weaker unless you stay warm," smiled Ameleana. She
was a tall, dark blue-haired faery with intense, yet cheeky,

light blue eyes that matched the little wings that continuously fluttered behind her.

"Thank you, but I do feel stronger. I think I can manage."

"Very well," she answered, taking a little step backwards and watching as he leaned on a post temporarily, "Just a little dizzy. I haven't been on my feet for quite a while. Don't worry, I'm fine," he added as he adjusted the weight on his feet.

Noticing the looks on the two faeries faces, he smirked, "honestly, I'm okay. I just needed to get my balance, that's all."

"As long as you're sure?"

After nodding, Zalea led them out of the simple room in which he had spent the last few days. They followed closely behind, walking away from their homes and deeper into the silver forests of Moharth.

After just ten minutes of slow ambling, he stopped for a moment, leaning on the nearest tree as the two faeries turned and smiled at him.

"Yes, you should rest for a moment. Do not worry though, we have almost reached our destination," said Zalea, pointing to an unusual silvery blue willow in the distance. "We are nearly there."

Keen to get there, the man without a name gently pushed himself away from the soft silver fern covered tree and smiled at his companions with a nod before they continued on their way.

Although the view of the sky was mostly blocked out by the huge array of trees in wildly different shades of silver and grey, it wasn't dark. The colours around them offered an almost consistent source of light, as if the trees were covered in a million beautiful faery lights. The effect was nothing less than dazzling.

As they approached the weeping willow, a small figure slowly stepped out from beneath it.

26

Dressed from head to toe in black and leaning on a crooked old stick, she stood waiting for their approach. "Sheharazalea and Ameleana... what a welcome surprise. And you bring a guest, how lovely, how lovely. How is your father, my dear?"

Zalea approached the old lady and gently hugged her before offering her prettiest smile, "He is very well... very well."

"You were never very good at hiding the truth, my dear. He may well be in good health, but your sister's disappearance sits dreadfully on his heart. As it does yours, my dear, as it does yours. But I have some news. I can tell you she is alive and well... and, I do believe her heart is somewhat lighter. She has friends. So please, worry not about her. Just know she is well."

Zalea quickly wiped away a tear from her eye as the old lady turned to hug Ameleana gently, before focussing her attention to the man standing before her.

"So you must be the one with no name. The one with no memories?"

Nodding, the old lady took his hand and squeezed it, her eyes closing as she did so. He watched as her eyeballs moved at high speed beneath her closed lids before suddenly opening her eyes wide.

"You must come in and sit down. Come, have some willow juice."

Entering through the long dainty branches of the large tree, the man was surprised to find a warm and welcoming home filled with knick knacks and items from the forest that had been sculpted into pieces of art.

As the four of them sat around a gently burning fire in the centre, the old lady handed them all wooden cups filled with a clear liquid that tasted fruity and sweet.

"I'm sorry. I completely neglected to introduce myself, didn't I? Well, I am Gwynethea, the old wise woman

27

around here," she chuckled. "I also have a few tricks up my sleeve," she added with a twinkle in her eye.

"So you're not a faery?" asked the man while she shook her head, removing her cape to prove it.

"No... just a very, very old lady who can help you recall who you are... Jackson."

The man nearly spilled his drink at the mention of that name. A name that stirred something in his very soul, making him positive she was right. Jackson *was* his name.

"Jackson," he whispered. "That's me. That's my name. Jackson.... yes, Jack for short! How did you know? he asked as she merely smiled and stood to pour him some more juice.

"Your soul spoke to me when I touched your hand. You told me your name... now we just need to see if we can find out a bit more."

"How? How do we do that?"

"Well, it's not going to happen immediately. It's going to take some time. Ladies, are you okay staying here this evening?"

Zalea nodded but Ameleana shook her head, "I must go back to Xander. He said he would wait for my return."

Gwynethea smiled, "Xander is a good partner for you, my dear. I wish you the brightest future together. You should go... he is waiting by the cherry tree," she chuckled.

Zalea stood up with her friend, "I'll walk you out. I'll be back soon... Jack."

After the faeries had left, Gwynethea knelt by Jack's side and took both of his hands in hers.

"There is much for you to learn about this world, Jack, before you can understand how to return to yours. All is not what it seems... there is much to fear, but I believe you have already encountered that part of our world."

"I... I don't understand."

28

"You may not understand what I am saying now, but it will soon make sense, my child. Did Sheharazalea explain about her dear sister?"

"Her sister? No, what happened?"

As Gwynethea let go of his hands, she plopped herself down onto the ground and sighed.

"Some time ago, her sister disappeared from Argentumalea and hasn't been found since."

"What do you mean, disappeared?"

"I mean just that... one day she was here, the next she was gone. But she is alive. I can still sense her and I do believe she is being cared for. She is safe, for now anyway."

"Have you searched for her?" he asked, intrigued.

"Of course. But there are certain parts of our world we are not to wander anywhere near. But I don't believe she is trapped there."

"Do you have any idea where she is trapped then?"

"Before I answer any-more questions, I think we need to discover your truths, don't you think? I just wanted you to know about Tiffanimelicomelea, Sheharazalea's sister, before she comes back. She feels your sorrow because she is experiencing it herself. Now, take my hands and close your eyes. I want you to clear your mind."

Doing as he was told, Jack focussed on the old lady's voice, thinking of nothing but the soft gentle sounds coming from her mouth.

With no memories to think of, his mind soon became blank while he felt Gwynethea enter deep into his subconscious.

"I can see... I can see into your mind's eye... you have been through hell these past few years, my dear Jack. Oh my...." She suddenly dropped his hands and opened her eyes wide in shock, just as Zalea walked back into the room.

"Gwynethea! Are you all right?" she said, rushing to her side as Jack opened his eyes in confusion.

29

"I...I...I saw the...the..."

"What? What did you see?" asked a totally blank looking Jack.

"Oh my... I'm sorry, my dear. I just need to take a moment. Just a moment."

As the three of them sat down and stared into the softly flickering flames of the fire, Zalea held the old lady's hand tightly and waited for her to calm herself down.

After a couple of minutes of silence, Gwynethea turned to look at Jack, her face hiding whatever feelings she had experienced. With her other hand, she took his and squeezed tightly.

"Jack, I don't think you're going to want to remember.... but I understand you must. Your most immediate recent memories should appear first. You must let them re-appear slowly before we start going further back in time. But..." she said, turning to face the flames, "some of them might not want to return. Some might stay locked away forever..."

Jack nodded, still completely unaware of what she had been witness to.

"Sheharazalea, are you sure you want to be a part of this?" she asked the young faery to her other side who nodded vehemently.

"Very well. Then we shall begin."

- Chapter Six -

Oliver could hear giggling as he knocked on the front door of the old wooden house Lilly called home. A moment passed before it was opened by Moira who greeted him with a smile and a kiss on the cheek.

"Come on in, Oliver. The girls are just packing up their things."

"Oh... are you going somewhere?" he asked, surprised. Lilly swooped into the living room at the sound of his voice, straight into his arms, almost knocking him to the floor... something that was becoming a bit of a habit.

"We're going to December's for the weekend."

"What? Down to Seattle?"

"Well, technically it's not Seattle exactly, it's the outskirts," she replied with a cheeky smile. Oliver's smile dropped. But before he had the chance to say anything else, Lilly giggled again, "and then December's coming back.... to stay... for good!"

"Oh wow, that's awesome," he laughed just as December appeared from the bedroom struggling with a large backpack.

"Let me get that for you," he said, taking the bag from her with ease. "Would you like me to put it in the car for you?"

"That's kind of you, Oliver, thank you," answered Moira who was stood by the kitchen door with a drink in her hands. "Would you like a cup of tea?"

"No thanks, I just had a coffee up at the Lund Hotel," he replied as he quickly walked out of the room to Moira's hire car.

As he returned, he tried to straighten his hair from the blustery conditions outdoors. The girls, who had been joined by Sammy and Tiffani, were eagerly waiting for him.

"What happened in Lund? We forgot you were heading out that way this morning? Did Chris go with you?" asked December.

Nodding, Oliver told them about the search and of the impending storm.

"In fact you girls ought to get going before the weather takes a turn for the worse. I wouldn't want you to get caught up in the worst of it."

"He's absolutely right, of course. We should leave right now before it's too late. There's not a lot I can do to help if it hits en route," said the glamorous red haired ghost who suddenly appeared out of nowhere.

"Mom, there's nothing you could do... at all, anyway. But yes, are you girls ready to go? We should really leave now."

As the girls nodded and Lilly ran back into her room to make sure she hadn't forgotten anything, Moira went and sat in the car, leaving them to say their goodbyes in private. She was soon followed by December.

"Erm, thought I'd better give the two love birds a moment on their own," she winked, climbing into the back with her dead grandmother.

Ten minutes later, the four of them were en route to Moira's home near Seattle, leaving Oliver with Sammy and Tiffani. The three of them stood looking out of the window as the wind began to howl through the forests beyond. All of them were thinking about the poor missing cheerleader who was out there somewhere, alone. And it was about to get much worse.

#

Water gushed from the top of the hill, culminating in a heavy downpour that looked more like a waterfall than rain. But it had been pouring non-stop for over five hours and it didn't look like it was going to stop any time soon.

Carmelo, Jo and Chris crouched beneath a tall brown tree temporarily protected from the onslaught of water by its overly large leaves. They were soaked through.

"We've searched everywhere. I just can't think of anywhere else that would make a suitable hiding place for Jemima. I can't sense her either."

Jo looked at her fiancé. She wasn't ready to stop searching for her old schoolmate. Not just yet.

Suddenly springing into action, they were alerted to the fact they weren't alone as a combination of scents filled the air. They jumped up, their eyes scouring their surroundings.

Carmelo was the first to laugh at the sight of their two friends, Tabitha and Zoltan, who had almost managed to creep up on them.

With a slap on the shoulder, Zoltan grinned, showing a set of razor-sharp white teeth, "We nearly had you there."

"Nonsense... we knew you were there the whole time," Carmelo replied as he playfully punched his buddy on the back.

"Anything yet?" asked Lilly's cousin, Tabitha.

"No... you?"

The two shook their heads in dismay.

The darkened sky was given a temporary reprieve from the blackness of the clouds as a massive fork of lightening lit up the evening sky, followed seconds later by a deafening clap of thunder that seemed to go on for ages. Once the deep reverberating sound had quieted down, Jo spoke softly, "Wherever she is, whatever she is, Jemima will be terrified. We have to find her. I refuse to stop until we do."

Tabitha lifted her rain splashed eye lashes up to her friend and squeezed her hand as she looked into her eyes. "We'll find her, Jo, we will."

Another massive clap of thunder almost shook the ground beneath their feet as the lightening continued to

shoot bright forks across the sky, lighting up the small islands that sat calmly in the rough waters beyond.
"That's it!" yelled Chris, all of a sudden. That's why we can't sense her. She's not here on the mainland... she's over there... buried beneath one of those islands."
"Chris, you're a genius," yelled Carmelo as he stepped out into the open air, where the rain splashed off his face.
"Duran knew we wouldn't be able to hear her. The surrounding water is blocking out all the sounds. Anybody ready for a swim?" he said with a grin, looking around at his friends.
"Well, we're already soaked to the bone. What difference is a bit of ocean water going to make?" laughed Zoltan as the five of them ran towards the water. Not one hesitated as they dived straight into the rough, freezing cold water of the Pacific Ocean and began swimming as fast as they could.

#

As Jemima laid curled up on the floor in foetal position, she thought about the short life she had led. She was an only child. Loved. No, adored by her parents who had spent so many years and money on fertility treatments to have her. Her mother had been forty-four when she'd given birth to her nearly seventeen years ago and her father was fifty at the time. They doted on her. Always had, always will, thought Jemima. And now they must think I'm dead, she sobbed hopelessly.
For what seemed like days she had thrown herself against that door in futile attempts to get it open. She had even taken to clawing at the walls to try and dig her way out, but there was no use.
Jemima had given up. Now she wanted nothing more than to curl up and die. But why hadn't she? She knew she should be dead by now and the fact that she hadn't

frightened her. She knew, deep down, that she was no longer the person she once was. That beast had done something to her.

As her thoughts swirled around her head in an endless stream of images and memories, Jemima heard a faint sound. Crawling to her feet, she cocked her head listening to what it might be. She put her ear against the wall and slowly moved along until it became stronger. She banged hard where it was at its loudest and screamed for help for what seemed like hours. When she felt she could shout no more, she slumped to the floor and dropped her head to her knees. At the same time, the noise grew louder. Suddenly, something sloshed onto the back of her neck. She rubbed it and looked up. Something dripped onto the top of her head. Scrambling to her feet, Jemima rubbed her palms along the wall until she found a damp patch. "Water!" she yelled, clawing at the area to try and loosen it. Sure enough, after hours of scratching at the wall, water began to gently pour out of the small hole she'd created. Although she didn't physically feel the need to drink, she desperately wanted to feel human again, so she swallowed as much as she could. A simple act that made her feel mentally stronger, so she continued to scratch at the hole in the wall.

But when the water began pouring out, Jemima's high pitched laughter turned sour when she realised her feet and ankles were submerged. The water was pouring in... but it had nowhere to go.

"Help me!" she screamed. She was going to drown and nobody would rescue her. Her body would rot in the water and nobody would ever know.

Jemima thought of her parents, the pain they must be going through and the pain that would stay with them for the rest of their lives, never having known what really happened to their daughter.

Sobbing, the sixteen year old cheerleader who was one of the most popular girls in school, always happy and sweet to everyone, just sat in the water, doing nothing but watch it slowly rise. She was giving in. She would let the water take her.

As minutes turned to hours, the water filled the room. Soon there was nowhere left for her to breathe. Taking one last breath, she let her body fall beneath the water. Slowly drifting down to the bottom, her long hair spread out around her. She cast one last look at her surroundings before the pain in her lungs became too much to bear and her body involuntarily breathed in the water in place of air. She fought it but it was no use. Her arms and legs kicked out in protest but soon she was calm. The look of panic was replaced with one of peace. The young girl everyone had grown to love over the past sixteen years was gone.

"Here!" yelled Zoltan as the others followed behind at a super fast pace. "I have her scent."

The werewolf began to dig with his hands until he hit something solid. A heavy steel door.

"Let me," said Carmelo as he jumped as high as he could and came down on the door with such force that part of it instantly ruptured. Repeating the movement several times, the door finally broke through and Carmelo found himself within a small flooded room. He saw the body of a petite girl floating beneath the surface, and so he grabbed her and pulled her into the open air where the rain was granting them a temporary break.

"Jemima!" screamed both Jo and Tabitha in typical girlie fashion.

"Is she dead, Carmelo, is she dead?"

"Please just calm down and give me a moment," he replied as he gently placed her body on the ground and checked her over.

"I'm sorry to say this young girl is no longer with us..."

36

Jo sobbed, "No...oh no, Jemima. I'm so sorry."

"But, she is far from dead," he added.

Looking up at him, Jo turned to face the girl and saw her pretty features had changed since she had last seen her. She was far more beautiful than ever before. Even after spending weeks beneath the ground, trapped without food, and then drowned, Jemima the vampire was born.

"She is going to need to feed. Zoltan, can you and Tabitha find her something to feed from? Perhaps a rabbit or something like that? That should keep her going until we can get her back to the mountains."

Zoltan and Tabitha disappeared into the forest as Jo gently squeezed her old friend's hands, waiting for her to return to consciousness in her own time.

"It's better we don't rush her. Her body probably needs a little more time to adjust after the drowning. But don't worry, she will be fine."

"Apart from the fact she's a vampire now and she can't ever see her family again," replied Jo, shaking her head. "They'll have to be told she's dead. They're going to be heartbroken."

"I know darling, but they simply cannot know about our existence. You know that," he replied.

~ Chapter Seven ~

Moira placed the telephone receiver back on its old fashioned holder and looked to the top of the stairs where Lilly and December both sat in their pyjamas eagerly awaiting news.

"That was Jo. They've found Jemima. She's alive."

Both girls squealed with delight and jumped up, running down to the bottom of the stairs where they threw themselves on her.

"But she's no longer human," Moira added slowly, "Duran turned her into a vampire."

The squealing stopped abruptly as the three looked at each other, not knowing what to say.

"At least she's alive," said a voice from the shadows. "That's more than can be said for me."

"Oh Mother, honestly. But, I suppose you're right. I just hope that poor girl can come to terms with what's happened to her over the past few weeks."

"What happened?" asked Lilly eagerly.

Looking up at the grandfather clock as it began to signal five o' clock in the morning, Moira shook her head and started to walk towards the kitchen.

"Come in here, I'll make us some hot chocolate while I tell you what Jo said."

".... and she thought she was as good as dead," said Moira after relaying what she had been told.

"Well, she would have been if she wasn't a vampire. Goodness only knows how long she was unconscious in the water. The poor girl. She must have been terrified. She must still be terrified. Where is she now?" asked Ruby.

"Jo was calling from your house, Lilly. They were just freshening themselves up before heading back up to the Elders."

"B... but surely she's a real danger to everyone at home? When Jo was first turned, she had to be restrained..." said Lilly, jumping up and heading back towards the phone. Moira stopped her before she could get any further, "Honey, there's nothing to worry about. Jemima is incredibly weak. She couldn't hurt a mouse. That awful craving that usually happens has been dampened down to such an extent because of what she's been through. There's really no danger at all. Please don't worry, honey. Your family and friends are perfectly safe and besides... Carmelo is there and so is Zoltan. They are very strong," she smiled.

"Oh... okay.... Sorry, I guess I panicked a bit. I just worry about them, you know?"

"Of course you do. We understand. Plus, this is the first time you've been away from them all since you moved to Canada. It's only natural. You can call them later on if you need to but let them get some rest for now, okay?" Lilly nodded and walked back into the kitchen where she sat herself up to the counter next to December. They watched Moira finish making another hot chocolate before handing each a cup. December mumbled her thanks, followed by a wide yawn.

Like a domino effect, Lilly yawned too, causing Moira to open her mouth for more oxygen. The three of them giggled as Ruby over exaggerated her effort to yawn, making a long loud yawning sound in the process.

"It's been so long since I needed to do that... oh how I miss it," she said with a wink.

Later that morning, after they'd returned to bed for a couple of hours, the girls had woken up to the smells of a cooked breakfast being prepared in the kitchen. After they'd showered and dressed, they'd rushed downstairs, with tummies rumbling loudly, to find Monty in the kitchen waiting for them.

"Morning girls! I trust you had a good night's sleep?" he asked as he began to serve the delicious eggs and bacon with toast and tea.

"Mmmm, this smells gorgeous Monty, thank you!" said Lilly tucking into it as December opened one of the cupboards, taking out a bottle of Brown Sauce and proceeded to pour loads of it onto the side of her plate, followed by curry flavoured Ketchup.

"Urgh, December... you have such weird tastes. That looks horrible. Curry flavoured ketchup for breakfast? With Brown Sauce? You're just too weird for words," she laughed as she shook her head.

"Our December has always had eclectic tastes in food. Even when she was a toddler, she used to love Yorkshire pudding with jam and ice cream. Mind you, her Aunt Penelope never allowed it. We used to sneak it to her after she'd gone out."

"Eww, December!" laughed Lilly as December pretended to ignore them.

"Where's Mom?" she asked eventually, after the giggling had stopped.

"She had to pop out to buy a few things for the spell. She said she wouldn't be gone too long. Oh, and Lilly, she said for you to feel free to use the phone if you want to call your family."

Lilly nodded in thanks while she took the last few gulps of her tea before hopping off the stool, placing her dirty dishes into the dish washer before she headed into the hallway where she picked up the phone and promptly dialled home.

All was fine, of course. Lilly had just missed Carmelo, Jo and Jemima who, according to Sammy, was totally out of it.

"It was almost like she was on medication or something. She is in serious shock and she hasn't come to terms with everything that has happened yet, but I guess that's to be

40

expected. It's so sad. Tiffani and I are going to go up and spend some time with her when you guys come home. Maybe you could come too. I think she's going need the support from people she knows."

"That's a good idea, Sammy. We'll definitely come up with you. Poor Jemima. Is she feeding okay?"

"She's actually quite disgusted at having to drink blood but she can feel she needs it so yeah, I suppose she is. She's going to need some serious looking after though, Lilly."

"She needs to be with the Elders right now. It's the best place for her. Jo will make sure she's okay too. I'm just so glad she survived... well, in a manner of speaking."

"Yeah, I know what you mean."

The sound of a car door slam made Lilly jump.

"Oh, that must be Moira. I'd better go. Give Tiffani my love and we'll see you next week, okay?"

"Okay, Lilly. Have a great weekend. Take care. Bye."

"Bye."

Just as Lilly replaced the receiver, the front door opened to reveal Moira dressed from head to toe in emerald green.

"Wow, you look amazing in that colour, Moira."

"Thanks, honey. You're so sweet. Did you manage to talk to Jo?"

"No, I just missed them but Sammy's assured me everyone's okay though."

"Well, that's all that matters," she replied, closing the front door behind her, "if you and December have finished your breakfast, we ought to go downstairs and get started."

Lilly nodded and called for her best friend who had been chatting to her dead grandmother. They both walked into the hallway as they heard Moira's voice. Well, December walked into the hallway. Ruby floated.

"Hi my darling," said Ruby, "did you get everything you need for the spell?"

Moira smiled and nodded, "yes, I can always rely on Melina for times like these. That woman's store is amazing. I could spend hours just browsing all her stuff. I love going there."

"Yes, I remember Melina when she was a little girl in that store. She used to spend every waking hour with her mother and grandmother in there learning all about the craft. How is she?"

"She's okay, she still has bad days but that's to be expected. It's only been nine months."

"What happened nine months ago, Mom?" asked December as they walked down the stairs into the basement while Moira flicked on the light to reveal a simple room painted entirely in purple.

"It was so sad, such a tragedy," whispered Ruby as Moira turned to the girls, "Melina's mother and grandmother died in a fire," she said.

"Were they.... were they.... w....witches?" December whispered.

"Oh my," said Ruby, swooping down to her grand-daughter's side, "They most certainly were witches. Very good ones at that... but stop that thinking right now, my dear. It was an accident. They died in an accident. They were most certainly not burnt because they were witches, if that's what you were thinking. That sort of thing doesn't happen any-more. It's been centuries since the last witch was burnt at the stake."

"That's true," added Moira. "It was just a terrible tragedy and I'll b.... oh, honey, are you okay?" she asked after noticing December had slipped down the final step onto her bottom and was clutching her head.

Holding her head tightly, December let out a slow moan as Lilly and Moira helped her up from the floor and carefully walked her over to the only place she could sit: a small single bed.

"I... I think I'm all right, thanks. It just suddenly came with such force that time. They're not usually that intense so quickly," she said, continuing to rub her forehead.

"Honey, would you do me a favour and run upstairs and bring us a damp kitchen towel?" asked Moira as Lilly nodded and hopped up the steps two at a time.

Moira opened the purple ornate wooden wardrobe at the side of the bed and pulled out a small box. Inside were a number of perfectly placed stones of different colours and sizes. Moira picked up a pretty green stone and handed it to her daughter.

"I want you to hold onto this for a while. Green is the colour of healing. It should help your headaches during the spell, and hopefully afterwards too."

December inspected the smooth stone under the dim light. "What is it?"

"It's quartz, my darling," answered her grandmother. "These stones have been in the family for many years so they should be very strong and powerful by now. But stop thinking too hard. Just hold it in your hand and relax. Here's Lilly with the wet cloth... it will work wonders, I'm sure," she winked.

After a few minutes of lying down with the wet towel on her forehead, December's colour began to return to her face. Trying to get up, Ruby hovered to her side. "Not so fast, my darling. Stay lying down for now. We're not going anywhere so you just stay there and get some rest." December did exactly as she was told as Lilly sat beside her with a glass of water.

"Here, have a sip of this," she said, handing it to her best friend.

The girls then sat back and watched as Moira prepared the spell to find out what these headaches were all about.

"Do you have any idea what she's doing?" whispered Lilly.

Shaking her head slowly, December responded, "Nope."

"Have you been down here before?"

"Once, when I first arrived. Mom brought me down here to be welcomed home... by all my ancestors."

"Huh?"

Stifling a laugh, December winced. "I've no idea how but the voices of my ancestors came out of nowhere to welcome me home. It was amazing."

"So you didn't see them?"

"No. It was just their voices. Apparently Mom can summon them whenever she really needs them but that time they just wanted to say hello, I guess."

"So she's going to summon them to help us?"

"I guess so. She hasn't really told me what she's doing yet. I know about as much as you do."

The girls were quiet as they watched Moira light the white candles that surrounded the large ornate book which sat in the middle of a simple tall white table in the centre of the room. She then lit a number of carefully placed incense sticks around the basement. The light switch was flicked off and they sat in the dark candlelit room and listened to Moira and Ruby as they whispered the words of the spell that would summon the help of their ancestors.

"In this sacred space and time
We call now the Old Ones from our family
Those long passed and always cherished
We call upon you to show yourselves before us."

"Why doesn't it rhyme? I thought spells always had to rhyme?" whispered Lilly.

"Shhh, my dear girls. We need silence for the spell to work," shushed Ruby, but before they continued their chanting, she added, "You've been reading far too many fairy tales. Spells have very rarely had to rhyme. That's just for the enjoyment of children," she winked.

The two women continued their chanting as Lilly and December remained quiet, watching and listening as the atmosphere became calm and inviting and the scents of the incense wafted throughout their eerily calm surroundings, waiting for something to happen.

"In this sacred space and time
We call now the Old Ones from our family
Those long passed and always cherished
We call upon you to show yourselves before us."

A few minutes later, the sounds of whispering could be heard. It was a sound December recognised instantly and she smiled and squeezed Lilly's hand while her other hand continued to grasp hold of the green quartz.

The whispered sounds became louder until they were more easily recognisable.

"Ruby, Moira, December.... and another not of our family... Lillian... welcome.

It is rare we are summoned in the presence of another, yet we can feel you are equal to one of our family. It is our pleasure to meet you.

Our names are Constance, Fidelia, Genevieve, Theodosia, Millicent, Ethel, Perpetua, Valeria, Evelyn..."

"My dear ancestors, we cast the spell for you to show yourselves. Would you mind?" said Ruby matter of factly.

A woman with a mass of red curls appeared out of nowhere. She wore a simple loosely fitting brown tunic which was clearly from a long gone era.

"Ruby, I know I am the one you seek. The others are not needed on this day."

"Millicent?" asked December who now stood directly in front of the strange woman.

45

"Aye, December, I am Millicent. I believe we have a strong bond."

Both Ruby and Moira stood speechless, while Lilly continued to sit on the bed, eager to learn more.

"Yes, I believe we do too!" she squealed. "But we thought perhaps I was you, reincarnated."

Millicent chuckled. "Why, my dying words perhaps reflected that, but no. We are alike you and I. We share the very same gifts. One of which is why you have summoned me here today, I believe."

December nodded while her mother stepped forward. "Hello Millicent. Thank you so much for coming when we called. I had hoped you would be the one to help us but I wasn't entirely sure, which is why I summoned you all."

"My dear Moira. I am always most happy to help you, and any of our kind, for that matter. How wonderful it must be to live in this place and time when we are not burnt at the stake or drowned in the river."

All the girls nodded in agreement as they watched the petite spirit hover a few inches from the ground.

"I do believe that book over there has one more spell that could be of great use to us in this endeavour to find your Lost Soul," she said pointing to the spell book that sat amidst the slow burning candles. As she spoke, the pages flipped over, finally stopping as Millicent let out a sigh.

"How do you know about the Lost Soul?" asked Lilly, nervously.

"With such a strong connection to December, I know of every event with which she has been involved lately, Lilly. Might I add I am so pleased you girls found each other. I would have given almost anything to have such a friend when I was alive. But that was not meant to be."

"Oh I see... the spell which gives a spirit her body back, albeit temporarily," said Ruby, reading over her daughter's shoulder.

"Will this work?" asked Moira, "I thought it only worked on spirits that had recently passed away."

Millicent nodded, "You are correct, Moira. It has only ever worked on the newly dead but I have nothing to lose... plus, with such strong witches among us today, what's the worst that could happen. I could die?" she said with a girlie giggle.

A long laugh erupted from Ruby's mouth, "Millicent, I just knew we would get along."

After it was decided they would carry out the spell to bring Millicent back from the dead, Ruby stayed with the spirit of her ancestor in the purple basement while Monty drove Moira, December and Lilly to Melina's store in town.

"Wow. It's like nothing I've ever seen before. It's beautiful."

"It certainly is, honey. I could quite easily spend hours and hours in here."

Lilly listened to mother and daughter as all three walked in to the witch's equivalent of Aladdin's Cave. Instantly welcoming, the shop's store front contained hundreds of crystals which glistened as the sunlight hit the window, making tiny rainbows that shot in all directions, reminding Lilly of Oliver. The little crystal angels he had given her on her first birthday in Canada still hung in her bedroom giving the very same effect. Several large wooden bookshelves were laden with books of all sizes, new and old, while behind the main counter sat countless glass jars filled with all manner of herbs, spices and other cornucopia. Shelves filled with crystal balls, large and small, surrounded the shops interior. The smell of burning incense took Lilly right back to the purple basement, making her feel warm and comfortable and at ease.

The shop also contained ornaments of all sizes, featuring dragons, witches, warlocks and more. There were cauldrons; some very small, some huge and heavy. Another section of the store was dedicated entirely to jewellery; Celtic style pagan rings, necklaces and bracelets as well as charms and tiaras which led to another room that was filled with clothes... cloaks, scarves, skirts, tops, dresses all in beautiful shades of purples, greens, oranges, blacks, etc.

Lilly wandered in and out of the different sections of the store, eyeing up the stacks of CDs containing Celtic music to meditation sounds and music for relaxation. There were headphones where you could sample the different sounds. Lilly put them on and listened for a few moments to the sounds of dolphins and whales in the wild. She clicked the button to change the CD to hear the sounds of gentle running water and the rainforest. It almost gave her the urge to go to the toilet. With a smile, she clicked the button a second time and almost jumped as the sound of a woman's voice began to tell her to 'relax, breathe, let the negative energy exhale from your bones with a long sigh....'

Lilly took off the headphones and looked around for December. Her attention was interrupted by the sight of a woman who looked remarkably like the singer from Fleetwood Mac. What was her name? She jumped as someone put a hand on her shoulder, "Have you seen her? She looks exactly like Stevie Nicks," said December's voice in her ear.

"I was just thinking the same thing... even her clothes are identical."

Lilly was only familiar with the band since December had arrived from England. Moira was such a big fan that she had all their albums and listened to them frequently. Suddenly the woman turned to the girls and grinned. Even though she hadn't been in hearing distance, the woman nodded. "Thanks girls... I get that a lot," she said

48

with a wink before turning her attention back to the book she was so interested in.

Both girls blushed crimson and turned to walk in the opposite direction where they were faced by a huge owl, making them jump.

"Don't worry girls. It's actually stuffed. It's kinda sad, I know, but he belonged to my grandmother and she was so sad after he died that she decided to have him preserved. Oh hi, by the way. I'm Melina! You must be December... and you must be Lilly?" the pretty young woman with the cropped blonde hair asked.

Wendy's Wonders had been there for years, having been opened by Melina's grandmother in the 60s. Her daughter, Shannon, had joined Wendy to work in the shop as soon as she was old enough and she had loved it. She never missed a day, not even when she was heavily pregnant with Melina twenty years ago.

"Hi, yes, how did you know?" asked December, before realising she knew the answer already as Melina laughed and pointed to her hair.

"You are most definitely your mother's daughter. And she's told me a little about you and your best friend. Welcome to Wendy's Wonders."

The girls laughed.

"Thanks. It's an awesome shop. I've never seen anything like it. I could spend hours in here."

"Most people say that. Thank you. My Mom and grandmother were very proud of it. And so am I," she said.

"We're very sorry about your family, Melina."

Melina just smiled. "I feel like they're still here with me in this shop."

"I see you met my girls, Melina," interrupted Moira who had appeared from the back of the shop with a large basket filled with goodies, "Thanks for letting me into the back. I know a lot of this stuff isn't available to regular customers," she smiled.

Ever since Wendy's Wonders had opened to the public, Wendy had kept a separate room in the back for serious witches, where all kinds of weird and wonderful things were for sale for the more unusual spells. Perhaps not 'eyes of newt' or 'puppy dogs tails' but close.

"If you girls have finished browsing, we ought to head back home."

~ Chapter Eight ~

As Gwynethea took Jack's hands in hers, Zalea sat quietly to his side by the softly glowing orange flames of the fire in the centre of the room.

"It's dark, there is nothing but blackness all around you. You can see nothing. You can hear nothing. Just the sounds of your breathing. Your breath is quick and short. You are afraid. You try to stand but you are being held against your will. There are chains around your ankles and wrists. You cannot move. The pain. There is pain all around you. Oh," Gwynethea recoiled from Jack, temporarily dropping his hands. When she opened her eyes, they are not her eyes that Jack and Zalea saw. Her eyes were no longer blue but bright green, like a cat's eyes. Jack jumped and Zalea screamed. "Gwynethea!"

Suddenly, she closed her eyes once more and when she re-opened them, the old lady's blue eyes had returned.

"I am fine, young one. This is nothing but a memory. It might flash in my eyes, but fear not, it is just a memory. Come, we must return. Jack must remember."

Taking his hands, she reverted back into the trance.

"You are not alone. There are others chained like you. You can hear them but you cannot see them. There is a light in the distance, it is coming closer and closer. It is a torch. It is being carried by someone. Wait, you gulp back the fear. It feels like it's stuck in the back of your throat. It comes closer and closer. It is not human. It is... Nephilim."

Suddenly, Jack let out a low groan and a sob, "I remember the beast," he whispered," I remember. No.....no," he sobs.

"That's enough, Gwynethea!" yelled Zalea, jumping up and trying to unlock their hands.

When Gwynethea opened her eyes and looked around, she released Jack's hands.

"You were with the Nephilim, Jack. I am amazed you survived."

"But who are they?" asked Zalea, rubbing away a falling tear from her cheek. "Who are the Nephilim? Did they take my sister?"

"My dear, Sheharazalea. We are here to recall Jack's memories. I cannot tell you if they have your sister. But for now, we need to concentrate on what he has blocked from his mind, okay?" she said soothingly as Zalea nodded and returned to her seat by the side of the fire. "I'm sorry," she said.

"It's all right, my dear. You are clearly anguished. We will get to the bottom of this. Now we must speak of the Nephilim."

"Nephilim," whispered Jack quietly, "who are they?"

"They are demons, my dear, demons. And they live not far from Argentumalea."

"There are demons close to us? Why do we not know about this? We cannot live near to demons," screeched Zalea.

"Shhh child. The Nephilim and the Faeries have lived close to each other for thousands of years. It is just the way it is. No doubt you have all been told not to venture far from home. Well, the Nephilim are one reason why. But they can never come close to your home. They are trapped, you see."

"But how did they get Jack?" she whispered.

"I'm not sure. To discover that, we will need to go back to the trance, to remember."

"Then we must. I need to remember everything," said Jack.

"Then take my hands and we will return. We will try to go further back in time."

As Jack took hold of the old woman's hands once again, a shiver went down his spine as he recalled that awful dark, damp place where he had almost perished.

"The beast is close. He is looking for something, someone. He makes his choice and releases the chains of someone close to you. It is a man, an old man. He yells for help. All you can hear are his sobs as the Nephilim carries him out of the cave in which you are trapped. Your face feels wet. You are crying. Another memory is coming through. You are in a dark place. You are alone. There are no chains but you are trapped in a dark room, a black room. There is no way out. You are drained, so drained and so weak. Suddenly you see a light in the room, it's like water, no... a....a vortex. You step into it. You know it's the only way you can escape this room. Then there is nothing, just a whirling and you fall right into the hands of the Nephilim. You try to run, you are surrounded by the beasts. You are too weak. You fall to the ground. You feel like you are falling to sleep."

Zalea watched the rapid eye movement of Jack's eyeballs beneath his closed lids, but she knew she must let them continue, knowing it was the only way for him to remember himself and what happened to him. How he came to be in Argentumalea in the first place. She wondered if he might have any memory of her lost sister, Tiffanimelicomelea.

"You wake up. You are in a small cage surrounded by many others trapped in similar cages. When you turn your head to look around, you find a female Nephilim watching you. She hungers for you, you can tell by her eyes. You ask her what she wants. She says nothing. You shout and she stands, laughing at you. She moves closer to you, so close you can feel her breath on your face through the bars. You yell obscenities at her. You feel disgusted. But she does nothing but laughs a cruel, evil laugh. But wait, that laugh, it reminds you of something.

53

You remember someone. A beautiful woman who has harmed you in some way. Who is she, Jack? Remember her. Focus on this beautiful woman."

Jack winces and speaks, "Vivian. I remember now. I know who I am."

~ Chapter Nine ~

The spell worked. December, Moira, Ruby and Lilly looked on in utter shock as Millicent appeared to them in earnest. Not just a floating spirit but a woman with a body.

"Oh, get the woman some clothes, already. She'll freeze to death in here standing there naked like that. And after all of this, we certainly wouldn't want to lose her to the cold would we?" said Ruby, floating around her ancestor in shock.

"Yes, yes, of course. I'll run upstairs and get something for her to wear," muttered Moira, who was having some difficulty believing the spell had actually worked.

"I'm human again... after all these years. I can barely believe it," whispered Millicent, pinching her arms and jumping up and down.

"Woah there. Can you wait 'til you've got some clothes on before you start doing all those gymnastics" sniggered December with a grin.

"Oh, sorry... I'm just excited. It's been a long time since I felt like this. Well, since I actually felt at all."

After Moira had hurriedly returned with an outfit, Millicent struggled to put on the jeans. But when she did, she looked just like one of the family.

Finally, December hugged her ancestor and squealed, "I can't believe it. I just can't believe it."

Lilly remained seated on the bed, not quite sure what to do or say.

"Let's all go upstairs and get something to eat and drink. This calls for a celebration, don't you think?" said Moira, leading Millicent up the steps and out into the bright light of the hallway and into the kitchen.

"You sit yourself down and I'll just go to the garden to tell Monty about our guest and then we'll have something for lunch."

Millicent couldn't stop touching things. The kitchen worktop, the toaster, the sink, the tap (the feel of the running water particularly excited her), the fluffy towels... it was as if she was feeling everything for the first time. But then, she probably was considering she was originally from the 1200s.

Just as the excitement was building for them all, December fell from the stool to the ground, clutching her head in pain.

"Call for Moira please Lilly," said Millicent, deftly picking December up from the floor and helping her into the living room where she placed her carefully on the sofa.

"Now this is what you called me here for, December. You must trust me when I tell you I know exactly what you are going through. I need you to focus. I know it is not easy but you must focus on the pain. The pain is trying to tell you something. Can you focus on it? It will eventually go away but you must find out where it's coming from. Who it's coming from."

The others rushed into the room and watched as Millicent calmed December down, calmly talking to her and getting her to focus all she could on the pain.

"Now close your eyes. Do you see anything?"

December gently shook her head and winced.

"It's all right, December. You can talk. Don't move your head, just talk to me. What do you see?"

After a few moments, December spoke, "I see a man."

"That's good. Can you describe him?"

"No, it's too dark. I can just see his outline."

"Can you see where he is?"

"It's so dark."

"Can you hear anything?"

56

December focussed hard on the vision behind the head-ache while everyone in the room was silent.

"I can hear something, it sounds like, like chains. And sobbing. He is sobbing. I think he's being kept prisoner."

"That's good, December. Is there anything else you can tell us?"

"It's warm... I don't know how I can tell, but it just feels warm, really warm."

"That's good, December. That's enough for now. Open your eyes and focus on me. Look at me and breathe slowly. Just look at me. Is the pain fading?

December nods, "Yes, it's going, it's going."

"Excellent. Now close your eyes and rest for a while. We'll be right here."

Millicent took December's hand and held it tightly. She turned to Moira and said, "Well, I can tell you this. December is going through the exact same thing I did. She has somehow developed a connection with this man."

"Do you know who or where he is?"

"Well, I can't really answer that."

"What about when it happened to you? Who was it? And where were they?" asked Lilly eagerly.

Millicent closed her eyes for a second before turning to look out the window.

"It was very unusual. He was a man who was from our world but he had somehow become lost on another," she tried to explain.

"You mean he was on another planet?"

"I don't believe so."

"Well then, what do you believe?" asked Monty.

"I think you'd all better sit down..."

After they'd all made themselves comfortable, Millicent began to tell them the story about how she began communicating with a man called Badrick.

"The headaches began when I was quite young, but I
didn't learn to control them until I was 20. It was then
that I began to have the visions of the young man. He too
was trapped in chains in a dark place surrounded by evil.
It took a while but eventually we managed to actually
converse, strangely enough through space and time. He
told me his name was Badrick and he was just a normal
man. I didn't quite believe that, of course. I think he had a
secret of some kind. But that secret he took to his grave.
But anyway, he had been born, grew up and lived in
England with his young wife, two daughters and a son.
One day he was working the fields when he saw a strange
light. When he walked towards it, he was sucked into it
and when he woke up he was chained to the wall of a
dark cave. He told me he felt like he was deep
underground. There were others chained there too and
every now and again, the beasts would come and take one
away. I never found out what the beasts were doing to
them, whether they feasted upon those poor souls or
killed for entertainment. Badrick did not know until...
until they took him and once they did, I never heard from
him again. I know deep down they killed him."
With eyes wide open with shock, Lilly asked, "But who
are these beasts?"
Millicent closed her eyes once more, looking out the
window again to calm her.
"Nephilim. They were the Nephilim."
Moira and Ruby gasped in unison.
"Nephilim," said Monty, "I thought they were just
mythical creatures?" he asked.
"I used to think witches and vampires were mythical
creatures. How wrong was I?" replied Lilly without
thinking.
"The Nephilim are real. They are most definitely real."
"But what are they?" said December sleepily, who had
been listening to everything with her eyes tightly closed.

58

"The creatures I've read about are the offspring of demons who mated with women. It is believed they were cast to the depths of the earth where they've been trapped for thousands of years. However, over time they have continued to try to lure men and women into their grasp so they can have their fun with them before they cast them aside."

"But that's just myth though, right?" asked Lilly, confused.

"That's what I thought until Millicent told us otherwise. Are these the same creatures, Millicent?"

Looking across at her family and friends, the young woman sighed, "I'm afraid to say so, but yes, these are one and the same. These mythical creatures you speak of are the Nephilim."

"But how do they lure their prey?" asked an intrigued Ruby.

"Badrick told me he saw this strange light and he went into it. That is all I know."

"So, a kind of vortex, then?" asked Moira, fiddling with the ring on her finger nervously.

Millicent nodded, "quite possibly, yes."

"So now we just need to figure out who this man is and how we can rescue him," said December as she sat up, looking straight at Millicent who patted her on the hand with a smile.

"You mean, *if* we can rescue him," added Ruby quietly.

- Chapter Ten -

"Who is Vivian, Jack?" asked a startled Zalea as both he and Gwynethea opened their eyes simultaneously.
"She's the woman who ruined my life. She killed my wife and teenage daughter and put a spell on me before kidnapping me and my newborn baby. She kept me trapped for years and I couldn't do a thing. Not a damn thing about it..." Jack said before he broke down and sobbed for what seemed like hours.
Gwynethea and Zalea just sat beside him, letting him release the intense grief that had been locked within him for so long.
Eventually, he could cry no more and he looked into the flames, "I need to find my daughter. I need to find Lilly."
"We will do everything we can to help you, Jack. But for now, I suggest you get some sleep. You must be exhausted after such an intense experience."
He nodded and yawned at the same time.
"And it wasn't so long ago you nearly died, remember? You're still not as strong as you could be. Take some time to relax and let your body and mind heal," added Zalea, patting his shoulder gently.
He looked across at the beautiful faery who had brought him back from the brink of death. He owed her everything. He owed her his life, yet she wasn't interested in that. She was just happy he was finally safe and that he'd finally remembered.
Looking into her eyes, he was saddened to see the heartache that lie beneath them. She was almost mourning the loss of her sister and he was determined to find out what had happened to her. She had helped him and now he wanted to help her.
But first, they both needed to rest. He was well aware of that.

"I think it best that both of you remain here and sleep this evening. I will make us some food before we turn in," said Gwynethea, standing and stretching her arms and legs with a stifled yawn.

"You are exhausted too, Gwynethea. Let me help you," said Zalea as she stood and stretched.

Jack looked on as the woman and faery prepared a broth from strange looking vegetables. When they were finished and he was handed a bowl, the first mouthful was like a firework in his mouth, hot and spicy and absolutely delicious. He smiled and the bowlful was soon gone. His eyes became heavy and before long he was curled up in front of the fire gently snoring.

Gwynethea smiled across at her faery friend, "The poor man was exhausted."

"Yes, grief does that to you," replied Zalea with a yawn.

"I know you too are grieving, my dear Sheharazalea but you must not. I believe that Tiffanimelicomelea's life essence continues to be strong."

"But what if she has been taken by the Nephilim? What then, Gwynethea?"

"I believe Jack will help you find her, my dear. You were his saviour and now he intends to be yours," she said with a smile, watching the young faery lie down and close her eyes. Her breathing slowed until eventually sleep overtook her.

Startled awake by what seemed like a jolt out of the blue, Jack sat bolt upright. For night time, the light was unusually bright. He looked around to see both women fast asleep to his side. He climbed up from the ground and tiptoed to the entrance of Gwynethea's home. Pushing the hanging branches of the willow tree aside, he looked out at the night and marvelled at the orange sky above. It was like nothing he'd ever seen. Bright and fiery. Even the silver forests looked tinged with an orange hue.

It was quite spectacular. Jack wondered where exactly he was. It was another world.

Am I on another planet? he wondered. Or another dimension? I hope I can find my way home, he thought as a sudden pain in his head caused him to wince and curl to his knees.

He was suddenly reminded of his time with the Nephilim. Whilst trapped, he had found himself connected to someone back home. A young girl. A friend of Lilly's. She had somehow managed to communicate telepathically with him and then....yes, the memory was returning, he had spoken to his own daughter when she was in danger. But how? he wondered. Jack realised he had to find that connection again. It was the only way he knew of finding his way home back to his family.

- Chapter Eleven -

It felt like an electric shock. A shock which jolted
December awake in an instant, forcing her to sit bolt
upright in bed. The moment she opened her eyes, she had
to shield them from the intense bright light from the full
moon that shone in through the bedroom window. She
had never seen such a beautiful moon before. But it
wasn't just the beauty of it that made her breathless, it
was something else. It almost felt like the moon had
jolted her awake.

As she sat looking out of the window, with Lilly fast
asleep in the bed next to hers, there was a gentle sound of
footsteps approaching and her bedroom door was pushed
open.

"You felt it too, didn't you December?" Millicent asked,
tiptoeing to the window as they both looked out at the
bright light above.

Nodding, December watched Millicent's face almost
gleam in the moonlight. A smile burst forth from her lips.

"It's a sign, you know?"

"What do you mean," she whispered.

"I'm not sure, but it has happened to me before."

"Do you think it has something to do with the
Nephilim?"

Millicent nodded, "I do, absolutely."

"Hmm, what's going on?" said a muffled voice from
beneath the blankets.

"Wake up and see," giggled December to her best friend
who finally poked her head out of the covers.

"Oh wow... it's almost blinding me."

"Here, put these on," laughed December quietly, passing
her a pair of dark sunglasses.

Lilly took them and put them on, sitting up in bed to look
out at the enormous moon.

"It woke us both up."

"What do you mean, it woke you both up?" she asked.

"It somehow gave us a shock, a jolt. It felt like electricity," whispered December as Millicent nodded, even though she was unsure what electricity felt like.

After a few moments, Millicent said, "I'm thirsty."

"Me too," said December and Lilly in unison.

The girls all tiptoed out of the bedroom and downstairs, careful to avoid the creaky step as to not wake up Moira or Monty.

As they entered the kitchen, December opened the refrigerator and took out the milk.

"Milk or hot chocolate?"

It was a no brainer. She began to heat the milk so the three could enjoy a cup of hot chocolate in the moonlit kitchen.

All was silent while December quietly poured the hot drink into three cups before they all sat at the counter and did nothing but sip and look out of the window.

"Room for one more?" said a voice out of nowhere, making the girls all jump, almost spilling hot chocolate all over the counter.

"I couldn't sleep," said Ruby, floating into the room and hovering in front of them, the moonlight shining right through her.

"That's probably because you cannot sleep, Ruby. You're dead, remember?" giggled Millicent.

"Why Millicent, you sound exactly like my daughter," she replied, raising her eyebrows. "So what's going on? Come on... do tell," she said, pretending to lean her elbows on the counter top and batted her eyelashes.

"The moon woke us up," said all three seriously, before Millicent explained exactly what had happened.

"My, that's fascinating and yet, bizarre. But you're quite right, there must be something going on here. We need to find out a bit more about these, these Nephilim characters, and not forgetting your Lost Soul, of course. I think we should return to Powell River and head on up to the Elders, don't you?" she asked.

#

Several days had passed since the girls had been awakened by the moon. They were back in Powell River, where December was spending a few nights with Lilly while Monty, Moira and Millicent were busy decorating the new house.

"I can't believe Mom wouldn't let us go straight up to the Elders," huffed December as they sat eating sandwiches during their school lunch break.

"I guess she was right though. We have missed some school lately. We need to catch up for a bit first. The Elders have been told what's going on. They're looking into it for us, so they should have news for when we get there on Friday night."

"I guess you're right... I just want to get to the bottom of all this, you know?"

"Yeah I know but I'm sure it can wait a few days. Now I've stopped working for Ben, we've got our evenings free to do a bit of our own research," smiled Lilly, watching her best friend open her sandwich up and take out its contents, eating the ham before the cheese and then the sliced tomato and pickles. Finally she dunked the buttered bread into her coffee and popped it into her mouth.

"Eww, December, that is so gross."

December raised her eyebrows and smiled, "Was Ben okay with you stopping work for a while?"

"Yeah, he was fine. He understands I have some catching up to do with my very best pal," she giggled.

"Hey g..g..guys," said a voice approaching them, "we're doing a c...c...collection so we can buy a special wreath for J...J...Jemima's memorial service on Thursday. Can you give anything towards it?"

65

Sydney Jones was one of Jemima's classmates. He was the geek everyone loved, the perfect person to organise a collection.

"Sure Syd... here's five dollars," offered Lilly as December smiled and opened her purse.

"Have you met December? She's new here?"

December and Syd smiled at each other, as she passed him another five dollars.

"It's g..g...great to m..m..meet you, December. Thank you for th..th...the money. The service is at th..th..the local church. Hope you c...c...can make it," he smiled, placing the money in a brown envelope in his satchel.

"He seems sweet," said December.

"Yeah, he is. Everyone loves Syd."

"Are we going to go to the service? It'll be kinda weird won't it? I mean, given the circumstances."

"Of course we're going! We have to," said Lilly, "it'll look weird if we don't go. Nobody else here knows what we know," she added in a whisper as December reluctantly nodded in agreement. "What's really weird is the fact she's supposedly being buried first. But there's, like... no body."

"Shhh December," said Lilly as a group of fellow classmates walked past and said hi. They waved back.

"Apparently there's been some kind of... spell... to make them think they're burying their daughter but it's not going to be her in the casket."

"It's not?" asked December astounded.

"Well, of course it's not."

"No, I didn't mean that. Obviously it's not going to be her. But if it's not Jemima being buried, then who is it?"

Lilly shrugged her shoulders, "I don't know. All I know is the Elders are dealing with it. It's best if we don't think about it."

Lilly looked at her watch and gulped back the last of her drink. "Time's up... we need to get to class."

"It says here the Nephilim are the 'sons of God and the daughters of man'," said Lilly's aunt Rose later that afternoon as she sat at her computer reading while the girls sat drinking tea by her side, all Rose's cats purring while they slept in various different locations throughout the room.

Walter, Rose's husband who also happened to be a vampire, paced from one end of the room to the other. "Yes, that's what I've heard about them too. The truth is, I never for a moment thought they actually existed. Silly really considering what I am and what I know. I should have known they are as much a part of our existence as angels and sirens," he said more to himself than to anybody else.

"And here it says the Nephilim were cast into a place of total darkness where they would be trapped for all eternity," said Rose, continuing to read to herself. December, Lilly and Millicent looked at each other, recalling Badrick's comments at being chained in a place of darkness.

"So where do you think this place is?" asked Lilly to her aunt. "Does it say anything about that?"

"Hm... I'll keep reading and see."

"I'm thinking along the lines of caves, something like that," added Walter, finally sitting down in the old comfy armchair usually favoured by his wife.

"Well, you might be on to something because here it says they were cast deep into the earth, away from the temptations of man, where they would be trapped to live in darkness for all of eternity."

"If that's the case then how did they manage to lure man to them in this darkness deep beneath the earth?" asked December, swigging back the last of her tea before she picked up the teapot to see if there was any-more left.

"I'll make some more," said Rose who stood up and stretched her arms after sitting at the desk for so long. December smiled and took her place while Millicent looked on in awe.

"I still can't quite believe you have all of this information at your fingertips. It is truly astounding."

Lilly laughed, "This is the 21st century, which reminds me, I keep meaning to ask. How come you don't talk like you've come from the 13th century?"

Millicent laughed, "If I did, you would not understand me. Plus, I've had several hundreds of years in the spirit world to understand the real world has changed somewhat. I learn from watching the world."

"Oh," responded Lilly innocently, "cool."

"When you try and find out where the Nephilim are hidden, there are signs all over the world. They could be anywhere. Look, here it says caves in Malta, here in Romania, Missouri, Scotland..."

"Perhaps there are so many of these beasts in existence that they were cast into lots of different locations?" questioned Millicent.

"That's highly likely, young lady, and a very valid point. Perhaps we should be looking at any suitably deep caves?"

"The Elders caves are pretty deep," pondered Rose, "Sorry, that's just me thinking aloud. I guess the Nephilim caves would need to be a lot deeper than those?"

"Absolutely... I believe we're talking much deeper into the earth," added Walter.

"Can I just point something out here?" asked Lilly as she looked around at all the excited faces as they nodded.

"This is just stuff we're reading on the internet. We shouldn't get too carried away... it could all literally be myths and things people have made up."

"Of course, that is possible, but look at the hidden truths about us, Lilly. We are women that can change into cats...

you can read up about that on the internet. Walter is a vampire, look at all the articles online about that and then of course you've got werewolves, Yetis, angels, spirits... there might just be some truth in all of this. It's worth looking into, don't you think?" asked Rose matter of factly.

Lilly nodded with a smile, "Actually, I was hoping that's what you were going to say."

- Chapter Twelve -

It had been a few days since Jack and Zalea had visited Gwynethea, recovering his memories in the process and now he was even more eager to get started on finding his way home, as well as finding Zalea's sister.

They had left Gwynethea and her warm, cosy home within the willow tree behind. He couldn't thank her enough but he didn't want to put the old lady in any danger so he had insisted she stayed where she was, safe and sound. Although it had been a long time since she'd had an adventure, she knew she would just slow them down so instead, she gave them a small bag containing a couple of items that just might come in handy.

After they had said their goodbyes, Jack and Zalea had returned to Zalea's home where they were met by her father and best friend, Ameleana.

"My dear daughter," said the Chief of the Malean Faeries as he engulfed her in a long tender hug. Did you accomplish what you set out to do?"

"Yes, father. Jack has recovered his memory."

"Then you must tell me what happened. How did you find yourself in Argentumalea amid the forests of Moharth, my lad?"

"Perhaps you ought to sit down, father," suggested Zalea as she led him to the nearest soft spot on the ground where they all sat comfortably.

"Jack was taken from his homeland by the Nephilim."

"Blistering Buzzards!" he yelled loudly. "The Nephilim... the Nephilim. How is that possible? And survived? And, Sheharazalea... you were not to know of the Nephilim. They are not spoken about among the Maleans."

"I know Father but Jack lives. If these beasts have taken my sister, your daughter, then perhaps there is a chance we can rescue her."

"Rescue her? From the Nephilim? It is impossible, absolutely impossible."

"No Father... I do not believe it and I am going. I am going to find Tiffanimelicomelea and if that means going into the lair of these beasts, then so be it."

The Faery Chief looked at his daughter so tenderly, he stroked her cheek softly, "You are so like your mother, you know that, my dearest daughter. But I lost her such a long time ago, and then your sister. I cannot... will not lose you too," he said, turning away and brushing a tear from his eye.

"But Father, please," she pleaded.

"No, and that is my final answer. You are not to leave Moharth. Do you understand?"

Zalea looked down at her feet, her wings fluttering in the breeze behind her and nodded. "Yes Father."

"I promise I will find her, Zalea. I can do it alone. Don't worry."

"You are a brave soul, Jack. And I thank you. If you would like, I can send some of my best faeries with you?"

"No, I think I should do this alone. I don't want to endanger any of your kind. But thank you for your offer. I will leave at nightfall."

When the golden orange skies turned a deeper shade, Jack decided it was time to say goodbye to the Malean Faeries, thanking them for saving his life and taking care of him. He was saddened everybody turned up to wave him off, except for the one faery he wanted to see the most. He had grown fond of Zalea during the time they'd spent together. Considering the way their friendship had blossomed, he found it hard to believe she couldn't say goodbye. But he understood. Saying goodbye was such a difficult thing to do.

The community of faeries all stood and waved farewell to the strange man who had appeared out of nowhere. They stood watching him walk away, with the large leather bag on his back and his temporary walking stick. He turned one last time and waved just before he walked out of sight, gone.

Jack had been walking for several hours before the feeling he was being watched overcame him. He jumped to the side and hid behind a nearby silver tree, carefully looking around to see if he was being followed. He could see no-one behind him, so he stepped out from the tree and continued on his way, but the sense remained with him. His stomach soon began to rumble so he eventually sat down beside a softly flowing stream. The faeries had told him all the water in the kingdom was safe for consumption, so he dropped his bag to the ground and leaned in, cupping his hands so he could take a sip. As his thirst was quenched, he sat down and took a small piece of bread from his bag. Biting into it, he heard a gentle thud behind him and then a splash.

"Oh!"

Turning, Jack found the culprit. The person who had been following him was none other than Zalea. She had been carrying a small bag herself which she had accidentally dropped and it had rolled into the water.

"You'll never make a spy," he chuckled, standing and retrieving the bag from the stream. "Your father won't be very happy."

Looking down at the ground, Zalea lifted her eyes to look into his, batting her eyelashes in time with the movement of her lilac wings. "I know, but I had to do it. I couldn't just sit back and let you go alone. I need to find her, Jack."

"I know, I know," he said as he took her into his arms in a soft hug. "And we will. We will find her. But why didn't you just tell me you were coming with me."

"You would not have let me. You would have told my father."

He smiled, "No, Zalea. I wouldn't have told him. But I would have tried to stop you from coming. This is going to be dangerous."

Zalea shrugged her shoulders, "I know."

"Do you know these forests?"

"Yes, but I have never left them. I have only ever been to the edge of the forests of Moharth. I have never ventured further."

"Well, tomorrow you will. But for now, let's get you some food and then we will continue walking. It's going to take us quite a while to walk to the edge of the forest, then we can rest for a few hours before we go beyond your borders," he said, looking across at the miles of silver trees in the distance. Eyeing a few small mountains beyond the forest, he wondered what lay in wait.

That night as they lay side by side beneath a thin cotton blanket, Jack's head began to ache. It was a familiar sensation he'd had before. It was the headache that came before the girl had communicated with him.

As he sat upright upright, Zalea stirred and opened her eyes, "What is it?"

"I think someone is trying to talk to me?" he whispered, rubbing his forehead.

"What do you mean, Jack?"

Explaining what had happened while he was in captivity, Jack stood up and paced up and down, waiting for the girl's voice in his head, but nothing came.

"Try speaking to her?" suggested Zalea.

"I'm not really sure how, to be honest."

"Try focussing on nothing but her and say a few words. Ask her if she's there."

Jack did as she suggested and sat down next to her, "Okay, I'll try."

He sat motionless for a few moments before he closed his eyes and spoke, "Hello, are you there? Can you hear me?"

After a minute of waiting, Jack dropped his hands to his side.

"No, nothing. Maybe it's just a regular head-ache."

"Keep trying. Focus on her, on nothing else. Pretend I'm not here, Jack," she said, laying back down and pulling the cover over her body.

"Hello... it's me. We spoke before. Are you there? Can you hear me? Please, please hear me."

~ Chapter Thirteen ~

It happened during the last class of the day. December and Lilly were in the middle of World History when December suddenly yelped in pain.

The rest of the class turned and the spotlight was on her. "December, are you okay?" whispered Lilly as Mr Motley rushed over to see what all the fuss was about.

"Is everything all right over there, girls?"

December winced and held her head tightly.

"It's these really bad head-aches. She's been getting them a lot lately."

"Well, the class is almost over, you'd better take her home, Lilly."

"Yes, Sir."

Their classmates watched in silence as Lilly helped her friend stagger out of the room. They walked slowly out of the high school until they were in the fresh air when December asked to sit down for a while.

"Some fresh air will help, I think," she stuttered.

"What happened?"

"I'm not sure... but it felt a lot like the last few head-aches."

"Remember what Millicent said, she said you need to focus on the vision."

"No, I don't think it's a vision this time, Lilly. I think he might be trying to communicate with me again."

"I don't understand this at all. You never used to get headaches before. I thought the headaches only came with the visions? said Lilly.

"Yes they did but something's changed. I don't know what though. But I need to get home, I need to speak to Millicent."

Lilly thought for a moment. "Can you orb?"

"I don't think so... not with this pain, I wouldn't be able to concentrate."

"Well, either we call someone for a lift and wait for them to turn up or we walk."

"Let's do both... can you call my Mom and we'll start walking too."

"If you're sure?"

December nodded as they both stood, but the second Lilly started dialling her cell phone, a car drew up in front of them.

"Monty! How did you know?" asked a relieved Lilly.

"Millicent told me you needed a ride so I came down as fast as I could."

"Monty, you're a star," muttered December as the pain came back again and she winced. Monty hopped out of the driver's seat and helped her into the back of the car. Millicent was waiting outside the front door as the car drove up the driveway. Her blue jeans were covered in paint splatters of all different colours and her white T-shirt was no longer white but more of a tie-dye effect. Lilly chuckled at the sight of her.

"Thank you Millicent."

"That's quite all right, Lilly. I felt it straight away... I think he's trying to communicate with her again. This is good," she said, following Monty into the house, who held December in his arms.

"Oh darling, darling. Are you all right? Whatever happened?" asked a concerned Ruby as she was placed carefully on the daybed in the newly decorated living room.

"She got one of the bad headaches again, right in the middle of World History," relayed Lilly, stumbling in, carrying both of their school bags. As she dropped them on the floor, she sighed and plopped herself down onto the new fluffy cream carpet as Moira came rushing in, drying her hands on a towel.

"Millicent believes he's trying to reach you, honey. Did you hear him?"

December shook her head but the pain prevented her and she cried, holding on tightly to the green quartz stone she now kept with her at all times.

"Focus on that pain, December. Remember you can control it. Don't let it control you. Focus on the pain.... on the pain, nothing else. Moira, perhaps a cup of sweet tea might help?"

Moira scuffled out of the room into the hallway, almost falling over the boxes that still hadn't been unpacked from the move and into their new kitchen which was twice the size of their old one.

"Tea... tea, where did I put the tea?" she yelled to no-one in particular.

"Moira, why don't you go and sit down with your daughter and I'll make the tea. It's all right, I'll find it," said Monty, carefully turning her around so she faced the kitchen doorway, gently pushing her out of the room. Absent mindedly, she wandered back into the living room and sat down, watching as Millicent tried to make her daughter focus on the pain.

Colour returned to December's face and her grimace turned to a smile.

"I can hear you. Can you hear me? Where are you? But more importantly... Who are you? she asked as the others waited with baited breath to finally discover the identity of The Lost Soul.

- Chapter Fourteen -

Jack laid down beneath the soft blanket smiling. He couldn't quite believe it. He'd finally managed to get through to the girl, which had enabled him to recall another missing memory. The memory of when his daughter had been trapped within a falling cave. He had somehow managed to speak to her, keeping her awake until help had arrived.

"Your name is Jack?" the girl had said almost hyperventilating. "Jack.... Tulugaq?" she'd asked. Nodding to himself, Jack responded as Zalea looked on in fascination.

"Yes, that's me. When we communicated before I never got the chance to explain who I was. How did you know?"

"I'm... I'm with your daughter," she'd squealed into his head. He could almost feel the excitement that grew within her.

"Lilly? Is she okay? Tell her I'm sorry. I miss her. I'm trying to get home to her..." he'd mumbled trying to get all the words out at once.

At the mention of his daughter, Zalea had sat up with a grin, wishing she was able to hear both sides of this bizarre conversation.

After a few more minutes of speaking to the young girl whose name was December, Jack's head began to throb. As the pain became too much to bear, he'd had to stop the communication. Both had agreed to try again in a few hours time, after they'd rested.

As he held his head in his hands, Jack couldn't stop smiling. He was elated.

"Tell me, Jack. Tell me everything," Zalea said, watching him rub his eyes.

"The girl, December, she's my daughter's best friend. She has special abilities, actually she said she's a witch. A good one, mind you. She recently had visions of me in the caves so they somehow tried to get through to me and it worked, Zalea, it worked. My daughter, Lilly, she's fine. She's more than fine, actually. She's great. She's in Canada with my family. I can't believe it, I can't quite believe it. After everything that's happened, she's managed to escape that evil woman and is back with my family. My family. My father..."

"Slow down, Jack," laughed Zalea.

"I'm just so excited."

"I know, I know. But you need to rest so you can try and speak to her again, and you need to gather your strength ready for the rest of our journey."

Jack nodded, looking out at the darkening orange sky. He felt different than he had that morning. Something else filled his body. It was hope.

As the sky lightened to a yellowy orange colour, Jack sat waiting for Zalea to stir from her sleep. He had managed a few hours but the excitement of speaking to December had been too much to bear. The thought of getting back to his daughter had filled his mind and prevented him from relaxing sufficiently for sleep. But he didn't feel tired. He was just eager to get back in touch with her and eager to continue on the journey to find Tiffanimelicomelea and his way home.

The thoughts in his head were soon busy focussing on the shooting pain than ran from the base of his skull to his forehead. He could feel December trying to get through to him. He did as she had suggested and focussed entirely on the pain, until the throbbing became more of a dull ache and the sound of her voice filled his mind.

"Can you hear me, Jack?" she said.

"Yes, December. How are you both?"

He heard her giggle, "We're great. Lilly is sitting beside me. She so wishes she could talk to you."

"Tell her we will have a lifetime of talking to do when I get home," he smiled.

He waited a moment for her to relay his message.

"We think it's important to tell you what we have discovered," she said before continuing, "We believe you were taken by the Nephilim..."

Jack interrupted her immediately, "That's right. They kept me captive in their caves. Somehow I got away. I don't know how... it's a memory I seem to have lost. All I know is that I was found by the Faeries. They say I was on death's door but they saved me and nursed me back to health..."

"The Faeries?" asked December.

"Yes, I know it sounds bizarre but it's true I can assure you. I have one of them with me now. She is helping me find my way home, while we also search for her sister who is missing."

December was quiet for a few moments, presumably as she spoke to Lilly.

Her voice was different when she spoke again, "Did you say your faery friend's sister is missing?"

"Yes, that's right."

Again, a pause.

"Jack, I'm with a group of people at your father's house. It's all very complicated to tell you about them now as our time is limited but I can tell you there is a faery currently living here. Her name is Tiffani, oh, hang on a sec.... no, her real name is Tiffanimelicomelea. She got lost from her home a while ago and the Elders found her."

Jack laughed aloud, "I don't believe it," he whispered.

"Zalea... it's your sister. She's with my family. She's safe."

Zalea broke down in tears, real tears of joy.

"Jack, I can't talk for much longer. The pain is getting worse, I need to rest. We and the Elders are trying to find out where you are. We're trying to find a way of getting you home and Tiffani back to her home. I'll try and speak to you again when we have news," she said, her voice cracking under the pain.

"I understand. We'll continue our journey... we're trying to find the Nephilim. Perhaps we can find our way out from there. Don't worry, I will speak to you if we discover anything."

As Jack said goodbye to December, after she had told him repeatedly to be careful, he turned to find Zalea still sobbing. He held her in his arms until eventually she was able to speak.

"Thank you, Jack. I would never have known she was alive were it not for you."

"It's okay... December told me Tiffani is very well. She's actually living in my father's home with Lilly."

"It's so strange how this has all happened, isn't it? she asked dreamily, "this connection you have with December, how you found yourself here and my sister found herself there. I wish I could understand how our worlds work together."

Jack nodded, not knowing what to say. It was a coincidence, just a bizarre coincidence but he was relieved they no longer had to search for Tiffani. Now they knew she was safe and well, their only mission now was to find their way home.

- Chapter Fifteen -

Lilly found it difficult not to smile as she donned her simple black dress, opaque tights and boots. She was dressing for a funeral for a girl who wasn't actually dead. Well, technically she was dead but very much alive in the vampire sense. But the smile was for her father.

After all this time of not knowing if he was alive or dead, she now knew. He was alive and well, albeit he was still in danger.

After December had spoken to him, Lilly had been so overwhelmed with emotion that she needed to be alone so she could run with nature in her other form.

Leaving Moira's house, she had run home before shedding all her clothes and heading into the forest, where, the moment she was out of sight, she relaxed her muscles and allowed the transformation to take place. Her fingers snapped back to become claws and her pale skin became covered in a sheath of black fur. Her eyes widened into their true feline shape and in a split second, Lilly had become a beautiful black mountain lion.

Letting out a low growl of contentment, she jumped from tree to tree, scratching her dark claws, sharpening them against the bark, arching her back gracefully as she moved. Turning to look at her surroundings, she put her nose to the ground and took in the thousands of widely differing scents of the forest that had become so familiar. Her favourite being the smell of the damp trees, so fresh and clean.

Running, she felt truly liberated by the knowledge that her father was okay. She wondered where he was and how we had got there. But her thoughts soon turned darker as she remembered the Nephilim and what Badrick had told Millicent. They somehow took people and tortured them before killing them. The Nephilim were pure evil. An evil she needed to know more about. From now on, Lilly decided her sole purpose was to learn enough about them to be able to rescue her father from their clutches. He had told December he was trying to find them in order to find his way home. She shuddered again. I need to get him home before he walks right into their lair. Before it's too late, she thought, turning back and running as fast as she could towards her home.

As Lilly finished getting ready, she stepped out of her bedroom and into the living room where Oliver stood in a smart dark suit.

"You look gorgeous," she said, wrapping her arms around his neck and kissing him gently on the lips.

He chuckled, "I was just thinking the same about you... although all this black reminds me of when you first arrived."

"And that is why I'm also wearing this," she said, tying a bright orange scarf around her neck. "December lent it me, but you probably guessed that already," she laughed.

"Is everyone ready?" asked Zoltan who appeared from the room he shared with his girlfriend, Tabitha.

"Almost!" yelled Tabitha, hopping into the room wearing black jeans and a deep red blouse, one black boot on and the other in her hand. "Yeah, yeah, I know. I ought to be wearing all black but I just thought, you know, she's not really dead so...."

"It's okay, Tabitha, we understand," said Rose who had just walked through the front door with Walter in tow. Both wore black trouser suits. Behind them stood Chris awkwardly, who was wearing a suit that was a tad too big.

"You look great, Chris. You're almost the same size as Ben," said Lilly with a wink and he smiled in return.

"Okay then, let's go. Everyone else is meeting us there," said Zoltan as he picked up the car keys and headed out the door, leaving Tiffani and Sammy behind, who wouldn't exactly be welcomed into the church with their ample wings on display.

"... We beseech Thee, O Lord, in Thy mercy, to have pity on the soul of Thy handmaid;
do Thou, Who hast freed her from the perils of this mortal life, restore to her the portion of everlasting salvation. Through Christ our Lord, Amen."
"Amen" repeated everyone who stood by the final resting place of Jemima Dickson. Well, or so most people there believed.
Lilly looked around at the sea of black that surrounded her. A sea of grieving faces. If only the people knew the truth about the supernatural world, then this kind of thing would never have to happen, she thought to herself as she watched Jemima's parents drop two red roses atop the casket before it was lowered into the ground. Her mother's face was one of utter devastation and her father's was completely blank, as if the truth about his beloved daughter's death hadn't quite sunk in. No parents should ever have to bury their children. But they wouldn't have had to if they could accept the truth. The truth that vampires exist. As do werewolves, faeries, elves and all other so-called mythical creatures. We are real, she wanted to shout out loud.
She felt someone's hand on her shoulder. Turning, she faced her Aunt Meredith, who had lost her own husband not so long ago. Meredith had a knack of reading the thoughts of those dear to her and just then, at that time, it was no different. She knew exactly what Lilly was thinking and she sympathised with her.
"I know, my dear, I know what you're thinking but it can never happen," she whispered, turning away to watch as people began to disperse from the graveside.

Lilly approached and looked down at the flowers and wreathes that lay waiting to be placed atop the gravestone. The biggest and most beautiful had a simple note attached that said, "We will miss you, Jemima. You were one of the brightest lights at our school. Rest in Peace, PR High School."

Taking out her camera phone, she took a quick picture of it so she could show Jemima later.

"She'd like that," said Meredith simply before she walked away arm in arm with her youngest son, Cormac.

"I ch..ch..chose the flowers," said another voice from behind her.

Lilly turned to find Syd standing aimlessly with a tear-stained face. He rocked back and forth on his toes.

"They are beautiful, Syd, they really are."

"P..p..p..pink was her favourite c...c...colour. I can't believe she's g..g...gone, she's really gone."

Lilly just smiled sadly as Syd's closest friends came and took him away without saying a word.

"Well, that was awkward," whispered December who had been standing right at the back of the group. Lilly just nodded as they linked arms and walked back towards the rest of the family but not before turning to take one last look at Jemima's grave.

Almost everyone had left, just one person remained. A young woman who wore a bright red scarf around her head. Lilly didn't recognise her. She certainly wasn't a student at the school, and she wasn't anyone she knew from town.

December followed her gaze.

"Oh, she's stunning," she said, "I've never seen anyone so beautiful. Do you know who she is?"

Lilly shook her head, "She must be one of Jemima's relatives or something. From out of town, maybe?"

"She looks like a supermodel," concluded December as the girls turned away from the cemetery without a second glance.

- Chapter Sixteen -

They had been walking for about six hours and were exhausted. Zalea eventually gave up and asked Jack if they could take a break when she noticed the small river just up ahead.

"Sorry, you should have said something sooner. I never even noticed how tired you look."

"That's okay... I know you're eager to find this place."

He smiled as they wandered over to the water's edge and knelt down to take a few gulps. Zalea followed suit and used her small hands to scoop up the water to her mouth.

"The water's quite warm," he said.

"Oh, that's better. I was starting to get so hot. Actually, I think I'm going to have a swim," she said as, without a seconds thought, she dived gracefully into the water, fully clothed.

"It's wonderful," she giggled, swimming with the grace of a dolphin.

"Come on in, it's quite refreshing," she said as she gently splashed him before he jumped in by her side.

They swam quietly for a few minutes before Jack stopped to lean back on the riverbank and take in their surroundings.

As they had walked from the forests that morning, the silvery colours had eventually given way and revealed trees of lush golden browns that twinkled beneath the orange sky.

They were gradually getting closer to the mountains they had spotted from the distance the previous day but there was still a long way to go. It was there Jack believed he would find the caves where the Nephilim resided. He didn't know how we knew, he just had a feeling it was where he needed to be.

As he lay back on the soft golden sands, Jack turned his attention to the beautiful faery that swam in the warm waters of the river. The water twinkled off the back of her lilac wings and she swam on her front before she turned over and began floating on her back, every now and again kicking the water with her strong long legs to help keep her afloat.

When she noticed Jack was watching her, she turned to face him and smiled, "It's a beautiful spot, isn't it?" she sighed.

"It certainly is. I wish we knew where we were though."

"Sorry, but I only know of Moharth. I have never learned of any other place within Argentumalea. When I return home, I am going to tell my father the faery children should learn about this world. Had I known more about it, we would be at an advantage."

"I agree you should all know more about where you live. The children of my world all learn about the world's geography in school."

"Tell me about your world, Jack?"

"Hmm, well, it's very different from this one."

"How?"

"Well, we have a blue sky for one. And a bright yellow sun that lights up the sky and warms us during the day and when it goes down in the evening, the moon appears. Sometimes it is a huge glowing white sphere in the sky and other times, it is barely visible. It is a sight to behold though."

"A blue sky? It must be an amazing sight."

"I guess we have always taken it for granted."

"Tell me more. Your world sounds fascinating"

"My world is a complicated one. At times it is truly magnificent, it has sights that are breathtaking, places of such beauty that they take your breath away. And yet we are destroying it," he said.

88

"Destroying it? But that's terrible. Why would you do such a thing?"

"Like I said, it's complicated. Suffice to say we are using up all of the earth's valuable resources at such an alarming rate and in the process we are polluting our world."

"Can it not be stopped?"

"Some people are trying to slow it down, to save the planet but others simply don't care. It's sad, really."

"Sad... and tragic, so tragic."

Jack smiled at her while he watched her rub gently at her eyes as if wiping away tears.

"Tiffani must be heartbroken."

"What do you mean?"

"Ever since she was a little girl, sadness has made her cry. She bursts into tears at the smallest thing.... even if it doesn't affect her. If she sees someone else is sad, she will cry for them."

"Perhaps you share a little of her emotions," he suggested as she rubbed her eyes again.

Zalea smiled at him, "I think perhaps I am a little more discreet," she smiled.

Turning to swim a little more, Jack noticed a few bubbles pop up from beneath the smooth water. Bubbles that changed in size and quantity until the surface of the water erupted.

"Zalea!" he shouted. She turned with a smile, which froze on her face as she noticed what was happening.

"Jack!" she yelled back, but it was too late. She was being dragged into the centre of the river and pulled downwards.

Jack dived head first into the river, swimming as fast as he could to reach her. Arriving at the place the bubbles had appeared, he ducked underwater and searched for her. His eyes immediately fell upon the tail of some kind of red scaly fish. He swam until he reached and grabbed it, pulling it with all his might.

As the beast turned to face him, Jack recoiled in shock as the face of a beautiful woman looked straight at him, baring sharp ugly teeth. Zalea struggled in her arms, trying to loosen herself from the grasp of the strange creature.

As Jack pulled her tail, he managed to draw her closer to him, close enough to take a punch. The force of which caused her to loosen her grip on Zalea who swam free while he and the beast continued their battle beneath the water.

Needing to take a breath, Jack felt himself begin to weaken. He knew if he didn't get to the surface for air he would surely drown. So he kicked as hard as possible and propelled himself through the water until he was able to breathe. But the second his face reached the surface, he was grabbed and pulled under. His weakening body prepared itself for the intake of water, but the moment he thought he was about to drown, his mouth was covered by something, or someone, who breathed air into his lungs. He opened his eyes wide and saw another beautiful face. She looked right into his eyes and smiled, pulling him up from the depths of the deep river until they both surfaced.

"Jack!" yelled Zalea, "behind you!"

"It's all right, Zalea, she saved me," he spluttered.

The beautiful creature pulled him across the water until he was able to drag himself out of the water, coughing and spluttering. Zalea helped him out, pulling him far from the water's edge, away from danger.

"Forgive my sister," said the creature, "She was once tricked by the evil doers of this world and she now believes everything to enter these waters is evil. But I could see she was wrong on this occasion. Do not think badly of our kind. We are not evil."

"Who are you?" asked Jack as he finally managed to calm himself down.

"My name is Dacius and my sister down there is Arapea."

"Thank you for saving me, Dacius. I am Jack, and this is Sheharazalea."

The creature nodded her head and smiled, "I am sorry my sister tried to harm you. You are not injured are you?"

Jack turned to Zalea, who shook her head.

"No, we are fine thank you. May I ask of the evil doers you mentioned? We are on a journey to find the Nephilim and wondered if that is who you were referring to?"

Dacius visibly cringed at the word, baring her scary looking teeth in the process.

"I take that as a yes, then," he said.

Nodding, Dacius continued, "They are the epitome of evil but they are trapped within their caves. You should be safe from them provided you stay away from those caves."

Smiling, Jack said, "Oh, but we need to find their caves. It is the only way I can find my way home."

"In that case, if you could breathe underwater, I could take you directly to them but that is clearly not possible. However, if you follow the river towards the mountains, you will find an entrance to their caves deep beneath the high waterfall that begins where the river widens. I wish you luck, Jack and Sheharazalea, but you will need more than luck to survive the clutches of the Nephilim," and before they could say another word, the creature had vanished deep beneath the water.

~ Chapter Seventeen ~

"I am so very sorry to learn of your daughter's fate, Mrs Dickson. Please accept my condolences."

Mrs Dickson shook the woman's outstretched hand with one hand and nodded as she wiped her eyes with a silk handkerchief with the other.

Lilly watched her as the beautiful woman then walked into Mr and Mrs Dickson's house where they were holding a wake for their only daughter. She was the woman from the funeral. Lilly became even more intrigued now she knew Mrs Dickson didn't know her at all.

The woman spoke to no-one, ate nothing and drank nothing. She merely hung around and watched the people as they mingled and talked to one another.

"Have you noticed something strange, Lilly?" whispered December.

"What's that?"

"Look at all the men in here."

Lilly did as she was told and turned to look at them all.

"They're all staring at the mystery woman. So, she's beautiful. What's so strange about that?"

"Really look at them, Lilly. Look at their eyes."

It was then that she knew December had a point. The men looked like they were under a spell. The only ones free of the spell were Chris and Walter - the only vampires in the room and Zoltan, a werewolf. Even Oliver was blatantly ogling the young woman, which really irritated Lilly.

"That woman is not all she's cracked up to be," she whispered.

December nodded and pulled her friend outside.

"Maybe she's a witch?"

"She's not a witch," replied December.

"How do you know that?"

"I don't know... I just do. Maybe we should get the others together and go home?"

"Definitely. I'll go get Oliver and Chris and the rest of my family. You go and get Moira, Millicent and Monty."

The two girls split up, both going back inside the house but in different directions.

"Oliver, it's time to go home,"

"Huh?"

She tugged at his sleeve but he would not take his eyes off the woman. She tugged again, but nothing.

"Oliver!" she said louder, "I'm tired. Can you please take me home?" she said through gritted teeth.

When he ignored her for the third time, she tugged his sleeve so hard he spilled his drink down his white shirt, breaking the apparent spell.

"Huh? Sorry, what did you say? Oh no, my shirt. Sorry Lilly, what did you want?"

Lilly rolled her eyes at him and then noticed all the men had returned to normal. Looking around, she couldn't see the woman anywhere.

#

"Hi Jemima. How are you feeling?" asked Lilly after they journeyed to the Elders a couple of days later.

"Like hell," she answered, "but it's really good to see you," she continued, standing to give her former school friend a long hug.

"I'm so sorry about... everything that's happened. You don't deserve this."

"Does anybody?" she asked almost bitterly.

"You'd be surprised how many paranormals there are, you know. Once they've come to terms with it, they tend to cope okay with it. I'm just sorry about, you know, your family and your friends."

"Did you go to my... funeral?"

93

Lilly nodded, "It was almost like everyone in Powell River was there. The kids from school organised a beautiful wreath for you. I took a photo... I guess in hindsight that wasn't such a great idea."

"No, I'd like to see it," she said as Lilly took her phone from her handbag and scrolled through the pictures until she found it.

"It's really pretty. Thanks... for taking it. It means a lot."

"That's okay. How are you finding it up here?"

"Under other circumstances, I'd probably be awe-struck. It's incredible. I guess I just don't feel like being impressed right now. Rather a lot to come to terms with. Being kidnapped by a guy who was so evil, you know? Being hurt by him and his friends, being made into a vampire, being trapped alone for so long... drowning... I could go on."

"Well, if it makes you feel any better, I'm not entirely human either," she said attempting to smile.

Jemima raised her eyebrows. "Maybe a little," she smiled, "What happened to you?"

"Basically, my Dad and I were kidnapped by an evil witch when I was born, she murdered my mother and sister, then kept Dad under a spell in London and basically kept me prisoner, then my Dad disappeared, the witch went off somewhere and left me alone. I was sent over here where I found an amazing family I never even knew existed, then they told me I could turn into a mountain lion. The witch returned, nearly killed my grandfather and my cousin, who ended up having to be turned into a vampire to survive. I then found out my best friend is a witch (a good one!), then an evil vampire who killed her grandmother came out of nowhere and began killing and turning people into vampires... I guess you know the rest. Oh I forgot the part about my Dad being taken by the Nephilim," she said with barely a breath.

94

"I had, like, no idea, Lilly. I'm so sorry for you too. Wow... this is one seriously screwed up world, isn't it?"

"You can say that again," laughed Lilly, "I should introduce you to my friend, December. She's the witch I mentioned. She moved here from Seattle, actually first she moved to Seattle from London but now she lives in Powell River."

"Hi, Jemima, It's great to meet you," said December cheerily, who had been standing back waiting for Jemima to feel a bit more at ease. She stepped forward and held out her hand.

Jemima stood and shook her hand, "It's really nice to meet you, December." So you're a witch, huh?"

Nodding, Jemima smiled, "You'd be amazed at how many of us there are around here. And when I say us I don't just mean witches."

"Yeah, I'm kind of understanding that now," she said, looking around at the weird and wonderful characters that lived within the Elders caves.

"I'll get used to it.... I am getting used to it," she laughed, although it didn't quite reach her eyes.

"It'll take a little bit of time. Hey Chris, come and meet Jemima," yelled December, but the moment Chris stepped out of the crowd of people, Jemima shot backwards with a hiss, her teeth bared and her eyes shining red.

"It's okay, Jemima. Chris was being kept against his will by Duran. He wasn't one of them," shouted Lilly, trying to calm her down.

"Carmelo... we've got a problem," yelled December, as he ran through the throng of people to the end of the grand hall where the four of them stood, Jemima ready to pounce.

"Jemima, calm down, remember what we taught you. Control those emotions. Chris is completely innocent just like you. Duran and his buddies murdered Chris's family and then turned him into a vampire. You're safe here. Completely safe," urged Carmelo as he held her arms and gently tried to pull her back down to the sofa where she had been sitting.

"I'm... I'm sorry, Jemima, I'm sorry for what he did to you but they did it to me too. I didn't want this either. Please believe me," pleaded Chris who stood motionless waiting for her to calm down.

Jemima's protruding fangs retracted into her gums and she broke down, sobbing.

"I'm sorry, I'm so sorry..." she said repeatedly.

Chris approached her and knelt down by her side, "It's okay, it's okay. I know what you're going through."

She looked up at him and he took her hand and squeezed it.

Lilly looked across at December and smiled but the smile wasn't returned. Instead a pained look momentarily crossed her eyes. Rushing to her side, she took her hand and pulled her away from the crowded main hall, into the room they used whenever they stayed there.

She pulled her until they were both sitting on the soft old green leather sofa with its fading arms and comfortable cushions.

"Is Dad trying to communicate with you again? Is it a headache? Remember what Millicent said about focussing on the pain?"

December smiled, "No, no, it's nothing like that. No headaches or anything,"

"Oh, then what happened. You looked like you were in pain?"

"Did I?" she asked innocently.

"December, this is me, remember? I know when something's wrong."

Her best friend put her hand through her shoulder length red hair and smiled a sad smile.

"I guess it was because of Chris."

A look of confusion crossed Lilly's face.

"He and I have been close since we met, you know. I really like him."

"Well, that's obvious. He really likes you too."

"Perhaps he does, but not as much as Jemima. I have to face the facts. He's a vampire. Who am I kidding? He needs to be with his own kind? And Jemima is now a vampire, a beautiful vampire the same age as him who he can spend eternity with."

"Oh December, you do have a point, I guess."

December gave her friend an angry stare. "That should have been the time you tell me he likes me more than any other girl, that not even a vampire could compete with me, blah blah blah...!" she said crossly.

Lilly chuckled, "I'm your best friend, I'm not going to lie to you, December. You realised it the second he took her hand. Perhaps they are meant to be together. If anyone has ever had a real connection, it's those two. You two can still be friends. I mean, it's not like anything ever happened between you two, is it... or did it?"

Shaking her head, December tried hard to smile, "No, we only ever held hands. It just wasn't meant to be, was it? Oh God... I'm such a moron. But, but he was so cute. Is so cute. He's just a lovely guy, you know?"

"Yes, he's cute and yes he's a lovely guy and yes, he's a great friend and if you were a great friend, you'd accept this and let him move on with his life which could possibly mean a relationship with fellow vampire Jemima, who, I might add, could really use our support right now. It's not like she's stealing your boyfriend, December, because he was never your boyfriend in the first place. He was just a really good hand holder," she laughed as she stood pacing from one end of the room to the other. Suddenly she was pelted by a multitude of cushions. "Hey!"

"Sorry, I just remembered the last time we were in here... I was hitting you with a cushion then, so I figured I'd do it again."

"Stop using those magical powers on me right now, December or I'll... I'll..."

"You'll what?" she giggled as the cushion kept tapping her on the head, "You'll turn into a mountain lion and eat me for dinner?"

Soon the two girls were flopped out on the sofa giggling so hard that they got stomach ache.

- Chapter Eighteen -

"What were those things?" asked Zalea.

"I think there is a very good possibility they were mermaids."

"Mermaids? But I thought mermaids were supposed to be good?"

"They *were* good... that first one only grabbed us because something really bad happened to her before, at the hands of the Nephilim. It was the Nephilim that made her that way. It's kind of sad."

"Yes, it is very sad. I shall never want to go bathing in a river... ever... again."

Jack laughed heartily, "I know what you mean. I'm sure we can still bathe. We just need to be quick about it and keep a look out. There was one good thing that came out of that encounter though," he smiled as Zalea looked at him quizzically.

"The Nephilim? Dacius told us how to get there."

"Oh yes, of course!" she chuckled. "All we need to do is to follow the river towards the mountains and then enter the cave through the waterfall where the river widens. Is that right?" she asked and he nodded in return.

"Absolutely."

After the couple had rested and dried off, they picked up their bags, threw them onto their backs and continued on their way along the riverside, in silence.

"Tell me about your daughter, Jack?" Zalea said quietly. Taking a deep breath, Jack pouted his lips and turned to look away from her.

"I'm sorry. If it's too difficult to talk...."

"No, it's not that. It's just.... just that we went through hell for years, you know. I feel like I lost her and she had such a terrible childhood. And I couldn't do a damn thing about it. I couldn't help her. I wanted to, you know, God how I wanted to. But there was just nothing I could do..." he croaked.

Zalea patted him on his back, "I understand."

"No, I don't think you do, Zalea. I don't think I really understand what happened either. That woman, that evil woman, she put me under that spell for years... so many years. Lilly must be 15 or 16 by now, and I wasn't there for any of it. Not really."

"I'm sorry, Jack. It must have been unbearable for you."

"I just hope Lilly is okay, you know? I mean, really okay, deep down. No child should ever have to go through what she went through. Losing her mother and her...s...sister like that," Jack turned away again as a few tears escaped from his eyes. He rubbed them away and turned back, attempting a smile at his new friend. "Sorry, I just miss them, I miss them all so much...... Is that a bird?" he asked suddenly looking upwards to see where the gentle sound of flapping wings was coming from.

"A bird?" Zalea asked, "What's that?"

"You don't know what a bird is?" he asked astounded as she shook her head.

"A bird is a small creature with wings... but, if you don't have birds in your world, then what is that?" he asked as it suddenly dawned on him that they could be in danger as the large winged creature swooped down towards them.

"Run, Zalea... hide behind those rocks!" he yelled, astounded at what he saw.

The flapping wings slowed down significantly at the sound of Jack's voice and the creature swooped down just metres from them.

As Jack prepared to protect them both from harm, the creature opened its mouth and squawked loudly, making them jump. It then lowered its head for a moment before peering back up at them as if waiting for a response.

"I... I think it's communicating with us," whispered Zalea, tiptoeing out from behind the huge boulder and bowed her head in response.

"No Zalea, No!" yelled Jack, "If that's what I think it is, it's dangerous."

"But it seems friendly," she whispered, approaching the strange looking winged creature with her arm outstretched.

Jack rushed to her side and yanked her away from the beast until they both hid behind the boulder.

"Why did you do that? It looks friendly."

"But we don't know that... and it looks suspiciously like a... like a....." he stuttered.

"Like a what?" she asked.

"Like a Pterodactyl. But that's impossible. They're extinct. They haven't been around for millions of years."

"In your world," corrected Zalea.

"Well, there is that, I suppose. I just wish I knew more about your world," he added, peering round to see the winged creature still standing in the same position.

"It's still there."

"Then let me approach it," she replied, pulling away from his grip and attempting to walk up to it. "See? It's quite all right," she said as it gently nuzzled at her hand.

Amazed, Jack followed, watching the faery giggle as the creature repeatedly licked her face.

"I see you found company, Oprah" said a voice out of nowhere.

Jack leapt to his right and scoured the area to identify where the voice had come from. Looking upwards, he saw a man on top of a ledge some 40 metres or so above them. The two watched in awe while he scaled down the side of the jagged cliff with absolute ease, his strong arms taking his full weight as he took the final few metres in a jump, landing firmly on his feet.

The winged creature hopped away from Zalea and headed towards the man, who patted it softly on the head with a smile. Both turned to face the strangers.

"I would ask 'friend or foe' but I can see perfectly well I have nothing to worry about. Oprah here is a good judge of character," he said smiling, approaching them with his hand outstretched.

"I'm Nickolaus Pryce, please... call me Nick," he said as Jack took his hand and shook vigorously.

"Jack Tulugaq and this is my friend, Zalea."

"It's really good to meet you Jack and Zalea," he said, eyeing up the beautiful pair of lilac wings that jutted from her upper back.

"I am a faery from the Moharth forest," she offered.

"Ah yes, of course. I've never spent much time within Moharth, Oprah here prefers to be out in the open. But I have heard of your kind. But you," he said turning towards Jack, "are not from around here. That I can tell... quite easily," he smiled, revealing a set of perfectly aligned teeth that were a little stained. "Let me guess... you're from the States? Or Canada, perhaps?"

Jack's eye lit up at the mention of his home, "But how... how did you know?"

"Because I, too, am from the States," he said with a wink, before adding, "How long have you been here?"

Jack's mind went into overdrive imagining how this man could finally help him get home. "Honestly, I don't know. I was trapped for some time before I was rescued by Zalea and her people. We've been travelling a few days now."

"And where are you heading?" he asked as Oprah nuzzled the ground between them.

"To the Nephilim caves," answered Zalea.

"Woah there. Are you crazy?" he asked.

"Possibly," replied Jack, "but we believe it's the only way to get home. How long have you been here?"

"Believe me, you don't want to know."

But when Jack continued to look at him with raised eyebrows, Nick's expression changed to one of sadness and he shrugged his shoulders,

"Maybe 15... 16... years."

Jack gasped, he felt winded and took a step backwards as if he'd been punched in the stomach.

Nick stepped forward, thinking he might have to catch him if he fell but dropped his arms to his side when Jack steadied his balance.

"Perhaps we ought to go and sit down and have something to drink?" said Zalea as the two men nodded in agreement.

"...and then when I woke up, I found myself here. Well, I found myself in those awful caves you're so desperate to find."

"But weren't you chained up?" asked Zalea, picking at the strange looking bumpy brown fruit Nick had given them to eat.

"No, but I did see others were in chains," he choked, "I saw those beasts, the Nephilim, taunting them. I don't know how I got there but I sure as hell wasn't going to stick around."

"So you managed to escape?" asked Jack eagerly.

"In a manner of speaking. I hid within those caves for days on end, trying to figure out what to do, I couldn't find a way out, it was like a never ending maze of caves. Eventually I stumbled upon a river running through them. I knew I'd die if I didn't get out, so I threw myself in and hoped to God it would lead to safety. I swam for as long as I could under the water. And just when I thought I was going to drown, something miraculous happened. An angel appeared and breathed for me. Then she held onto me and we swam beneath those caves until eventually we were free. She let me go and I swam to the surface. When I turned back to her, she was gone," he said in awe.

"It was one of the mermaids," said Jack.

"Have you seen them?" he asked.

Nodding, Zalea answered for him, "One of them attacked us and then her sister saved us."

"Why would one attack you?"

"Apparently she was harmed by the Nephilim so now she fears for her life every time someone goes into the water."

"That's... understandable, I guess. But tell, me, what happened to you? And why do you think the Nephilim caves will help you find your way home?"

"Well, that's kind of a long story...."

- Chapter Nineteen -

"We've decided to postpone the wedding," announced
Carmelo and Jo at dinner that evening. "I know, I know,"
he said, looking around at the hundred or so faces that sat
quietly watching him from around the enormous table in
the centre of the grand dining hall, "but Jo and I feel the
wedding would not be the same without her Uncle Jack.
And in light of the latest information about the Nephilim,
we feel we are much closer to bringing him home. So
I'm sure you will all understand our big party must wait a
while. Enjoy your meal everyone."

Jo squeezed his hand as he sat down and a hum of voices
returned to the hall as people began talking to their
friends and family as they ate and drank deep within the
Elders' caves.

Later that evening, Lilly was still beaming as a small group
gathered in Carmelo's quarters to discuss Jack and the
Nephilim.

"Thank you," she said to Jo who was the last to arrive,
closing the heavy long drapes to the room behind her.

"It wouldn't be right to have such a celebration of love
without your Dad being here, Lilly, especially when we
are able to communicate with him now. Well, December
is able to, anyway."

The cousins hugged each other and sat down, while
Carmelo stood facing December, "I want you to get as
much information as possible this time, December. The
more we know about where Jack is, the better it is for us
to figure out his true location."

December nodded and lay down on the only sofa in the
room, as the rest gathered around her with notebooks.
Millicent sat by her side and held on to her hands.

"Remember what I told you, December. I know there is
no headache at the moment, but if you focus purely on

Lilly's father, you should be able to obtain a connection. Don't worry about how long it takes, we're right here for you."

Turning to look at her mother, December returned her smile and closed her eyes.

"Everybody should remain silent, please," said Millicent as December's mind began to focus on the Lost Soul, Jack.

Soon enough, a faint throbbing entered her head and she winced. Millicent squeezed her hand to reassure her and so she continued to focus on the task in hand, until the ache came as strong as it had before.

Minutes later, she spoke out loud, "Are you there, Jack? Can you hear me?"

A smile crept upon her lips as she listened to the voice within her head.

"He's here," she said softly to the others.

"Get him to describe his whereabouts to you," said Carmelo who sat with his hands clasped from behind his desk.

"I'm with the Elders. We want to get as much info as possible about where you are. Okay? Yes. You have? Who is he? Hm Hm? Just a sec, let me tell them. He's met another man who's been there for years. His name's Nickolaus Pryce, from Tucson and it happened to him on 18th August 1997. They want you to look into the dates and see if there is a connection."

Carmelo jotted down the name and the date and waited for more details.

"It's very what, sorry... oh, okay. They say the sky is very orange, it does get darker but it's always tinged with orange. There doesn't appear to be a sun or a moon. The landscape where they are at the moment is kind of like the Grand Canyon but on a much smaller scale, and there is a river. He says to ask Tiffanimelicomelea about Moharth... it might help. There's what there?" she

106

suddenly said even louder, "erm, okay. Apparently there are creatures very much like Pterodactyls but they appear to be gentle. Hm? Mermaids. Okay, there are mermaids too. He says that's pretty much it, at the moment."

Gabriel, who had been very quiet until then, suddenly spoke, "December will you please tell my son we WILL get him home, and... and I miss him terribly," he croaked.

December smiled and passed on the message. "He says he misses you too and he knows. He says he's coming home to you and Lilly.... Raven's Promise."

Gabriel smiled and patted at his eyes as December whispered goodbye to Jack before sitting up and holding her head in her hands.

"Thank you, December. I understand how much it hurts and we really appreciate you are willing to continue to put yourself through the pain," said Gabriel kindly.

"That's quite a lot of interesting information that should help us to pinpoint where he is. We'll get on to it straight away," said Carmelo, standing and passing on a few notes to a younger man who stood eagerly awaiting instructions. "I want you to look into the dates this Nickolaus was taken and the date Jack disappeared. There might be something useful there. And then please pass on these notes to the other Elders."

The young man took the pieces of paper, nodded and exited the room without saying a word.

"We have been doing some research on these Nephilim and we can confirm they do exist, I'm afraid," he said to the group, "and we have been able to discover they do in fact live in caves throughout the world. It is believed these caves are hidden deep beneath the surface of our world."

"So all we need to do is work out where they are, so we can go in and rescue him, then?" said Lilly more to herself than to anyone else.

"Well, it's a little more complicated than that, I'm afraid, Lilly. The Nephilim are known to be extremely dangerous."

"How dangerous?" asked December.

"That we still have to determine. But rest assured we are working on it,"replied Carmelo.

#

Later that night, December and Lilly lay awake looking up at the cave walls in two single beds positioned next to each other.

"Do you really think we'll be able to find him, December?"

"Of course I do. We've got some amazing people on our side working everything out. I don't doubt it at all. Why? Do you?"

Turning her head to look at her friend, Lilly drew in a breath, "I honestly don't know. I guess I'm scared about what might happen. These Nephilim sound so terrifying that I'm just worried about will happen if they catch him?"

"You mustn't think like that. Just concentrate on him coming home safely. The power of positive thinking, it is pretty amazing."

"That's easy for you to say, you're a witch."

"And you're a witch's best friend," smiled December as she turned over and lay on her front, "now let's get some sleep. We've got a long journey home tomorrow," she added, blowing out the candle that had been flickering in between them.

- Chapter Twenty -

"I have to say it's so good to have some company," said Nick as the three of them bedded down for the night, with Oprah lying some distance away from their small camp fire.

"How long has it been?" asked Jack.

"I have met others over the years but never anyone from my world. The only humans I've ever seen were corpses."

Jack's ears pricked up, "Corpses?"

Nodding sadly, Nick continued, "When I was trying to find my way out of the caves, I tripped over them. A pile of bodies, dead bodies. The stench was unbearable. I think they were being prepared to be dumped somewhere."

"I think that's how I got out... I don't remember exactly how I got there but I was dumped, presumed dead I suppose. When I came to, I was lying in a large pit next to a corpse. There were probably more, but I don't really remember. I was so weak, I passed out."

"It's not something you really want to remember," sighed Nick, "but if you could recall, it might help find a way in."

"I've thought about it over and over but I just don't remember anything about how I got out. There is one thing that confuses me though."

"What's that?" asked Zalea and Nick at once.

"Why are they dumping the bodies so far from their caves? How are they transporting them all that way?"

The three of them remained silent, looking up at the orange tinged sky.

"Nick, you've been here for years, have you never seen them?"

He shook his head, "Never. I don't think they ever leave the caves."

"Then how are those bodies being dumped?" he repeated.

"They must have someone working for them on the outside," whispered Zalea.

"Surely I would have seen them if they had," asked Nick quietly.

"Maybe you did, maybe you just didn't realise it at the time. Think back to all the times you have seen anything out of the ordinary."

"Erm... anything out of the ordinary? Have you looked around you, Jack? Everything is out of the ordinary here."

"Yeah, I know. Sorry. How on earth have you survived here all alone?"

"I'm lucky I found Oprah pretty early on. She was just a baby when I found her next to her dead mother. She kind of gave me something to live for..."

"That's why she's so tame," said Zalea smiling as Nick nodded to her side.

"Yes, I have come across others that aren't quite so friendly but when they see me with Oprah, they tend to disappear. She protects me as much as I protect her."

Jack chuckled, " I have a daughter too."

Nick laughed, "Yes, you could say she is my adopted daughter. How old is yours?"

"She'll be about 15 or 16 now."

"You don't know exactly how old she is?"

"It's a long story, but suffice to say that since she was born, our lives have been somewhat hazy... there are lots of things we are both trying to forget."

Nick looked up quizzically.

"We were kidnapped when Lilly was born. Turns out the woman who took us, also murdered my wife and eldest daughter..."

"Jesus, Jack, I'm so sorry."

"... and the woman wasn't even a normal woman. She was a witch. She put a spell on me for years, she took my blood..."

"There are witches up there?"

Jack laughed, "You're surprised? Look around you. Look at what took you from your home, Nick. This world is full of weird supernatural beings. I mean, look at Zalea. Would you ever have known faeries existed?"

"I guess not. It's all surreal. If I ever get home, nobody will ever believe me."

"You're right about that, Nick. If you tell people about this place, you'll be put in a loony bin."

"What is a 'loony bin'?" asked Zalea.

"It's where crazy people are locked up," answered Nick with a chuckle, before asking "How did you know about witches and stuff, Jack?"

"My family has always known about such things. There are lots of, let's say, 'special' people back home, Nick. People with special abilities that must keep it a secret. My family is one such family."

"Do you have special abilities?" he asked, stunned.

"Not personally, but some of my ancestors were able to transform into ravens."

Nick started to laugh, "You're a laugh a minute," he said, amused. But when Jack said nothing, Nick turned to look at him. "You're actually... serious?"

Jack merely nodded.

"Ravens? Well I never."

~ Chapter Twenty-one ~

As the family and friends gathered their belongings in readiness for their journey back down to Powell River, they were asked to head into the main hall.

As everyone bustled into the huge cavern, Lilly wondered what was going on as she grabbed hold of December's hand and they walked in together.

"We have information," said Carmelo as he stood and beckoned for everyone to sit down, "regarding the Nephilim."

December and Lilly turned to look at each other as they hurried to the front of the room where Jo sat beside Tiffani and Sammy, "What's going on?" whispered Lilly.

"Listen..." replied Jo.

"We have managed to find out a number of things regarding the Nephilim, which we believe may help us in our search for our dear friend, Jack. When we last communicated with him through December here, we were told he had found another man who had been taken some 15 years ago. The dates of their vanishing shared something in common. Both disappeared on the night of a Full Moon. We have since had our computer whizzes, witches Emilie and Margot, looking into disappearances on the nights of full moons and we have discovered many people have vanished on such dates. It's nothing concrete, of course, but it is a start. However, there is more. We have been in touch with our worldwide contacts and found out there have been recordings of strange mirror-like anomalies during the phase of the Full Moon over a number of years..."

Suddenly there was a hiccup and Tiffani stood up, wide-eyed, "That sounds like the strange thing I saw just before I found myself in your land."

"And what happened, Tiffani?"

"I thought it was so beautiful that I walked into it and found myself... here. That's all I can tell you, I'm afraid."

"But that's very useful information, my dear," smiled Gabriel.

"It sounds like some kind of vortex," shouted a voice from the crowd as people began to whisper to each other. Carmelo nodded and quietened everybody down, "Yes, you're quite right Seamus, it does. But we don't know for sure. What we do know is the Nephilim are behind this and the only way we are going to get to the bottom of this is by finding out more about them. So, I am asking you to reach out to your contacts and try and find out as much about the Nephilim as possible. We must bring Jack home... and of course, at the same time, return Tiffani to her own home to her own family. Please keep me up to date. Thank you everyone."

As Carmelo stepped down, he approached Lilly with a smile, "Are you all set for your return home?"

She nodded, "I wish I could stay here and help you find out more about the Nephilim."

"Don't worry, we will keep you informed. You must get back home ready for school on Monday."

"Carmelo, you sound just like Gabriel," she laughed.

#

"It's good to finally have you back," said Oliver as he sat in front of the TV with one arm around Lilly.

"I've not been gone that long," she smiled, snuggling into him.

"You went down to Seattle, came back briefly and then up to the Elders. I hardly saw you," he scolded.

"I did ask you to come with us."

"I know, I know, but I can't keep taking time off work, I'll end up losing my job," he replied, ruffling her hair.

"Speaking of jobs, has Ben found a replacement for me yet?"

113

Oliver was silent for a moment before he changed the subject, "So, how are Carmelo and Jo?"

Lilly turned to look at him, "You didn't answer my question!" she said, "And Carmelo and Jo are fine. Well?"

"Well what?"

"Has Ben found a replacement?"

Again, he was silent for a few seconds before he looked away from her.

"Oli!"

"Yes, yes he has."

"Why was that so difficult to tell me?" she said, shaking her head. "So, who is it?"

"Who is what?"

"Grrr, what's the matter with you tonight? Who is my replacement at the vet's?"

"Erm, just some girl."

"Who?" she demanded.

"Someone from out of town, you don't know her."

"Well, what's her name?"

"Her name?"

"Yes, Oliver, her name? What... Is...Her...Name?"

"Babe, there is no need to be funny."

"I'm not being funny... you're being weird."

"I'm not being weird. You are!"

"Oh My God... Oliver this is getting ridiculous. Are you going to tell me her name or what?"

Oliver's cheeks turned a little pink as he opened his mouth to speak, "Okay, okay. Her name is... Calliope." As he spoke, his eyes glazed over momentarily.

"Oliver... is there something going on with you and this... Calliope?"

Oliver's face turned deep red as he looked straight at his girlfriend, "Lilly... no way. I don't even know her. She's just, just... someone from out of town who accepted your old job with Ben. There's nothing going on, honestly. All

114

I know is her name..." again his eyes glazed over while he spoke, "... Calliope."

Lilly's heart hurt. She knew there was more to this girl and it was clear Oliver was head over heels for her.

"I think you'd better leave, Oliver."

"B...but why? I haven't done anything wrong," he said deflated.

"You haven't done anything right either. I'm tired. I'd really like to go to bed now. Goodnight, Oliver," she said as she turned away and stormed out of the lounge, leaving him sitting with his mouth open in shock.

"What just happened?" he whispered to himself before he put on his coat and walked out, quietly closing the front door behind him.

- Chapter Twenty-two -

The more they walked, the further away the mountains seemed to get.

"It's been days and we don't seem to be getting any closer. It's weird," said Jack as they planted their belongings down on a couple of large rocks and approached the river to drink some of the refreshing water.

"Do you think it's safe to bathe in the river?" asked Zalea, who was getting increasingly hotter.

"If you stay by the water's edge and are quick about it. Don't worry, we'll keep an eye out for Dacius's sister," said Jack with a wink as Zalea walked slowly and carefully into the cool water, dipping her head back so her hair was soaked through. After a couple of minutes, she walked out, feeling much better.

"Is it me, or has it been getting warmer the past day or so?" she asked the two men, who both nodded.

Oprah squawked behind them and Zalea jumped.

"It's okay, she just wants a drink, that's all," said Nick, leading her to the water where she lapped at it until she was satisfied.

"I was wondering, Nick, how come you never tried to get home?"

"Why did I never try to go back into those caves full of deadly Nephilim waiting to pounce? Plus, where there are loads of dead bodies?"

"Okay, I get your point."

"But honestly though, I've thought about it for years. I've come pretty close but I can just never bring myself to go back there. It's almost like there's something keeping me away."

Zalea smiled, "I wish you'd have come to Moharth. We would have made you very welcome, Nick."

"I wish I had done too, Zalea, thank you."

"Tell us about your home, Nick" she asked, sitting down by the side of the river, her fingers trailing in the water beside her.

"There's not an awful lot to say, really. I lived in a trailer in Tucson, Arizona."

"What about your family?"

"I didn't have a family."

"What did you do for a living?" asked Jack.

Nick laughed, "I guess you could call me a survivalist."

"No, I mean before you ended up here."

Nick laughed again and shrugged his shoulders, "I'm being serious. I was a survivalist when I lived in Tucson. I used to travel all over North America teaching people how to survive in certain circumstances... in the mountains, forests, and so on."

"So basically people paid you to do what you've been doing here for the past 15 years?" asked Jack, intrigued.

Nick nodded, "If it wasn't so tragic, it would be funny."

"Amazing, absolutely amazing. Had it been anybody else, they probably wouldn't have survived. Perhaps that's what's pulling you back, preventing you from trying to get home?"

"What do you mean?"

"Nick, clearly you are in your element in this place. Perhaps deep down you feel more at home here?"

With a smile, Nick stood up, "You're probably right, but 15 years is a long time to spend without the company of other humans. Meeting you has strengthened my resolve to get home. I *want* to go back, I know that now."

"Good," said Jack, smiling, "then let's get moving."

The three of them grabbed their bags, hoisted them onto their backs, Zalea with caution so she didn't do any damage to her delicate wings, and they began walking towards the mountains, all the while keeping the river to their left.

117

Oprah walked behind them, occasionally nuzzling their necks between short flights when she would disappear to find something to eat before returning to walk behind them again.

As they wandered through the large dry valley with huge cliff faces at either side of them and the river continued to flow towards the mountains, they came across what looked like a mass of giant mushrooms.

Nick took his rope and lassoed it around the top, tugging it to make sure it was strong enough to hold his weight.

"What are you doing?" shouted Zalea as she and Jack stood, astounded by Nick's sudden bout of energy and enthusiasm.

"An excellent source of protein can be found on top of these things. It'll be great for dinner!" he hollered from the top.

"Can't we just cut a bit from the bottom?" shouted Jack in response.

Nick poked his head out from the mushroom's top and shook his head. "No... the rest of it is kind of poisonous. You can only eat the top," he said, descending down the side, even faster than he'd climbed up it in the first place.

"How do you know?" asked Zalea, taking the little mushrooms handed to her and placing them carefully in Jack's bag as he turned around.

"Trial and error. I tried it once... and once was enough."

The trio continued walking until Jack spotted a small cave in the canyon.

"That might be a good spot to spend the night," he suggested as they headed over to have a look but before they got there, Oprah began squawking loudly.

"Wait," said Nick and he pulled his friends behind him. "We're not alone. Stay here while I go and take a look."

Oprah followed behind as they stood and waited for him to check out the caves.

A few minutes later, there was a loud whistle and Oprah was off like a shot towards the cave, to her master.

"Okay, it's safe for you to come in now," yelled Nick as he threw something with a lot of legs out of the entrance. Oprah pounced on it and began ripping it to shreds, eating every last bit of the creature.

"What was that?" asked Jack.

"Giant spider... Oprah loves them but they're not so good if they bite you," he said, lifting his leg and revealing a nasty red scar on his ankle. "This one got me shortly after my arrival here. I thought I was going to die. The pain was excruciating."

Zalea shuddered, "Are you sure there aren't any-more in the cave?"

"Don't worry, I'm sure. If there were, Oprah would be able to smell them and she'd let us know. So you can rest easy tonight."

Chapter Twenty-three

"You look terrible, what's wrong?" asked December as she met Lilly at the entrance to the high school the following day.

"It's Oliver. I think... I think he might be two-timing me," she muttered, pulling her school books close to her chest and breathing in deeply.

"No way, that's just not possible. Not Oliver. Not with you. Are you insane? Why would you think such a thing?"

Lilly explained about what had happened the previous evening.

"Perhaps she's just attractive and he felt like you were putting him on the spot?"

"No, you should have seen his face when he mentioned her name. It was like he was talking about someone he was madly in love with, December."

"No, it's got to be something else, hon. Oliver is mad about you. You two are like soul mates or something. There's no way on earth he would have feelings for anyone else. Believe me, I know. I am a witch," she whispered. "So who is this girl anyway?"

Lilly pulled a face and said, "Calliope, apparently," almost choking at the mention of the name.

"Cool name. I wonder what it means."

"Who cares what it means. I never want to hear it said again... EVER."

December laughed, "You really need to take a chill pill, Lilly. You're imagining this. Seriously, you are."

Lilly pulled the same face and walked ahead of her best friend who giggled behind her.

"Okay, okay, we'll go check her out. This... Calliope..."

"Excuse me, did you just say Calliope? She's just so.... hot..." said a random schoolmate December didn't even know. The boy stood motionless for a moment, mouthing the name in silence, "CALLIOPE...."

"Okay, now that is weird. Lilly, did you see that?"

"See what?" she said, still annoyed.

"I mentioned the name Calliope and that boy....."

"CALLIOPE.... wow what a woman...." said another random school student who stood fanning himself down just imagining her.

"Lilly, you're officially right. There's something going on here."

"See, I told you."

"Not really, you told me your boyfriend is having feelings for another girl.... not somebody named Calliope is causing strange things to happen."

"December Moon... did you just say Calliope? Have you seen her? Is she here? Where is she? I need to see her!" yelled Mr. Bacon, one of the teachers who almost pushed her against someone's locker trying to get information out of her.

"Wh...what? Mr. Bacon, what are you doing?" she asked loudly.

Lilly watched in shock as all the boys in the hall seemed to be acting bizarrely, all because they'd heard that one name. Calliope.

Suddenly, the school bell rang loudly and the boys returned to normal, acting like nothing had happened.

December turned to look at Lilly, "After school, we are so going to find out about this Cal....."

Lilly rushed to her friend's side, dropped her books to the floor and put her hand over her mouth, "No... don't say it aloud."

December nodded and bit her lip.

"After school, okay?" and the two then split up to go to their respective classes, both still reeling from the weird occurrence.

#

"I'm not going in there. I think we should peer through the window instead."

"Okay, but the windows are really high at Ben's clinic. We'll need to find something to stand on."

"December, you're a witch. Can't you do a spell to make us hover in the air or something?"

"The clinic is often full of innocent bystanders, Lilly, they might see."

"Point taken. We'll just find something to stand on."

The girls were deciding what to do as they walked from school out of town towards Ben's veterinary clinic. As they approached it, they put their bags and books down behind the nearest tree and searched around for something to stand on.

"Here, this should do it," said Lilly who found an old crate. As they carried it sneakily around towards the window of the room where Ben carried out most of his work, both December and Lilly jumped backwards, dropping the crate and falling onto their bottoms at the sight of another person doing exactly the same thing they had planned to do.

"Crystal?" Lilly whispered as the young woman blushed at being caught, "What on earth are you doing?"

Climbing down from the small stepladder she'd been using to peer into the window, Ben's girlfriend looked at the two girls suspiciously, "I might ask you the same thing," she said looking at the crate as they dusted themselves down.

It was then they noticed she'd been crying.

"Oh Crystal, what's happened?"

Breaking down with tears pouring down her cheeks, she could barely speak.

"It's...it's... Ben. He broke up with me."

"No way. But Ben adores you."

Crystal shook her head, "Not any-more."

"But why?" asked December.

"Because of her... that, that woman..."

"Wait, let me guess... Calliope right?"

Crystal gasped, "How did you know?"

The two girls shook their heads in astonishment.

"I need to see what she looks like," said Lilly, climbing up the stepladder Crystal had placed against the wall.

But suddenly, there was a commotion around the other side of the building.

December grabbed both girls and pulled them away from the clinic, leading them behind the tree where they'd hidden their school books and bags.

The three of them peered around and watched as a number of local men and high school students all arrived by the side of the building and pushed and shoved until they were inside.

"What the hell is going on?" asked December. "Is that... Oliver?"

"Where?" whispered Lilly as she watched her own boyfriend, straightening his jacket and brushing his hair backwards before opening the door and walking inside. "That... ba...."

"Okay, there's no need for language like that, Lilly. There's clearly something weird going on here and we're going to find out what it is. Crystal, what does this woman look like?"

"I took a picture through the window," she said, pulling out her cell phone and clicking through the images until she stopped on the one she was looking for.

"That's her, that's Calliope," she said pulling a face as if it pained her to speak her name out loud.

Lilly and December both gasped at the same time, "It's her. It's the woman from the funeral."

#

"What on earth is going on?" asked Crystal as the three of them sat down in Starbucks each with a Cinnamon Soy

123

Latte. "Who the hell is she? And why have all the men in this town gone weird?"

"We don't know, Crystal, but we first noticed she had a funny effect on them at Jemima's funeral."

"I couldn't make it so I didn't see. Did you see Ben there? Was he drooling all over her there?"

December tried not to smile, "No, we didn't notice but chances are he was because everyone else was. All the guys anyway."

"All the guys except Chris, Walter and Zoltan that is," added Lilly as she circled her coffee cup with her finger.

"Do you think she's one of us?" whispered Crystal.

"What? A witch? Changeling?" said December, "I really don't think so, but I guess it is possible. Wouldn't we know about her if she was?"

"Not necessarily, not if she's new in town."

Taking a long sip of her coffee, Crystal turned to look at the people in the café, "What did you say her name was again?" she asked.

Absent-mindedly, Lilly opened her mouth to speak but before she could say anything, a hand was placed firmly on top of it as December gave her a stare.

"Don't you dare... we don't want a repeat performance of earlier," she almost shrieked.

Lilly nodded and pushed her hand away, "Sorry, that was close. Here, I'll type it into my phone instead," she said showing Crystal the woman's name on the screen.

"Why, what happened earlier?" asked Crystal.

"You won't believe it....just the mention of her name makes all the men go insane. Even our teachers were swooning. Crazy, just crazy."

"I want to see what happens," replied Crystal before the girls even had the chance to shut her up.

"Calliope," she said at the top of voice.

Suddenly, the three men that had been sitting in front of the window not far from them turned and stared.

"Did you say, Calliope? Wow... what a woman. Is she here? Have you seen her? Where is she?"

"C.A.L.L.I.O.P.E... Mmmm"

"That woman is mine," said the third, causing uproar to begin.

"Girls... we need to go, now..." said December, standing quickly as the two male staff members rushed from behind the counter towards the three men.

"Oh no you don't... she's mine."

Just as the three girls closed the door behind them, they heard a loud crash as a nasty fight ensued.

"Okay... I get the drift now," cringed Crystal.

"Well, we did warn you," said December as they rushed away as quickly as they could and hopped into Crystal's car. "Come on, let's go back to my place... maybe my Mom can shed some light on what's going on."

~ Chapter Twenty-four ~

Nick cooked the mushrooms over a small fire he'd effortlessly prepared an hour earlier. Zalea and Jack looked on as the orange hues of the sky began to darken. "I almost forgot about the things Gwynethea gave me just before I left Moharth," said Jack, reaching into his bag, pulling out a small leather pouch.

"Whose Gwynethea?"

"She is one of the wise women that live in the forest. She helps us whenever we need someone to turn to. In fact she helped Jack to remember his lost memories shortly after we found him."

"She sounds amazing. What did she give you?"

As Jack opened the pouch, a few small items dropped out, one of which was a small dagger.

"That's beautiful," said Zalea, picking it up, inspecting the exquisite tiny jewels that were embedded in the handle before handing it back.

"Why would she give this to me? It must be worth a fortune," Jack muttered quietly.

"It might be worth a fortune for you, Jack, but things like this don't really hold any value in our world."

"But it's full of such beautiful jewels?"

"These might be jewels to you, but they're all around us here. Have you really not noticed them?" she asked with a laugh in disbelief as Jack's mouth dropped open and he shook his head.

"You've been here all this time and you've never noticed you've been surrounded by some of the world's most valuable stones?" asked Nick, adding, "When I first found myself here, I began collecting them, but then, after a few years when I realised I would probably never get home, I stopped. I figured, what's the point, you know?"

Jack, still in shock, nodded softly as Zalea and Nick
looked at each other in understanding.

Suddenly, as if realising that this could mean something
important to his family, he decided he needed to tell them
and the only way to do that was to try and get in touch
with December again.

"Excuse me for a moment... I need a few minutes alone,
if that's all right," and he stood and walked away from the
cave.

"Is everything okay, Jack?" asked Nick.

"It's fine... I just need a few minutes to myself. I'll be right
back."

Zalea gazed at her friend as he stood up and walked away,
but said nothing.

Walking around the corner away from sight, Jack sat
down on the nearest rock and concentrated hard on the
young girl who had become his only connection to his
old life. His only connection to his daughter.

Soon enough, a dull ache began to rock the back of his
neck. Pain shot through the base of his head until it
drilled through to his forehead.

"December?" he whispered, "Can you hear me?"

After a minute of nothing, he tried speaking again, "Are
you there, December? Please hear me. I just wanted to tell
you something. It might be nothing but then again it
might be something.... please answer me. Okay, perhaps
you are unable to speak to me but there is a chance you
can hear me. If you can, I just wanted to tell you we are
surrounded by valuable stones. I never really noticed.
God knows why, considering they're glittering away right
in front of me, I was so focussed on everything else that I
didn't see them. I know it sounds crazy, totally crazy, but
it just might help you understand where I am. I hope it
helps, I really do. I need to get home, you know? Look, I
know you're probably not hearing this, I'm probably just
talking to myself here but if you can hear me, please tell

127

Lilly ... that I love her and I miss her and when I get home I'm going to make it up to her, okay? Oh... and December. Thank you. If you can hear me... thank you..." Jack didn't know what else to say so he chose to say nothing more. He stayed sitting there in silence for a good twenty minutes or so, doing nothing but thinking about his daughter, hoping December, his family and the Elders could figure out where he was and help him get home before he found his way to the Nephilim. He hadn't said anything before, but the idea of reaching the caves of something so evil terrified the life out of him.

"Jack?" said a voice in the relative darkness, "Are you all right?"

Struck out of his solemn thoughts in a flash, Jack looked up to see Zalea approaching slowly, "I was getting worried."

Smiling sadly he stood and faced her, "I was just thinking about Lilly... I tried to get through to December but she didn't seem to be hearing me. I guess I just needed to be alone for a while."

"Oh, I'm sorry," she said turning quickly away from him, "I'll leave you."

"No... please don't go."

She turned back to look at him and he noticed her small wings fluttering as she moved. She smiled and took her hand in his.

"Thank you... for being here Zalea. I know you want to find your sister, but I appreciate the company."

When she shivered, he pulled her to his side and placed his arm around her shoulders, careful not to harm her wings.

"Let's go back and get warm by the fire and then I guess we should get some sleep. We've another long day ahead of us tomorrow."

- Chapter Twenty-five -

As December came to, she felt groggy. Her head wasn't quite as clear as it should be as she recollected the odd dream she'd had during the night.

She'd dreamed of a lone stranger trapped in a strange place where the atmosphere around him maintained an orange glow. He'd been talking to her, telling her about jewellery. No, that's not right, she thought. He'd been telling her about the place where he'd found himself. Everywhere he looked there were shiny stones glinting in the dusky light. Valuable stones. Valuable jewels.

Suddenly, December sat bolt upright in bed. It hadn't been a dream at all, it was Jack. Lilly's father had tried to communicate with her but, because she'd been asleep, he'd come to her in a dream instead.

He was trying to tell her something.

Bounding out of bed, she grabbed her purple nightgown and threw it on while she pulled her bedroom door wide open so fast that it banged hard against the wall.

Halfway down the stairs, she realised she was only wearing one slipper, so she turned back, running upstairs two at a time until she was lying flat on her front on the bedroom floor, looking for the missing shoe under the bed.

"There you are," she muttered to herself, grabbing it and putting it on her cold foot before hot footing out of her room once again, only to run slap bang right into Lilly on the stairs.

"Lilly, what on earth are you doing here? It's barely even seven 'o' clock in the morning!" she exclaimed, startled.

"Yeah, yeah, I know, I know... I've been up all night reading about the Nephilim and I think I might be on to something..."

129

"You're insane, you know that? You know what though? I really need a cup of tea... is Mom downstairs?"

"Yeah, she let me in."

"Okay, let me wake up first and then we can talk," yawned December, pulling her night gown tightly around herself, forgetting why she was in such a hurry in the first place.

"...and then I found another website that said pretty much the same thing, well, the same theory anyway..."

December yawned once more and rubbed her eyes before taking a long gulp of her hot English tea. Both she and her mother were sitting quietly, eagerly waiting for Lilly to finally get to the point.

Before Lilly could continue though, Ruby appeared out of the living room wall with a huge smile on her face, "Well hello, darling. It's lovely to see you here so bright and early. How is everything with you and your family?"

"Erm, hi Ruby. They're great thanks..."

"Mother, Lilly was just about to tell us something important, if you don't mind?"

"Well, sorry. Please go on, Lilly," she said, hovering around the room, clearly feeling a bit put out.

"Oh, yeah, the theory. Well, I then went on to find a load of other websites which claimed the Nephilim do live in caves..."

"Well, we already came to that conclusion, like ages ago," interrupted December.

"I haven't finished yet," said Lilly, before continuing, "They do live in caves beneath us."

"What do you mean beneath us?"

"Beneath the earth."

"What, this earth?"

Lilly rolled her eyes as she looked at her best friend, "Do you know of any other earth?"

Ruby chuckled.

"I guess not. So you reckon there is a whole new world underneath our own, then?"

"That's what these sites seemed to point at, so then I started reading about the centre of the earth..."

"It all sounds very far-fetched, though, don't you think?" asked Moira who was fluffing up the cushions on the settee.

"This coming from a woman who is a witch, who descends from a long line of witches that have always practised magic, whose daughter is best friend's with a changeling and has close friends who are vampires, faeries... should I go on?" asked Ruby who was relishing the conversation.

"Okay, I get your point," smiled Moira as there was a sudden crash from the basement.

"What on earth was that?" asked December who jumped up in surprise.

"Oh not to worry, it's just Monty," said Ruby with one of her trademark cheeky smiles.

"What's he doing?" asked Lilly.

"Probably trying to get out."

"Well shouldn't we go and let him out if he's locked himself in there?" she asked innocently.

"Oh my, we can't do that?" Ruby replied.

"And he hasn't exactly locked himself in there," said Moira, "We had to lock him in."

December gasped, "Mom! You can't do that."

"Yes, we can and we must...he's trying to get out to that Calliope woman," she concluded.

"Ohhh, we get it," said the two young girls in unison as they looked at each other.

"Did you manage to find out any-more about her yet?" asked Lilly.

"Unfortunately, we weren't able to get through to Carmelo last night so Crystal has gone with Tabitha and

131

Zoltan up to the Elders to discuss it. She said she'd call us when they had something to report."

"I can't believe Monty has been affected too," said December with a sigh, "Who the heck is this woman and why does she have such a hold on all the men in this town?"

"Not quite all the men, only the human men," corrected Lilly. "Zoltan, Walter and Chris have all been fine which would suggest whatever power she has only affects humans."

"So until we figure out what she's doing, we'll have to keep Monty tied up down there. But don't worry girls, Millicent is down there keeping him company for now and I keep on popping in to check on him," said Ruby, "He'll be fine."

The girls glanced at each other before returning to their initial conversation: the Nephilim.

"So what are we going to do about my Dad?" asked Lilly.

"First and foremost we need to verify whether there is any truth in the information you found. If there really is another world beneath our very feet," said Moira, standing up. "I'm going to get dressed for starters," and she walked out of the room as her mother drifted out behind her.

"I'm going to check on Monty."

"Why don't you go and get dressed and we'll go out for a walk, get some fresh air?"

#

As the morning sun rose slowly into the pale blue sky, December and Lilly walked through the forest wrapped up in their warm winter clothes, gloves, hats and scarves. There was a light dusting of frost on the ground, with the occasional icy patch hidden beneath their feet, causing them to tip toe carefully. Their warm breaths hovered in the air before disintegrating into cold.

"Did you ever read Jules Verne's *Journey to the Centre of Earth* when you were younger?" asked December after she'd been quiet, deep in thought for a while.

Lilly shook her head and looked at her friend questioningly with a smile. "But I've heard of it, obviously. What about it?"

She shrugged her shoulders and pouted her lips before speaking, "I don't know... I just wonder whether there is more to it than meets the eye, you know? Maybe Jules Verne knew more about our world than people know. Perhaps he really did travel down there?"

"Yeah, and maybe Alice really did visit Wonderland and James really did go into the giant peach," laughed Lilly. December stood still and raised her eyebrows, "I would expect you of all people to be a bit more open minded, Lilly."

"I know, I know, I was just messing with you. If you are right, if that book was based on fact, perhaps we should get a copy and read it, then try and get through to Dad. See if anything rings true."

"Good idea. Let's go to the library..."

"Erm, it's a bit early. They're not going to be open for a while."

"Well then, how about a coffee while we wait?"

Lilly nodded and the two turned around, walking out of the tall green trees and back towards Powell River. When they eventually walked into the town, there were few people on the streets as it was so early. Heading towards Starbucks, there was a note on the door saying 'Closed for renovation. Open again soon'. December peered through the window to see if anybody was about, but was greeted by an enormous mess. Broken tables and chairs were scattered all over the floor and the coffee machines were smashed to pieces.

"Oh dear," she sighed, moving aside to let Lilly have a look at the damage. "I guess we left just in time yesterday... those guys must have got really violent." Suddenly a police car sped past them, followed by an ambulance.

The girls ran behind to see what the commotion was and were faced with yet another fight between about five or six of the town's men.

"Oh no... I bet that woman's caused this too. Let's go and speak to the police," said Lilly, pulling her friend along by her arm.

As they approached, four female police officers jumped out of their vehicle and ran into the commotion, eventually placing handcuffs on all of the men who continued to curse and swear at each other, kicking out and spitting like wild animals.

Two female paramedics were soon on hand to tend to the wounded man who lay unconscious on the side of the road. The girls watched in shock as they placed his body on a stretcher before wheeling it into the back of the ambulance, climbing into it themselves and then speeding off towards the hospital.

A small crowd of women was beginning to develop by their side and the girls listened to what was being said.

"My John's gone mad too. Last night he told me he was leaving and he ran off into the night. He didn't even say a word to the kids. I don't know what to do," cried one woman.

"Peter did the same thing. I've no idea where he is..." cried another.

"Evan broke it to me this morning. He told me he was in love with another woman. I can't bear it. What am I going to do?"

"I don't know what we can do, girls. It all seems so weird, don't you think?"

"Is there a full moon at the moment? Some people do strange things when there's a full moon," said a well known elderly lady whose husband had died a few years earlier.

"Break it up," shouted one of the police officers to the men who were still trying hard to get out of their cuffs and head butt each other.

"This is insane," whispered December as Lilly nodded and they crept out of the group, leaving the commotion behind them.

"I think we need to get the Elders down here... I'm not sure Crystal realises how bad things are getting," said Lilly as a half naked man ran through the town whooping and waving with glee.

"Holy Cow", yelled December, "He's gonna get pneumonia. We need to stop him."

"And how do you suggest we do that?"

"Come on," December yelled, runnning off after the poor man, Lilly in tow.

"What do we do?" yelled Lilly breathlessly as they followed him out of town.

"If we can corner him somehow, perhaps I can try a spell," she said quietly as they stopped for a moment to catch their breath.

But suddenly, the man turned from the side of the road right into the centre of it, just as a truck was coming. He didn't even see what hit him.

- Chapter Twenty-six -

They'd been walking for a couple of hours when Zalea collapsed to the ground without a word.

"Zalea!" yelled Jack as he rushed to her side and lifted her head carefully off of the dry sandy surface. "Nick, get some water."

After they'd tried to get her to swallow some water, Zalea stirred but didn't wake.

"What is it? What's wrong with her?" asked Jack while Nick shook his head.

"I've no idea. Perhaps she's over done it. Perhaps she needs to rest?"

"Surely she wouldn't just collapse like this if that was the case? She would have warned us if she wasn't feeling right."

Oprah trundled up to their side and put her head down to the faery's face. Sniffing, she gently licked her cheek and waited for a response. When there wasn't any, she lifted her head upwards and let out an extraordinarily loud long, deep groan.

Jack and Nick both placed their hands over their ears and waited for her to stop.

"What the hell was that?" asked Jack as Nick finally managed to get her to be quiet.

"I don't know, she's never done it before."

"Never? Not in the fifteen years you've had her?"

Nick shook his head in shock.

Turning back to face Zalea who moaned quietly, they watched her open her eyes, "Wh...what happened?" she asked.

Both men shook their heads in disbelief as Oprah once again leaned forward and licked Zalea's cheek.

"Ew... thank you Oprah, I think."

Lifting her up so was she in a seated position, Jack cradled her until she felt strong enough to hold her own weight.

"You just collapsed, and you wouldn't wake up. Well, you wouldn't until Oprah here managed to wake you. How are you feeling?"

"Honestly, I think I feel fine. A little light headed, but otherwise fine."

"Perhaps we should stay here for the rest of the day and let Zalea recuperate?" suggested Nick while he looked around at his surroundings.

"No, I'm fine, really."

"I have to agree with Nick. We should stay put for now." Zalea shrugged her shoulders and nodded, "All right," she conceded.

An hour later, both Zalea and Jack were feeling a little strange.

"I feel quite drowsy," said Jack, swigging water from the container Gwynethea had given him.

"Me too," said Zalea before she collapsed on the ground behind him.

"Oh God... it's happened again," muttered Jack, who felt increasingly weaker before passing out beside her.

Nick rushed over to them while Oprah let out a low groan. His head began to pound and soon he was on his knees beside them. All three had lost consciousness.

Oprah stood over them making loud groaning sounds until she heard movement from up ahead. Flying closer and closer were two of her own kind.

The moment they arrived, they touched down on the ground in front of her and hobbled over to her side. A moment passed between them where they seemed to communicate silently before they hopped from one side to the other and bowed their heads down to one another.

Then Oprah turned to Nick and shoved him eagerly with her nose. When there was no reaction from him, she turned and nodded to her friends.

They each stepped forward, delicately taking the people's legs in their beaks before gently pulling them along the ground away from the spot where they had collapsed. After about 10 minutes, the creatures came to a standstill and carefully put their human and faery friends down. All three creatures began to groan noisily. Halting, they waited to see if they would get a response. When none was forthcoming, Oprah nodded once again and all three placed their beaks by their friends and gently shoved them straight into the flowing waters of the river and waited patiently.

For a moment, the three bodies bobbed carelessly before they began to sink beneath the water. Oprah watched as they slowly disappeared from sight, letting out a low cry that soon became a desperate wail. Her two companions watched on before they turned away from her and ran away, taking to flight and flying off into the distance. Oprah sat waiting, her wails echoing in the valleys beyond.

Chapter Twenty-seven

It seemed like forever that December and Lilly had sat sobbing in Rose's house as both their families fussed around them, doing everything they could to try and make them feel better.

They'd seen vampires rip their enemies to pieces, evil witches cruelly commit murder, people turn into bizarre creatures, but this was the first time they'd witnessed an innocent man obliterated by a speeding truck. And the reason? Simply that he'd been under the strange spell of a woman named Calliope.

"The Elders are on their way, sweetheart, with Carmelo and Jo and the others," said Moira who sat beside her daughter gently stroking her red hair.

Lilly was still in shock, unable to speak while both sat next to each other, holding each other's hands as tears rolled down their cheeks.

Lilly's uncle Wyatt arrived and walked into the kitchen. He was as pale as a sheet.

"His name was Adrian Donovan," he said whilst removing the brown scarf from around his neck before taking off his woollen beige coat, "He wasn't from around here. Apparently he was just visiting some old school friends when... when it happened."

"I can't believe it, I just can't believe it," muttered Lilly.

"I know darling, I know," soothed Rose as she stood holding one of her many cats as it purred loudly in her arms.

Suddenly, December looked up, startled, "I've just realised something!" she said aloud.

"Hm... what's that sweetheart?" said her dead grandmother, who had been hovering around the room carefully avoiding the cats, who began to growl whenever she went near them.

"Wyatt... you're not under her spell. But I thought it was all men. But you're not... you're not, you know, erm, supernatural?" she asked.

"Oh my," said Rose, "she's right, Wyatt. Why aren't you affected? You must have the gene. You must have the raven gene. But you've never been able to change? That's strange."

Wyatt's eyes lit up, "I'm... I'm not sure. The change just never happened for me."

"But this means you've probably got it in you to change, Uncle Wyatt," said Lilly with a sad smile, "When was the last time you tried?"

He shook his head and went from one foot to the other, "Not for a long time. Years, maybe seven or eight."

"I think perhaps it's time you tried again, young man. How wonderful, another Tulugaq family member who can probably change into a raven. Oh how exciting," clapped Ruby.

"Mother, now is not the time for excitement... the girls are mourning here. There is a time and a place, you know," scolded Moira as Ruby immediately dropped her hands to her sides and looked to the ground like a child.

"Wyatt, yes it is very likely you can change but Moira is quite right, now is not the time for this. Perhaps you can concentrate on the raven gene later. Now there are two things we need to focus on. One is this Calliope woman and the other is Jack..."

Just as Rose was speaking, there was a tap on the door before it was pushed open to reveal Carmelo and Jo. They rushed to the girls' side and hugged them both.

"We're so sorry you had to witness something so horrendous. Are you both okay?" she asked, looking into their eyes sorrowfully.

After a few moments, December and Lilly both nodded.

"We will be... but now you're here, can we concentrate on finding out more about this woman?"

140

"I'll put the kettle on," said Rose, stretching her legs before she began filling the kettle with water and putting it on the heat.

"The others are right behind us," said Carmelo just as there was another tap on the door and it was opened to reveal Tabitha and Zoltan.

"Have we missed anything?" asked a panting Tabitha, pushing her hand through her spiky grey hair while Zoltan's face lit up questioningly.

"No, not yet," said Lilly as she hugged them both, "we're waiting for everybody else to arrive first."

"Well then, a nice cup of tea would go down nicely while we wait," said Tabitha with a grin as she watched Rose take a number of cups out of the cupboard. "I'll give you a hand."

#

That evening, when the final group of Elders, witches, vampires and other assorted 'people' had arrived, they all decided to move on to Lilly's house where there was plenty more space. It was also where Tiffani happened to be... a crucial link in tracking down Jack.

"Now we have all come together, we can finally discuss the two problems we are facing: discovering the location of Jack and the Nephilim and this strange woman who is causing havoc in Powell River," said Carmelo as he strode up and down the living room whilst the group watched and listened.

"I think we need to sort this woman out as a matter of urgency," said Moira, "All the men have gone totally crazy and our girls have witnessed such a gruesome event, that she caused."

"Absolutely."

"Yes indeed."

"There's no doubt about it."

"She must be stopped!"

"Do we have any theories?" asked Gabriel, who had made the journey down from the mountains and arrived after everybody else.

"At this moment in time, we have nothing concrete. We have researched back hundreds of years and there has been nothing written down that matches the appearance of this woman... and, of course, the way she has an effect on this townsfolk," said one of the witches.

"Could she be a witch?" asked Sammy.

"We're pretty sure she's not one of us. Of course, we can produce a spellbinding spell to enchant anyone at all, but we would have to be present, close to the men to have such an effect. We know for a fact she was nowhere near these men when they went wild, for want of a better word," said another.

"We have spoken to the witches of the North, South, East and West and none of them know this woman's work. Her picture is not familiar with any of them."

"So if we know she isn't a witch, what else could she be?" asked December.

"How about a Harpie?" piped up Ruby as she floated in and out of all the unusual people that sat and stood around the room.

"Hm... that's a possibility, I suppose," pondered Carmelo.

"What's a Harpie?" asked Lilly.

"Theh were believed to have bin winged spirits who stoole food from Phineas," said the tiny man that was sitting high on a stool brought in from the kitchen.

"Kieran!" exclaimed December, "I didn't see you come in."

The strange little man smirked and nodded to her, "Yer've got lots on yer mind sweet Decembah. Yer too, Lilly. But werry not, we are ere too elp yer," he chuckled to himself.

"Do you think she could be a Harpie, Kieran?" asked Lilly.

142

Sitting quietly for a moment, deep in contemplation, he eventually shook his head quickly from side to side, "Nah, I doon't. Harpies ave wings. Did yer see any wings?"

Lilly, December and Crystal all shook their heads.

"But they could have been hidden from sight," said Walter, taking Rose's hand who was sitting on his lap comfortably.

"No," said a sweet high pitched voice from the back of the room. "Hiding one's wings is not an easy thing to do... and incredibly painful. From what the girls have told me, this woman, Calliope, has no wings. Believe me, I know what that's like," said Tiffani, turning slightly to one side and letting her own wings flutter behind her.

A gentle chuckle flowed throughout the room before Moira spoke, "You do know the meaning of her name don't you?" she asked the group before continuing, "Calliope means beautiful voice... I wonder if it's got something to do with her voice. Is it her voice that is having this effect on the men?"

"It can't be, Mom, because she wasn't even there when we saw the kids in school go insane, and then that poor man in the street. I never saw, or heard her. You didn't either, did you Lilly?"

Lilly shook her head.

"But we shouldn't dismiss this idea though, Moira. It might still be a possibility. What else do we have?" asked Carmelo.

"Could she be a mermaid with human legs?" asked Zoltan. Tabitha gave him an odd look and he shrugged his shoulders, "Just thinkin' out loud," he said.

"No, she would look like Carla," replied Jo.

"Who is Carla?" asked Ruby.

"She's a mermaid who lives part of the time with us in the mountains and part of the time beneath the waters of the Pacific Ocean. On land, she grows legs, in the water, she grows a long tail for swimming."

143

"Oh yes, I remember her," said Lilly who recalled the first time she'd visited the Elders' caves," she had dark sparkly scales all over her skin."

Jo and Carmelo both nodded. "Proving Calliope is not a mermaid," added Jo with a smile.

"How about a Banshee?" asked Sammy.

Almost everybody shook their heads, "Far too beautiful for a Banshee, I'm afraid, Sammy," smiled Carmelo.

"She could be an Encantado," said another voice.

Jo smiled and turned to the source of the question, "That did cross my mind a couple of days ago so I contacted a few of our friends in Brazil and was told, no, it's impossible. The Encantados never leave the Amazon Rainforest, plus, they can only be seen in human form at night."

"But what are they?" asked Moira who had never heard of the word.

"They are beautiful creatures resembling dolphins who come out of the water at night and steal humans. Of course, in human form, they are particularly striking and highly seductive, apparently. But there's no chance Calliope is an Encantado. She's too far from home and she's been seen during the day. It's just impossible. Sorry, keep thinking!"

"I just had a thought... what about a Succubus?" exclaimed Lilly who recalled watching a fictional TV series about them recently.

The room went quiet as everybody gave it some thought.

"They do have the power for mind control and are particularly attractive," said one of the Elders as the others nodded, "You might be on to something there."

"When I was still alive, well, the first time round," said Millicent who had been silent until then, "I met a Succubus and you're absolutely right, she could control the minds of anyone but... she had to physically touch them to do so. And as the girls have said, Calliope was nowhere near these men and students when they went a little mad. So, I'm sorry to disappoint you, but Calliope is not a Succubus."

"Why don't we just go and ask her?" said Zoltan who was, as ever, eager for a fight.

Some of the others laughed out loud and patted him hard on his shoulder.

"Not this time, Zoltan. It's just too dangerous when we don't know what she is. When we don't know what we're dealing with," said Gabriel with another chuckle.

"Ah've got it, Ah've got it," yelled Kieran, the half faery, half elf who, as he jumped up and down on the high stool, lost his balance and fell with a thud to the floor. His miniature Wolf Hound, who had been snoring at the foot of the stool, immediately stood to attention and began licking his face.

"Ger off, Ger off," he shouted to his dog.

As the others rushed to his side and picked him up from the carpeted floor, he rubbed his elbow and his bottom at the same time.

"Ooooh me arse an me elbo..."

December and Lilly shared a secret grin and tried hard not to laugh out loud. No matter how hard they tried, it was always difficult not to laugh when someone fell over.

"Yer can laff, yer can laff... it wer actally a bit funny," he said, joining them to giggle at his unfortunate accident. Soon the entire room was full of laughter as Kieran's giggle was totally contagious. He was soon helped up to a lower, safer seat though, on the sofa next to the two girls. As the laughter died down and everybody wiped the tears from their eyes, bellies aching from laughing so hard, Kieran finally managed to say what he'd thought of.

"Ah shall try agin," he said. "Callupe.... praps she's a Saren?"

"What's a Saren?" asked Ruby.

"I think he means a Siren," corrected Moira.

145

- Chapter Twenty-eight -

Jack's eyes shot wide open after he felt oxygen flood his body. When he realised he was under water, he went rigid with panic. Looking upwards he soon discovered he couldn't tell top from bottom. The feel of a hand on his made him jump and he turned his head to face Dacius. She smiled before placing her mouth on his. She was breathing for him. Again, he felt another flood of oxygen in his lungs. When she pulled away from him, she pointed upwards, showing him the right way to swim to safety. When she released her grip, he nodded slowly, and began to swim away from her. He looked down and watched, repeating the same thing with Zalea who immediately came out of her unconscious state and followed him upwards towards the surface.

As they broke free of the water's hold, both gasped for air while they looked around to find the best place to swim to the edge of the deep river.

But as soon as they pulled themselves out of the water, Jack realised Nick was nowhere to be seen.

"Nick," he gasped and turned to look back down into the dark water but he could see nothing, not even Dacius.

"Are you all right, Jack?" asked Zalea who coughed and spluttered at the side of the river, her wings shaking off the little droplets of water that had accumulated there.

Nodding, he looked at her sadly, "but Nick?"

She shook her head.

There was also no sign of Oprah.

"What happened?" he asked as the two just sat side by side for a moment.

"I honestly don't know, Jack. I don't remember anything."

"Me neither. Are you all right to get up and walk for a while?" he asked her and she nodded.

146

Standing, he pulled her up and looked around. They appeared to have been dragged much further downriver, to somewhere unfamiliar. Their belongings were nowhere to be seen.

"Jeese... I don't believe this. What the hell happened?" he said to himself as Zalea began to sob.

"Don't cry, Zalea. We'll be okay. We'll figure it out. Shhh," he said, holding her hand and patting her shoulder.

Suddenly, the smooth surface of the water broke, bubbling slightly. After a few seconds, the face of a beautiful woman appeared. Dacius.

"Dacius!" yelled Jack, "Thank you for saving us... again. We are so grateful to you. But we have no idea what happened. Can you tell us?" he asked.

The mermaid swam to the edge of the river and pulled herself half out, so she sat on the riverside, her long tail swishing backwards and forwards in the water.

"It was the air you were breathing. It made you unconscious. You would have died had the beasts not dragged you away and pushed you into the water. They were the ones that saved you," she replied seriously.

"But what beasts? We have no memory of any beasts or any strange deadly air," sniffed Zalea.

"You have been travelling with one of them," added Dacius.

"Oprah?" Jack queried.

"The strange beast with the wings... there were two more. They pulled you away and pushed you into the river."

"B...but...where are they now? And where is Nick?" he asked.

"Nick?" asked Dacius, "That is the name of the other human?" while Jack nodded in response.

"Nick... my sister took him but fear not, she will not harm him. He is the one she has been searching for. She is finally happy...." she sang and dropped herself back into the water, swimming beneath the surface before they had a chance to say another word.

"What do we do?" asked Jack.

"There is nothing we can do. Dacius said her sister would not harm him. We must accept that and hope he'll be all right. And us? We must continue our journey without him. I hope Oprah is all right. She must have gone with her own kind," she said, turning away and beginning to walk some distance from the river.

"I'm sorry, Nick," whispered Jack as he too turned and walked beside her, continuing their journey towards the mountains to the Nephilim.

- Chapter Twenty-nine -

The following morning school had been cancelled.
December, Crystal and Millicent all sat on the bed in
Lilly's bedroom while Lilly hunched over the computer at
her desk, "It says that in Greek mythology, a Siren was
'one of a group of sea nymphs who by their sweet singing
lured mariners to destruction on the rocks surrounding
their island'. Or simply put, it says a Siren is a 'woman
regarded as seductive and beautiful'," she said, turning to
face them.

"It sounds about right... although Calliope isn't quite
dragging the men to their deaths on the rocks," said
December.

"No, but she's certainly luring them away from their
lives... some of them to their deaths," she replied, almost
choking on the final word.

"Oliver and Ben are okay... at least we know that much,"
said Crystal who had managed to briefly speak to Ben on
the phone, just to make sure they were still alive and well.

"For now anyway," added Millicent. "If she's a Siren,
goodness only knows what she's planning for them all."

"Well, Gabriel and Carmelo have told us not to worry.
That's why they're all here; to sort out the problem."

"I can't stand this. I feel like I need to do something. I'm
just so, so helpless. Not only with Calliope but my dad
too. It just feels like it's been dragging on for so long, you
know?"

The girls looked at each other sadly and nodded.

"We know honey. We'll get to the bottom of it soon
enough," said Crystal as she stood up and pushed her
hand through her short blonde hair. Walking over to the
mirror, she pulled out a lip gloss and deftly brushed a
little on to her full lips just as a prism of light glinted
across her dark skin in the sunlight.

"This is pretty," she said, looking at the little crystal angels hanging either side of her window.

"They were a gift from Oliver when I first arrived here," she said, gulping back her tears.

"Oh, I'm sorry. We can't seem to say anything right... but I know how you feel, Lilly. She's got Ben too."

"This is crazy, we are a house full of amazing and strong supernatural creatures. Surely we can sort out one stupid Siren," said December who suddenly stood up and stretched her arms and legs. "I say we go back and see if we can figure out just how powerful (or not) this Calliope really is."

All standing, the girls grabbed their coats and went to open the door.

"Wait," said Lilly, "the others aren't going to just let us go over there."

"They're not going to know, are they?" said Crystal with a glint in her eye.

"Some of them are vampires, they've got super human hearing. They probably heard everything we just said."

But Crystal shook her head, "They went out earlier when you were still asleep. They have no idea."

Giggling, the girls opened the door and walked right out of the house, stopping to tell only Sammy and Tiffani they were just going for a walk.

"Not so fast girls," said a voice by the front door.

They turned to find Zoltan and Tabitha smiling at them.

"We know you too well... and we know when something's going on. Come on, out with it," he growled with a cheeky grin.

"Okay, if you must know, we're going to check Calliope out. Find out how strong she really is," said Lilly matter of factly.

"Awesome... action at last!" he said as Tabitha grinned and they followed the girls out into the driveway.

"Come on, we can all squeeze into my car," Tabitha said as she unlocked her battered old red Chevy and they all climbed in.

"I'll drive," exclaimed Zoltan as his girlfriend headed towards the driver's door.

"Oh come on...you always drive."

"You expect me to get into this car full of girls and be driven by another one," he laughed shaking his head, "Give me the keys, Tab. I'm drivin'."

Tabitha threw her head back in laughter, "God, you are so predictable," as she tossed him her keys.

"And you love me for it," he added, catching the keys with one hand as they climbed in.

"Action... here we come," he growled as he put his foot on the accelerator and wheel spun out of the driveway. Driving through Powell River, it seemed like a ghost town. There were 'closed' signs across shops, cafés and even the large supermarket where most people did they grocery shopping.

"So this is what happens when all the men disappear, is it?" asked Crystal quietly.

"It's insane, it's almost like the world couldn't go on without man," added Millicent.

"Rubbish, absolute rubbish," said Tabitha, "of course we could survive without men. The women in town are just dealing with shock, that's all. The men have just suddenly upped and left. All they need is a bit of time to come to terms with what's happened and it'll be business as usual."

Zoltan laughed, "You're saying you wouldn't be bothered if Calliope had an effect on me too?"

"That's not what I said... but I could cope, of course I could. I'm a strong, independent woman."

"Yeah, sure you are babe," he laughed.

"What on earth is that?" asked Lilly as they drove over the brow of the hill and saw what used to be Ben's Veterinary Practice in the distance.

151

"Oh. My. God," said Tabitha, "What the heck has she done to it?"

As they approached, Zoltan pulled the car over to the side of the road and they all climbed out, mouths wide open in disbelief at what they saw before them.

The simple square brick building was no longer there. In its place stood a massive orange pyramid-like structure that spread over hundreds of square metres. On its pinnacle sat a large golden eagle. Not a real one, but one sculpted literally out of gold, glittering in the sunlight.

"I can't believe Ben would have agreed to this... it's just so....so....." uttered Crystal.

"Flashy?" suggested December and Crystal nodded, her eyebrows almost stuck together as she shook her head.

"It's like something out of an alien movie or something. It's insane. Totally insane," whispered Tabitha.

The group stood staring at the huge structure that was surrounded by hundreds of cars. Cars that hadn't been parked as such, just left where they'd stopped. Fortunately the clinic was located at the end of a lane. Had it been on a main road, the cars would've completely blocked it up.

"Come on, let's get closer," said Zoltan, turning and taking Tabitha's hand in his. The others followed behind.

As they approached, the soothing sounds of gentle singing could be heard.

"What is that?" asked Millicent.

"Someone's singing, I think," answered Lilly, "But it's not like any singing I've ever heard."

As they stood at the back of the building, December put her hand on the structure to feel what it was made of.

"What is it?" asked Tabitha.

"I don't know, but it's warm. Feel," she replied.

All six put their hands on the building, "It's almost like it's heated. Weird," said Lilly, "Let's creep around to the front."

As they rounded the pyramid's edge, all six of them gasped and quickly stepped backwards.

"Did you see that?" asked December.

"How could we not?" replied Lilly, "Oh God... this is crazy. Who is she and WHAT is she doing to our men?"

- Chapter Thirty -

Their journey so far had taken place over relatively flat
terrain, an open valley allowing them to continue on foot
in safety. However, as Zalea and Jack turned the long
winding bend in the river, the flat sandy earth beneath
their feet began to change as they faced a multitude of
jutting rocks coming at them from every angle.

The two stood staring in silence at what lay ahead.

"It is impossible to pass," whispered Zalea, gripping
Jack's hand tightly.

"You're right," he said looking around. "But there is one
way through," he said, pointing to the river beside them.
"We shall have to travel by water."

"But we cannot swim for such a length of time. We'll
drown."

Jack shook his head and released his grip on her hand,
"We can build a raft," he said turning back from where
they had come. "We passed some trees a little earlier and
these reeds will do to bind them together."

Zalea shrugged her shoulders helplessly, "I guess it's our
only option."

Several hours later, Jack stood wiping the sweat from his
brow, "I'm so glad I kept this dagger tied to my
trousers," he said as he held Gwynethea's sharp
bejewelled dagger out in front of him, a number of long
pieces of wood laying out before them. "It would have
taken twice as long to cut these trees down without it," he
smiled.

Zalea sat to his side, stripping the reeds apart and
producing long strong pieces that would act perfectly to
tie their makeshift raft together.

"We shall sleep here tonight and then set off when we wake in the morning," he said, finally sitting beside her to take a long well deserved break.

"You have worked hard today, Jack. I just wish I could serve you something delicious to nourish you," said Zalea. Smiling back at her, he shook his head. "We'll be fine, Zalea. We'll find food tomorrow. But for now, let's get some rest. Here, lie beside me, I'll keep you warm."

Neither of them slept particularly well that night. Without the soft cotton blanket that had been stowed in their lost belongings, they shivered as they curled up together beneath the dark night sky.

As the day approached and the sky lightened before their very eyes, they prepared to set off through the dangerous deluge of rocky outcrops all around them.

Travelling on the water was their only safe passage through.

Once the raft was strong and bound tightly enough to take their weight, the duo climbed aboard as Jack pushed them away from the river's edge towards the centre. Their makeshift paddles enabled them both to push themselves through the gently flowing water as they watched the unusual shapes carved into the precarious rocks around them.

"Nick would have enjoyed this," said Jack quietly. "He would have been in his element making a raft like this."

"Yes, but I do believe his would have been a bit more impressive," laughed Zalea.

Feigning hurt, Jack laughed and nodded.

"Hopefully this will take us to the Nephilim quicker than on foot, perhaps we should have thought of it sooner."

"I'm not sure I would have been comfortable before. I would have been frightened of Dacius and her troublesome sister," replied Zalea, looking down into the murky depths below. "At least now we know she has what she wanted all along."

"Hm," replied Jack, "I hope he's okay."

After a few hours of paddling through the water, Zalea suddenly pointed to something tall in the distance. "It's a Meliam tree. It bears the most delicious and nourishing fruit. If we can get over there and climb up those rocks, they would keep us fed for days," she exclaimed.

They continued in a straight line for a hundred metres or so, before they paddled to the riverside. Jack climbed off the raft first and held out his hand to help Zalea ease herself onto dry land.

Using a spare piece of the reed rope, he tied the raft securely around a long spiky rock that stuck out of the ground.

"We just need to climb up there," Zalea said, pointing to a rather dangerous collection of jagged rocks.

"Easier said than done," answered Jack as they tried to work out their best way upwards, "Wait a minute, Zalea. Can't you fly?"

She looked at him strangely before erupting into a fit of giggles, "Fly?" she said. "What makes you think I can fly?"

Looking a little embarrassed, he pointed to her wings.

"Oh," she chuckled and shook her head. "Only the Menukian faeries can fly, Jack," she said matter of factly.

"Then why have wings?" he asked sheepishly.

"Thousands and thousands of years ago, my ancestors were able to fly. Their wings were three times the size of mine but over the years the wings of my people have gotten smaller and smaller. We believe nature intends us to eventually have no wings at all."

"Evolution," he replied.

"I'm sorry?"

"It's an evolutionary process. Like me... my ancestors are believed to have looked more like apes..."

156

Zalea's eyes appeared wide and a look of complete confusion clouded them.

Jack laughed and shook his head, "Never mind, let's focus on the task in hand.... climbing up to that ridge."

Neither had much experience in climbing. Nick had made it look so easy but they just weren't getting anywhere. And the more they tried, the hungrier they became.

"Let's take a break and have a drink," suggested Jack as he bent over with his hands on his knees trying to catch his breath.

"I'm sorry, Jack, I'm sorry that I can't fly."

He shook his head and smiled at her, "I should be saying the same thing. After all, many of my ancestors were able to fly too... and some of my current family members. I wish I shared the gene to change. Imagine if I could become a raven, I could have just flown straight to those mountains."

"No, you couldn't have," scolded Zalea. "Then I wouldn't have been able to join you."

"I know, I wouldn't have left you behind. But if I could change, I could at least fly up there and knock some of that fruit down."

"Are you absolutely sure you don't have the gene, Jack?"

"I'm pretty sure. If the transformation doesn't happen by the time you're twenty then it usually means it's not going to."

"But did you ever try?"

He raised his eyebrows and squinted his eyes for a moment. "Honestly, I don't think I did after I turned twenty. I didn't feel the need to go off cavorting as a raven. I was so happy with my family life, that nothing else mattered," he said.

"So there could still be a chance?" she exclaimed but he shook his head.

"No, if there was ever a time I could have changed then I would have done so whilst I was being kept prisoner by Vivian."

Zalea stood in front of him and smiled, "But Jack, you were under her spell. She would have prevented you from doing any kind of magic."

"Possibly, but how about while I was with the Nephilim?"

Again she smiled, "Your memories were taken from you whilst you were there. You wouldn't have even known you were from a family of ravens, Jack. Don't you see? If you are ever going to find out if you can change, it's now. When you're desperate and hungry and... free from any evil preventing you."

Jack's shoulders dropped backwards, making him stand up straight, he lifted his head and smiled, "You're very good at this, Zalea. You're making me want to give it a go."

"Then do it, Jack, try to make the change. If it doesn't happen now, then at least you can rest assured it never will. At least try... just look up there at that juicy fruit."

He peered upwards and his mouth began to water.

Closing his eyes, he began to concentrate, thinking of nothing but his family and his raven ancestors.

- Chapter Thirty-one -

The small group had returned to Tabitha's car where they'd all climbed in, not saying a word. Zoltan quietly put the key into the ignition, had started the engine and reversed the car away from the pyramid before turning back towards Powell River.

As they arrived back at the house, Carmelo and Jo stood waiting their arrival home.

"Well?" Jo asked, "What happened?"

"Wh...what do you mean? We just went for a drive," said Tabitha as everyone stood, shoulders slumped forward.

"It's quite all right, you know. We are fully aware you went to Ben's. Presumably nothing happened or you wouldn't be back so soon," said Carmelo, patting Lilly on the back.

Nobody said anything.

"Crystal?"

The beautiful young woman brushed her hand through her hair and looked up at her friend before bursting into tears.

"There, there," he said, "Come, let's all go inside and you can tell us what you saw."

It didn't take long for the group to explain what they'd witnessed, much to the shock of the rest of them.

"It was a pyramid... like a real pyramid..." said Lilly before December continued, "and it was warm, when we touched it, it was warm."

"And...?" said Jo.

"All the men were there," added Zoltan. "And I mean, ALL of them. There were hundreds of cars just parked there, left in the middle of the road, doors open and then, when we walked around the corner..."

December coughed, making everyone jump, "...and we saw the men, all of them."

159

"Well spit it out, we're dying to know what's going on. Come on, do tell," said Ruby who was leaning in with her eyes open wide.

December continued, "They were all, you know, erm, like," she chuckled awkwardly, "erm... semi-naked."

"Did you say semi-naked?" said Ruby with a sly grin as the group all nodded at exactly the same time.

"So who's going back?" she said, "Whoever it is, I'm coming with you!" she laughed but nobody laughed with her. "Well then, perhaps I'll go alone..." she said, hovering away out of the room.

"Mother!" said Moira through gritted teeth as her ghost re-appeared, half out of the living room.

"What?"

"Oh... just go."

Again, Ruby smiled and was gone.

"What else did you see?" asked Gabriel.

"It was like something out of a film," said Lilly awkwardly.

"What do you mean, dear?" asked Rose.

"Erm, the few clothes they were wearing were kind of like, erm, like something from Egypt, like from Cleopatra," she said with an uncomfortable chuckle.

"This is so bizarre," said Millicent.

"Bazar... yeh, Millie, yer right there. Is this common wiv them Sarens?" asked Kieran.

"Unfortunately we don't know much about the Sirens, Kieran," answered Jo. "We're trying to track down a Siren expert at the moment but we're not having much luck."

"Which is why we decided not to approach Calliope until we know more. After all, we don't know how dangerous she really is," said Carmelo with his eyebrows raised, looking across at the group that had gone out that morning.

"Perhaps we could have....ouch....ow....oh......" said December, falling forwards onto the thick rug in the centre of the room, almost knocking her head on the coffee table.

Everyone rushed forward to help her as she held her head in her hands.

"It must be Jack," announced Millicent, "He must be trying to get through."

Carmelo took the young witch in his arms as everyone sitting on the sofa stood up to allow her to be gently placed there.

Moira held one hand, Millicent held the other and Lilly hurried to the kitchen to dampen a cloth for her forehead.

When she returned, the room was silent except for Millicent's soothing voice, calming her and helping her to get through to Jack.

After five minutes, it was clear he wasn't attempting to get through at all.

"I don't understand," said Moira, "I thought the headaches were purely to do with the communication?"

Millicent nodded, "They are," she whispered, her own brows knitted together in confusion. "Keep trying, December. He must be trying to get through."

As December winced and moaned at the pain, another person fell to the ground holding his head.

"Wyatt!" yelped his wife, Sonya.

"My goodness, what on earth is going on?" said Rose as Gabriel was the next to fall, "Gabriel!" she yelled.

And then, both Meredith and Lilly succumbed to the excruciating pain.

People rallied around them all, placing dampened cloths on all of their foreheads.

"What's the connection, Carmelo?" asked Millicent, "What connects all these people together?"

"It's Jack. He's Lilly's father, Gabriel's son, Meredith and Wyatt's brother. Jack is the connection. Could he be trying to communicate with them all?"

161

Millicent nodded, "It is possible, of course, but I think there's something else."

"Awww," yelled Wyatt all of a sudden as he fell off the chair and onto his knees. Everyone looked on in horror as his eyes began to darken and shrink in size right before them.

"Oh My God," said Jo, "It's not what you think it is...he's changing. Dad, you're changing. It's the raven gene."

"B...but how do you know?" asked Millicent in surprise.

"I have the gene, I've been changing for well over a year now. That's it, they're all changing," she said gleefully clapping her hands together.

And soon enough, Gabriel, Lilly, Wyatt and Meredith all sat in the living room looking around at their surroundings from a completely different perspective. They were no longer human, they were stunning large black ravens.

December was still wincing from the pain as she turned to look at the strange occurrence.

"Lilly?" she croaked as one of the ravens hopped up from the floor onto the sofa and sat beside December.

"Lilly? Is that you? she asked as the bird nodded its head. One after the other, people spoke to the family of ravens, identifying each one. Soon the room applauded and excited laughter broke out.

"I..I..I don't believe it, I j..j...just can't believe it," stuttered Sonya as Wyatt fluttered to her side and turned his head from one side to the other. He opened his beak and out came a loud squawk. She and Wyatt both jumped before he tried again, letting out a soft coo as she gently stroked his feathers.

"Mom?" asked Cormac, the astonished teenager who had always believed he had a normal mother just like everyone else.

162

Meredith gently tugged at his fingers with her beak as Rose approached the last bird who remained alone in the centre of the room.

"I always knew you could do it, Gabriel," she teased as he began to squawk uncontrollably and dance around the room happily.

The laughter soon died down as December continued to suffer aloud.

"Shhh, I'm sorry everyone, I know this is a very exciting time for you all, but December is still in a lot of pain and I know quiet really does help somewhat," said Millicent as Moira looked at her gratefully.

The room quietened down until her groaning became less and less and, eventually, she fell asleep.

"I'll carry her into Lilly's room," whispered Carmelo, bending down and scooping her up into his arms, carrying her as if she was as light as a feather. He placed her gently on Lilly's bed as Moira and Millicent sat down by her side.

"Thank you, Carmelo. We'll stay with her."

He nodded and quietly closed the door behind him.

- Chapter Thirty-two -

A long low groan escaped Jack's lips as a massive headache seemed to erupt deep within his head. It felt different this time.

He fell to the floor, holding his head in his hands as Zalea watched on helplessly. Turning her back on him, she rushed to the riverside and scooped up a little water in the wooden cup he had carved the day before. While she was looking away, Jack quickly removed his trousers, vaguely remembering something his father used to say about clothes getting destroyed in the change.

When Zalea turned back to him, she wasn't prepared for what she saw.

His large brown eyes turned darker and shrank while his slim legs became skinny and stick-like. His arms disappeared altogether and he howled uncontrollably. Zalea dropped the cup and ran to his side.

"What can I do, Jack? What can I do? I feel so helpless." she cried, tears falling down her cheeks, "I'm so sorry. I made you do this and now look at you, you're in so much pain..." she sobbed as his transformation continued, his cries of pain soon turning to the strange squawkings of a large black raven while he stood proud and pulled back his wings to reveal a beautiful set of black feathers.

"Are you all right?" she whispered and waited for some kind of response.

When he nodded, she let out a sigh of relief and wiped the tears from her eyes.

"Are you sure?" she asked and again he gave her an exaggerated nod before he turned to face the precarious cliff face that had given them so much grief.

With his wings outstretched, he began to move them up and down until he found himself lifting from the ground. If he could've shouted with glee, he would have.

164

Getting higher and higher into the air, he found himself swooping around, enjoying the freedom of flying. Flying, he was actually flying!

Eventually, when he stopped playing around, he glanced down to see Zalea jumping up and down, laughing and clapping her hands together.

He landed on the precipice facing the awkwardly positioned Meliam tree and flew up to the first oblong shaped brown fruit he could see, perching himself down beside it. He began pecking on the small branch that held it firmly until it began to loosen and the fruit fell to the ground.

He then swooped back down and began to roll it until it was on the edge. He peered over and made a loud squawk to let Zalea know it was coming down and then he pushed it as hard as possible.

Zalea stood to one side and let it crash to the ground, the fruit opening on impact to reveal several golden nuggets. She let out a loud, "Yes!" before picking it up and gently taking out one of the nuggets and putting it into her mouth. She savoured the flavour before slowly chewing it and swallowing it with a loud gulp, followed by a sigh of contentment.

Suddenly there was another loud squawk from above and so she moved away from the rocks and let Jack push eight more of the brown oblong shaped fruit to the ground.

As the last one fell, he threw himself off of the precipice and soared down to the bottom to stand beside her.

Now all he had to do was transform back into human form. But having never done it before, he had no idea how to.

"Okay, you can change back now, Jack," said Zalea smiling at him.

But when he did nothing but stand there, she began to worry. "You can change back, can't you?"

Jack didn't know how to respond so again he did nothing.

"Do you know how?" she whispered.

And that's when he shook his head from side to side.

"Oh no..." she sighed. "This is all my fault," she repeated again and again, bending her knees and flopping down beside him.

But Jack began hopping up and down shaking his head vigorously.

"I really don't know what to suggest, Jack..."

A loud slurping noise interrupted them and they both turned to face the water just as Dacius appeared, pulling herself onto the riverbank.

"Dacius!" exclaimed Zalea.

The mermaid smiled, "I see you have a problem. Perhaps I can help?"

Jack and Zalea turned to face each other and he nodded, hopping over to her side.

"I suggest you throw yourself into the water. The shock should turn you back into your usual form," she suggested.

"No!" yelled Zalea, bending down and picking up the raven, closely holding him in her arms, "It's too dangerous. He might drown."

"He will not drown. I will not let him."

Zalea looked down at her companion and he nodded his head. She turned from Dacius and took a few steps away from her, "But what if she takes you away like her sister did with Nick. I'm not sure I trust her, Jack. I... I'm frightened."

"Please don't be frightened of me," said a gentle voice from the water's edge, "I know my sister may have harmed you and she took away your friend but I am nothing like my sister. I would never try and harm you. I promise you that... you can trust me."

Jack nodded again and Zalea let him go. Holding her breath, she watched as the black raven flew higher into

166

the sky and then turned to dive bomb himself into the cool water of the river.

Crashing through the surface, Zalea rushed to the edge and watched him go deeper and deeper until she could no longer see him. Turning to look at Dacius, tears began to fall from her eyes.

"Please help him... please help him...."

Dacius smiled and pushed herself after him.

All Zalea could do was wait.

But the waiting didn't last long, soon the water began to bubble and before long, both Jack and Dacius burst through the surface. His face glowed with excitement as he swam to the shore and jumped out, rushing over to Zalea and picking her up before twirling her around with laughter. When he realised he was naked, he blushed and quickly located his clothes, getting dressed as fast as possible as Zalea turned away laughing.

"I can do it, Zalea, I can do it..." he exclaimed once he was fully dressed.

Dacius watched them and smiled before very quietly disappearing beneath the water and swimming away.

~ Chapter Thirty-three ~

The phone rang just as the Tulugaq family were returning to normal. Gabriel and Wyatt in Sammy's room and Lilly and Meredith in Tiffani's room.

They were helped by the Elders who gently coaxed them out of their transformations. It was easy for Lilly because she had been a changeling for some time. Although the sensations were quite different, the underlying transformation was the same. She was changing from animal to human.

Meredith struggled. Having only recently lost her husband, her transformation from raven to human wasn't quite so easy. It required intense concentration and relaxation... and she hadn't been able to relax for weeks. The mourning process prevented it from happening.

Moira was called in to assist. With her abilities as a witch and her gentle persuasive voice, the Elders knew she would be able to help.

"Hi Meredith," she whispered as she opened the door to the bedroom.

Lilly sat on the bed in a dressing gown, helplessly looking on as her aunt struggled with the change, pacing up and down on the carpeted floor, her claws occasionally catching on the woolly pile.

When she saw Moira, she hopped up onto the bed and squawked loudly.

"I'm guessing you're yelling 'help'?" she asked and the bird nodded in response.

"I know how difficult you're finding it to relax, Meredith, but you must know it is the most important aspect of changing back."

Again she nodded.

"So I think we'll try a gentle spell to help you completely relax. Is that okay with you?" she asked and Meredith nodded.

"I'll leave you both, then," said Lilly, standing up to walk out of the room, "You can do it, Meredith. Don't worry... good luck," she said as she closed the door behind her and headed to her own room where December was just waking up.

"Is she okay, Millicent?"

"I'm f...fine..." mumbled December from beneath the blanket. "What happened?" she asked, pushing it down and slowly sitting up.

"Don't you remember?" asked Millicent as December shook her head.

"Oh dear... that's not good. You have to remember these things, December. If you ever have these awful headaches, you must try and remain alert, relaxed, but fully alert."

December nodded while they told her all about the amazing transformations that had taken place that morning.

"You're a....you're a....." she stuttered and Lilly laughed and nodded, "Yeah, I know, a Raven Mountain Lion Human! Insane huh?!" she giggled.

"WOW... that is unbelievable and you caused it!"

"Me? I really don't think so. Considering the headaches, it must have been Jack who was responsible for it all," she said trying to recall if she had spoken to him but there was nothing but the pain.

"Maybe I ought to try and get through to him now it's over and make sure he's okay?" she asked, looking across at Millicent who stood looking out of the window at the forests beyond.

"Millicent?" she asked again.

"Hm? she said, turning around, "Oh, sorry, yes that's a good idea. Are you feeling strong enough?"

December nodded.

"Okay then, lie back down and I'll just go and see if Moira can join us," said Millicent who opened the door and walked out, closing it behind her.

"Are you really okay, December?" asked Lilly, bouncing on the bed and laying down next to her.

"I feel fine now but I do have this feeling we need to try and speak to your dad."

"Well I'm not going to argue with that... I hope he's okay."

The door opened and Millicent waltzed back, letting it shut behind her.

"Where's Mom?"

"She's coming, she's just having a chat with Meredith," she replied, sitting down on the wooden chair next to the bed.

"So Meredith managed to change back then?" asked Lilly while Millicent smiled back and nodded, "Yes, she's fine, just a little emotional that's all. Don't worry, her change will help her mourning process. Meredith is going to be just fine."

"Jack, are you there?" December whispered half an hour later with her eyes closed.

Waiting for a response, there was silence in the room.

"Jack, it's me December. I'm here with Lilly. Can you hear me?"

After a few more minutes of December wincing at the pain she was inflicting on herself, her face lit up.

"Yes!" she exclaimed, "You too? No no, it's just that it happened to a few others too. Hm?" December chuckled before continuing, "Lilly, Gabriel, Wyatt and Meredith. Yes, all of them changed. No, no, they're fine. And you? That's great. Oh, I'm so sorry to hear that. Yes, we're still working on it. There's just another problem here in Powell River that we need to sort out as well. Okay, we'll

talk again soon then. Yes, I'll tell her. She's sending you her love too. Bye Jack, bye."
Soon afterwards she opened her eyes and smiled at her friend. "He sends you all his love."
"What else did he say?" asked Millicent and Moira.
"Sadly, something happened to his friend, Nickolaus, and he's disappeared but more importantly, he changed, Lilly," she squealed, "Your dad changed into a raven too!"
Lilly jumped off the bed and began hopping up and down, shouting. "Oh, I need to go tell the others!" she said, walking out of the room while they climbed off the bed and followed behind.

#

"I understand you've been trying to reach our kind," said the mesmerising silky voice on the other end of the phone.
"Erm... I'm sorry? asked Jo.
"The Sirens," the voice whispered.
"Oh, erm, hang on..... Carmelo, the Sirens," she mouthed, handing him the phone.
"Hello, this is Carmelo, head of the Elders. Thank you for getting in touch. You are quite difficult to reach."
"We can only be reached if we so desire," replied the captivating voice. "We understand you have some...questions for us?"
Carmelo nodded, turned and sat on the chair that was positioned by the telephone stand.
"Yes, we would like to know more about the Sirens."
"And why would you like to more... Carmelo?" she breathed.
"Because we have an unidentified woman in our neighbourhood that we believe might be one."
"Oh, I see. If you can describe this woman, I can tell you whether or not she is one of us. We do keep track of them all. For our own security, I might add."

171

"Yes, yes of course, of course. This woman is really quite beautiful..."

"We are all very beautiful, Carmelo. Perhaps you should pay us a visit one day."

If it were possible for Carmelo to blush, he would have done. "I doubt my fiancé would be too happy about that," he laughed nervously as Jo looked up with raised eyebrows. "This woman is called Calliope and the mere mention of her name has the most bizarre effect upon the men in our community."

"Yet she has no influence upon you, I hear."

"No... it seems her effects do not stretch to the paranormal community."

"Aah, I see. Well I can tell you now that this woman, Calliope, is not one of us. We have no Siren that goes by the name of Calliope."

"But, could she be from another country, perhaps?"

"No, Carmelo. I am familiar with all of the sirens, worldwide. Plus... our kind could quite easily captivate even the paranormal community should we so desire," she breathed. "All it would take is for me to sing you a song, Carmelo, and you would be putty in my hands," she laughed softly.

"Erm, right then. Thank you... oh, I didn't get your name?" he asked.

"That's because I didn't give it to you... but I will just in case you ever want to... contact... me again. My name is Leilah. Goodbye Carmelo."

"Thank you, Leilah and if y....." but before he could continue, she was gone.

- Chapter Thirty-four -

After he had been reached by December, he could not get rid of the grin that spread across his face. The transformation had not only happened to him, but it had finally happened to the rest of his family too. It was a miracle, one which made the bond between them even stronger. He wished so badly he would be able to get home and soon.

Because of his eagerness to find their way back, he and Zalea had climbed back on to the raft soon afterwards with a renewed vigour to accomplish their journey. They took all of the delicious fruit from the Meliam tree with them.

Juice dripped down their chins as they pushed themselves through the water while they chatted, laughed and sang until they were too tired to continue.

That night they fell asleep effortlessly. The warm atmosphere enveloped them as they dreamed of their families, safe and well as they curled around each other, not for warmth this time, but for comfort.

They were woken by a huge explosion, a sound that shook the very ground beneath them.

"What was that?" shrieked Zalea, clinging to her companion.

"I don't know," Jack replied, jumping up and scouring the surrounding area.

"What's that smell?" she asked and he shook his head for the second time, "It smells like, like... burning. Something is really hot."

"It's beneath us, Jack. The ground is getting warmer." Sure enough, the ground was heating up and fast.

"Quick, get on the raft," he instructed as they both ran, hopping aboard before he undid the rope and pushed them away from dry land. There was a sudden eruption right where they had been sleeping and glowing lava began to pour out of the crack in the earth.

"Our oars...we left our oars behind," whispered Zalea as she watched them be devoured by the moulting liquid in a matter of seconds. "Will we be safe in the water, Jack?"

"I hope so," he leaned forward and tentatively dipped his fingers into what had been cool water just the day before. "It's warm, but not too hot. Hopefully, it won't heat up any further."

The two sat crossed legged staring out at the oozing lava as it covered the land beside them.

"We could try and get to the opposite riverbank," said Jack, but as he spoke, a gentle rumbling could be heard before another eruption occurred on the other side.

"I guess we'll just have to stay here and let the current take us. At least it's taking us in the right direction."

#

Several hours had past and the lava continued to pour from beneath the ground, flowing in the same direction as the river. Jack and Zalea lay on the raft carefully watching their surroundings, occasionally dipping their fingers or toes into the water to check the temperature which had risen a little since they'd first set off.

But as the water took them towards their destination, around a bend in the river, they were greeted by an altogether different scenario. The sound of falling water filled their ears. Sitting up quickly, both their heads turned towards it together.

"On no," said Jack, "It's a waterfall."

"But I don't see one."

"That's because we're about to fall in it."

They had two choices: face the waterfall head on or try and get to the riverside and risk their lives in the hot lava. There was no contest, they would have to hold on to the raft as hard as they could and go with the falling water.

Terrified, they sat for a few minutes while they drifted calmly along. When it began to get a little choppy, Jack pulled Zalea towards him. "Lie down," he said before he gently laid himself over her and gripped the sides of the raft.

"Jack, save yourself. You can fly... please...."

He smiled at her and shook his head. As they approached the falls, all other sounds were drowned out by the enormity of the falling water. It was deafening.

"Take a deep breath and hold on!" shouted Jack as they bobbed around on top of the water before they plummeted with the falling water below.

~ Chapter Thirty-five ~

"So we're back to square one again?" asked Lilly, pacing up and down the living room while many of the others were out checking out the pyramid.

She missed Oliver. God only knew what he was going through. Although, she thought, he's clearly enjoying himself, she seethed. Well, I'm not, she told herself. "What do we do now?"

"We wait for everybody to get back and see what they've found out," reassured Meredith who was looking decidedly more bright eyed.

"Meredith's right, Lilly. You need to chill out," added December, handing her a cup of tea.

"How can I chill out when that... that... woman has got my boyfriend dressed like some kind of Egyptian slave in the middle of February and goodness knows what she's doing to him. And every other man in Powell River for that matter," she screeched, almost spilling her tea all over the carpet.

"Lilly dear. We understand you're suffering but there are others who are suffering too," said Rose as she eyed Crystal who was sitting silently in the corner of the room, wrapped in a blanket with her fingers holding a hot drink.

"I know. I'm sorry. I just wish we could do something."

"I know dear."

When she heard the front door open, Lilly jumped up from her chair so fast that she banged her knee on the coffee, "Ouch!" she exclaimed before she hobbled out to see who had arrived.

"Chris! What are you doing here?"

Chris smiled and hugged her, stepping aside to reveal he was not alone. Someone slightly smaller stood closely behind him covered in a long cape that culminated in a long hood, completely hiding the person's identity.

176

When the front door was closed, the person turned and removed the hood from her face.

"Jemima!" Lilly screeched, "What the... what are you doing here? You can't *be* here. What if someone sees you? What if your parents see you? Chris, you're crazy for bringing her down here. Do you know what could happen if....."

"Lilly, will you please calm down," said a voice from the living room as December appeared in the doorway.

"Hi Chris," she said, pecking him on the cheek before turning to Jemima to give her a hug.

"It's good to see you but Lilly is right, you know."

Taking the long cape from her back and hanging it up on the clothes horse by the door, she smiled, "I know. But I needed to come down and do something. My family is in danger and I couldn't just sit back and do nothing."

"I understand and so does Lilly," said December with a roll of her eyes towards her friend, "She's just a bit on edge because Oliver is, you know, under Calliope's spell."

"Yes, we've heard all about it. We know she's got all the men over there. Do we know anything more yet?"

Lilly shook her head as they followed her into the living room where everyone stood to say their hellos.

"Unfortunately we've got nowhere."

"That's not entirely true," said Crystal, finally, "at least we now know what this woman isn't."

"So she's not a Siren then?" asked Chris and Crystal shook her head. "So where is everyone?"

"They've gone down to have a look for themselves, see if they can work it out. Understand who she is. I just wish we could stop her before someone else dies," answered Lilly.

#

Carmelo and his group approached the structure the same way Lilly and her friends had done earlier.

"Wow... it certainly is impressive," said Jo with a whistle. "How do you think she managed to get this built in so little time?" she asked.

"Well, with all those men as labourers..."

"Yes, but Carmelo... that would take weeks, months even."

"She's some kind of paranormal being, Jo. You should know by now that we can get things done amazingly quick with brute force or with magic. Either way, she's got her own pyramid on the edge of Powell River. Quite a feat? Yes, but impossible? No."

Jo smiled fondly at her fiancé before they moved at lightning speed to the pyramid's edge to get a closer view. Three sides of the structure were solid and closed to the elements but the fourth side, the one facing away from the road, was completely open, revealing the full extent of the pyramid's interior.

It had two floors, all open plan and the top floor was empty of items, but full of men sleeping on the floor. On the lower level there was a huge number of scantily clad men all bustling around as if in a daze. Far to the back of the room were four wide steps, on top of which sat a huge golden throne-like chair complete with intricate carvings.

Long tall columns were positioned throughout the room, and each one was surrounded by fiercely burning flickering flames shooting shadows across the walls.

"Do you see her?" whispered Walter from behind them.

"No, can anyone see her?" asked Carmelo as the group stealthily peered into the strange edifice.

"I don't think she's here," said Jo, "Look, the men are in a daze, just wandering about. If she was here, they'd probably be clambering to get to her. There's Oliver," she whispered, "Shall we grab him?"

178

"No, if she notices anyone has gone, she'll become suspicious. We don't want that. We need to take her completely by surprise."

"How about some of us men go in...you know, under cover?" asked Walter.

"Actually, that's not a bad idea. I doubt Rose would agree though."

"Rose knows I can look after myself," he chuckled.

"But what about the clothes, we would need to look exactly the same.

"Hm, yes. Perhaps we can get the witches to help. Jo, can you take some pictures?"

#

Later that evening, Walter, Zoltan and Carmelo, dressed in their finest Egyptian outfits, crept up to the pyramid and waited for an opportune time to enter the building.

"Remember, blend in as much as you can. The more we know about her, the better we'll be prepared to take her down," whispered Carmelo as they split up and began to wander around.

Calliope was still not seated at her throne so the two vampires and werewolf decided to see if they could find any of their friends.

It was eerily quiet, nobody said a word, they just wandered around doing very little except stare into space. It was as if they didn't know each other, these men who had grown up together and lived in the same town for years. The Chief of Police, the Mayor, old Mr. Daltry who had recently celebrated his 90th birthday, the Mayor's 17 year old son, these were just some examples of people the three recognised as they tried to blend into this bizarre crowd.

When Zoltan stumbled upon Ben, he expected at least a hint of recognition in his eyes, but Ben appeared to look right through him, continuing to wander through the hall.

"Ben," whispered Zoltan as he pretended to scratch his mouth, but there was no response. Nada, nothing, zilch. Occasionally, the men would gather in front of one of the fires and warm themselves up before they moved away again, blending into the crowd.

Suddenly the roar of an engine pricked their ears. The three of them grouped together. "It must be her," whispered Zoltan.

The moment the motorbike came to a standstill and the gentle sound of her boots could be heard tapping on the driveway, all of the men launched themselves forward towards the throne, sitting on their knees and placing their foreheads on the floor, as if in prayer.

The trio followed suit and waited for Calliope's arrival. They turned their heads slightly and watched as this relatively normal, yet beautiful looking woman walked through the crowd, wearing a set of bright red leathers, black and red biker boots and a matching helmet and gloves.

When she reached the first step, she took off her gloves and then undid the clasp on her helmet and pulled it away from her head, releasing a mane of thick dark blonde hair.

"Woah..." whispered Zoltan, "I'd forgotten how gorgeous she was."

Calliope slowly turned her head towards him and he bowed his head, almost kicking himself for being so stupid.

But after a few seconds, she looked away and proceeded to remove the biker leathers, revealing a simple black catsuit beneath.

"Robe," she commanded as a young man in his thirties seemingly appeared from nowhere, carrying a long golden robe which she helped her into and then tied a black sash around her waist.

She sat back on her throne and held her hand out at arms length, looking at it.

180

"Cream," she commanded and another man appeared carrying a pot of lotion he began to gently massage into her hands.

She sat back, made herself comfortable and closed her eyes.

Zoltan and Carmelo looked at each other questioningly. Both shook their heads as they waited.

"Bored," she said suddenly and the men on the floor began to stand. "Entertain me," she commanded.

The three outsiders crept to the side of the room as she pointed to a middle aged man with greying hair and freckles. "You and... you" she said pointing to a younger man who was carrying a little extra weight.

The man who had placed the robe on her, appeared with two swords, which the men withdrew from his hands and faced each other.

Calliope smiled before she flicked her wrist.

The sound of clinking swords echoed throughout the huge room as the two men began their battle and the others began to chant, "fight, fight, fight, fight, fight..."

Carmelo watched her face as the fight continued. It was then he noticed her green eyes had a slight feline look to them. He pondered it for a moment before her head suddenly whipped around and she looked directly at him. He turned his gaze away immediately and began to chant with the others.

But little did he know he was too late. He had given himself away.

- Chapter Thirty-six -

A familiar smell pervaded his nose, which he screwed up in disgust as he opened his eyes but was faced with darkness. A feeling of dread flooded his body.

"Zalea?" he asked, moving his hand to the side, feeling damp stones around him.

"Are you there?"

The sound of sobbing stopped him in tracks, "Zalea, is that you?"

"Jack...I'm so sorry...."

Relieved she had survived the waterfall, he tried to reach out but the sound of chains suddenly brought him back to another time. The time when he had been chained up in the caves. He pulled his arms forward but chains prevented him from moving.

"You could have escaped this if only you'd transformed," she sobbed.

"It's all right, Zalea, it's all right. We can get through this."

"But how?"

"You just gave me an idea."

Zalea was quiet. She knew what he was doing. So she said nothing while he tried hard not to make a sound as he made efforts to transform within the chains.

A few involuntary gasps escaped his lips before silence and then, the sound of chains as they dropped to the floor.

"Did you do it?" she asked eagerly and she was met with a soft squawk in her ear.

Jack's raven eyesight was near perfect in the dark and he was shocked at what he saw.

There were at least four of them. Two had been dead for a long time while the third only a few days perhaps. The fourth, however, appeared to be breathing but was either sleeping or unconscious. They were all adult men and all four were chained to the walls of the caves.

"What now?" she asked, knowing full well he couldn't reply. "Will you change back and try and release me?" she asked eagerly and he squawked in response.

But before he could do that, he checked out their surroundings, trying to find an escape route. Spotting several tunnels that went off in different directions, Jack flew a little down each one before deciding which route to take. Once he had made his decision, he returned to Zalea's side and began his transformation once more. It was getting easier.

"Okay Zalea, I'm back. There's another man here whose still alive. We need to try and release him too."

Zalea nodded even though he couldn't see her.

"I'll have to bash your chains with a stone..."

"What about Gwynethea's dagger? Will that help?" she said, feeling around on the ground where he had been chained.

"No, it's gone. I must have lost it in the waterfall. Unless... they took it when they brought us here."

Jack picked up one of the loose heavy stones and very carefully began bashing at the chain until, eventually, it broke, releasing her arm.

"Here, can you try and break the others while I try and help the man?"

She took his hand and squeezed it before the sounds of her hitting the chains with the stone reverberated around the cave.

As Jack approached the other survivor, he held out his arms until he could feel the man's arm.

"I'm here to help you," he whispered, "Can you hear me. Are you conscious?"

"I 'eard a bird," whispered the voice. "You ain't a bird?" he said.

183

"No, I'm not a bird. My name is Jack. I want to help get you out of here."

"I ain't 'eard a bird for a long time. What time is it? Is it time for tea yet, me dear?"

Jack sighed, this wouldn't be easy.

"Like I said, my name is Jack. You need to focus. You're chained up to these caves. How long have you been here?"

"Oooh, a long time, me thinks. They feed me though, they do. And they bring me water."

"When do they feed you?" Jack asked, concerned they would come face to face with their captors.

"Not for a while yet, Sir. I was just fed some fifteen minutes ago."

Jack shook his head, the man was delirious.

"Look, I need you to do what I tell you. Hold your hands out and keep them there. Don't move them. I don't want to hurt you. I'm going to bash the chains with a rock, all right?"

The man was silent.

"Is that all right?" he asked again and the man coughed.

"Where are we, Son?"

Jack sighed, "We are in the Nephilim Caves."

"Did you say Nephilim, my boy?"

"Yes, which is why we need to release you quickly."

"Then what are you waiting for? Get bashing, Sir."

Jack couldn't help but smile at the poor man's insanity while he began to bash until the chains were finally released.

The man slumped forward as Jack helped him up. Zalea rushed to his other side and they slowly began to walk through the dark tunnel out of the cave.

"Wait," said the man, "I need to say goodbye to Ronald," he said.

"Whose Ronald?" asked Zalea as they stopped for a moment.

"He was my friend, just my friend. Goodbye old boy. You were a good pal, Ronald. I shall miss our conversations. Farewell, old boy," he sobbed before telling them they could continue.

"What's your name?" asked Jack as they exited the cave.

"Me name, Sir? Me name's Eric."

"Well Eric, like I said before, my name is Jack and this here is Zalea."

"It's mighty nice to meet you Jack and Zalea," he smiled a toothy grin. Not that they could see it, mind you.

"It's so strange, we've been walking for what seems like hours and we've yet to see anyone," said Zalea.

"I just hope we're going in the right direction."

"Can we take a break, Sir, Jack, Sir?"

Laughing, he replied, "Eric, please don't call me sir. There's really no need."

"I am sorry... it's habit. I was a butler you know for years and it's ard to break a habit like that."

"I understand."

"I was a butler for royalty, you know?" he said proudly.

"Royalty? Really?" asked Zalea intrigued.

"That's right. Butler for royalty before I was ... I was ... you know, taken."

"What happened to you, Eric? How did you find yourself here?"

"Honestly, Si... Jack. I was doin' nothin' but mindin' me own business walking through Hyde Park in London when I sees this odd light. Like a mirror right in front of me. It seemed to beckon me in, if ya know what I mean? And then, the next thing I know, I'm 'ere in this rotten place. Taken by the... the Nephilim."

"How did you know they were Nephilim?" asked Zalea.

"I'd never even 'eard of 'em until I got 'ere. Ronald told me the truth. He knew all about them."

"What did he tell you, Eric?"

185

- Chapter Thirty-seven -

The fights continued well into the night, Calliope doing nothing more than sitting and watching. There was never any blood drawn, the fight would just continue until one of the opponents fell to the ground.

Calliope would then halt the proceedings, let them gather themselves up before she chose two more to continue the fighting.

At precisely 2 'o' clock in the morning, Calliope stood and all went quiet. The three outsiders looked across at the faces of the other men and they all appeared to be gazing up at her with smiles spread across their faces. It was the look you'd expect a man to give a woman as she walked down the aisle on their wedding day. A look of pure love and devotion. It was clear these men would do anything for Calliope and she knew it.

But Calliope was more focussed on something that was going on outside. She walked through the crowd and out into the freezing cold, staring up at the night sky... up at the moon, which was almost full.

She smiled and let out a deep throaty laugh that spread throughout the pyramid, a laugh that turned to a loud yell, echoing out into the night. When she returned inside, she didn't walk back to her throne, but she walked right into the throng of men and headed straight towards Carmelo.

"I wondered how long it would take you to join us... Carmelo," she said with a smile. "Welcome to my home."

"This isn't your home, Calliope."

"It is now," she said, dropping her head to one side and scrutinising him. "I rather like this place. Powell River. I hadn't intended to stay," she said, turning away from him and suggesting he walk with her.

"Then why did you come?" he asked stone faced.

"I was curious. I wanted to know why you were asking about me."

He flinched. "Why we were asking about you?"

She nodded, "Yes, you were asking questions and your friends were googling me. I wanted to know why so I figured I'd stop by and see for myself. Of course, when I came upon a funeral for a girl who wasn't even dead, my curiosity peaked."

"But...we'd never heard of you until you arrived here. So I don't understand why you think we were asking questions about you. I'm sorry, Calliope, you're wrong."

She shook her head as she sat herself down on her throne.

"No, Carmelo. I'm not wrong," she smiled, "and I'm staying here. I rather like it."

"What are your intentions Calliope?"

"Hm? I'm not sure... yet."

"One man has already been killed as a result of your games..."

"I have not killed anyone. No man has died at my hands" she said, looking down at her beautifully manicured hands. "Besides, man means nothing to me. He is here purely for my entertainment."

"What the hell are you?" yelled Zoltan from the crowd, approaching her.

"Zoltan the werewolf. I was wondering when you would introduce yourself. And Walter, while we're making our introductions, you might as well be included."

"How do you know who we are?" asked Carmelo through gritted teeth.

"I know everything about everyone," she said simply.

"Who are you? What are you?" asked Zoltan, scrunching his fists into tight balls.

Calliope dropped her head backwards and began to laugh, "You mean you still don't know? Oh dear... and here I was believing the Elders to be all knowing and all powerful, when really you're just the same as them," she said pointing to the men who continued to look at her lustfully.

"No, we're not the same, Calliope," as Zoltan jumped towards her, changing from a stocky muscular young man into a wolf. Before he had the chance to reach her, she merely held out her arms and flicked her wrist and Zoltan was bounced from one wall to the other before she finally let him crash to the floor.

"You were saying?" she asked.

Carmelo and Walter retaliated, trying to pounce on her but she moved even quicker than they could. The two vampires ended up crashing into each other.

Looking around for her, their eyes searched the room but she was nowhere to be seen.

"I'm up here, boys, but there really is no point in you trying to stop me. I'm stronger, smarter, faster, etc., etc. than all of you put together," she said from the second floor where a few men continued to sleep on the floor. "And if you continue your silly games, the death of all these men will be on your shoulders."

"What the hell is she?" growled Zoltan after he'd turned back into human form and donned the crazy costume he'd been forced to wear before to preserve his modesty.

"It suits you, Zoltan," she smiled down at him. "Don't mess with me, gentlemen. If you do, you will be sorry. Nobody messes with the Nephilim."

- Chapter Thirty-eight -

Zalea and Jack carefully helped Eric to the ground where they sat next to him leaning against the cool rock and huddled closely for warmth and comfort as the old man began to tell them all about the Nephilim.

"The Nephilim are pure evil, they are," he said slowly, "They're the sons and daughters of fallen angels who bred with man thousands of years ago. The fallen angels passed on their powers to these beasts, makin' 'em stronger, faster and meaner than anyone else on this 'ere earth. But their young'uns are also the most beautiful beings you'll ever see. They can entrap you with nothing more than a simple look of their eye, a flick of their hair or even the mention of their name. The Nephilim might be part human, but there ain't nothing humane about 'em. It is said God was so enraged when these fallen angels mated with man, that he cast their souls to live among the caves beneath the earth for all eternity."

"Is that where we are?" asked Jack.

"Aye lad. We're trapped with em, beneath our own world."

"Hang on a second... beneath our own world?"

"Aye... this is the centre of the earth, my boy."

- Chapter Thirty-nine -

As the hours passed by, December and Lilly finally got round to reading about Jules Verne's famous book, *Journey to the Centre of the Earth*, online.

"I really do think there is something about this theory, you know Lilly."

"Hm?" she replied, devouring every word that could be found about the popular book.

"I said, there's something about our theory. I have a feeling, you know, like a gut feeling, that the Nephilim live there."

Finally, Lilly turned her head away from the computer and looked at her best friend, "I know. I do too."

"So, what else does it say?" December asked as she stretched out her body on the bed while Lilly did all the hard work.

"Something here about there being dangerous gases and giant mushrooms..."

"Perhaps we ought to contact your dad again and tell him?"

"Shouldn't we wait for the others to come back first?" December rolled her eyes, "Okay. Read me some more while we wait."

Just as Lilly was about to read aloud, December sat upright, "Actually, look up how the characters got to the centre of the earth in the first place."

"Erm... it says 'the passage to the centre of the Earth is through the one crater that is touched by the shadow of a nearby mountain peak at noon during the last days of June.'"

"Right, well that's no help then."

"No, but we're not taking this thing word for word, are we? We're just accepting the theory that it is possible to get to the centre of the earth, where the Nephilim caves happen to be."

"Right," nodded December, "so, if this is the case then people are being sucked into some kind of mirror like vortex and getting stuck there."

Lilly slumped backwards into her chair, "But how? And why?"

"I don't know, I really don't know."

#

"It's been ages and none of them are answering their phones," said Jo a little later as she dialled again and it went straight to voice mail. "I hope there's nothing wrong."

"I'm sure they're fine, honey. They're undercover, they will have switched their phones off," said Sonya with a smile at her daughter.

"I don't know," said Meredith, "I'm getting a funny feeling myself."

"What kind of feeling, Meredith?" asked Rose, "We all know your feelings are usually the real deal."

"I feel like they've been discovered."

"Right, that's it. I'm going," said Jo, heading for the door.

"Woah, wait right there. You're not going alone," said Tabitha who rushed to her side, followed by a few of the Elders.

"What's going on?" asked Lilly as she and December appeared from her room.

"Meredith's had one of her feelings about the boys and so I'm not going to hang around here and wait for something awful to happen to them," replied Jo.

"We're coming with you, then," said December, rushing forward and grabbing her coat and hat, passing Lilly hers at the same time.

"Can you hold on to it, along with the rest of my clothes? I'd rather change into my raven form."

December laughed and nodded.

"Tiffani, you stay here where you'll be safe. I'm going with them," said Sammy, standing and putting a large cape over his shoulders to hide his wings.

"B...but...." she uttered before bursting into tears.

"Dear, please don't worry about everybody. I'm sure they'll be fine," reassured Meredith who went and sat down next to the delicate faery.

"I...I'm sorry," she whispered, "Is anyone else staying with us?"

Moira, Ruby and Gabriel all promised to stay with her as the rest of the group prepared to head out into the cold to find out what was going on.

Those that were capable of moving at high speeds travelled together, leaving the rest to travel by car.

It was the first time Lilly had the chance to fly outdoors. It was truly liberating, even more liberating than when she'd first made the change into a mountain lion. Swooping up and down between some of the grandest trees in the forest, she squawked happily, temporarily forgetting what was going on in her life, enjoying the moment of freedom, the wind rustling her feathers as she climbed higher and higher into the night sky, before turning to look down at the earth far below.

Lights twinkled within the scattered houses below as the moon shone upon them. Lilly was startled when something large suddenly appeared, flying upwards. As it came closer, she smiled to herself. Sammy. It was dark after all, so he was relatively well hidden.

She flew down towards him and together they continued their flight towards the pyramid, a structure which stuck out like a sore thumb in the landscape below. The sculpture of the golden eagle sat proudly on top of it. The two spotted the others gathered together several hundred metres away. December was gazing upwards, waiting for her friend's arrival. She held out her arm and

Lilly slowed down considerably, landing directly below her elbow. December smiled proudly.

"Do you want to change now?" she asked and the raven shook her head.

"Okay, your clothes are in the car. Let me know when you need them."

Lilly nodded her head forward and hopped up her arm so she sat comfortably on her shoulder.

"I feel like a pirate," she whispered as Sammy chuckled.

"Well, you don't look like one," said Jemima with Chris by her side.

"Jemima you really should keep out of sight."

"I'm fine, December. I doubt my father, or anyone else in there, will notice me, but I'll keep my hood up, just in case."

"Right, I want you all to stay here while I go and have a quick look at what's going on," said Jo, leaving them, moving so fast you could barely see her until she stopped beside the entrance to the pyramid. Peering around the structure, she watched as hundreds of men stood with their backs to her. They were looking at a woman at the front, sitting atop her golden throne, smiling.

Suddenly, the woman flicked her hand and every man in there fell to his knees before falling to the ground. Jo scanned the crowd for her fiancé but he was nowhere to be seen, neither was Zoltan or Walter.

"Come in, Josephine. Don't be shy," said a powerful female voice with a hint of laughter.

Jo scolded herself before she stepped out into the room.

"Calliope," she said confidently.

"Yes, I am Calliope. And you're Josephine, Jo for short, daughter of Wyatt and Sonya. Only child. Vampire, I believe. Oh and lest I forget, fiancé to Carmelo. I met him earlier. Nice guy, for a vampire," she said with a glint in her eyes.

"Where is he, Calliope?"

193

The woman laughed, "Oh we'll get to that later. Have some patience. Now, come closer."

Jo made a quick decision and ran at lightning speed towards Calliope but the moment she became close, she slammed into what felt like a wall, an invisible force field. Falling to the floor with a thud, Jo crouched, looking up at the woman. Her eyes had turned a bright blood red colour and fangs protruded from her full lips.

"There's no need to become nasty, Josephine," giggled Calliope, watching the vampire's temper increase tenfold.

"There is every need," she snarled, "Look at what you've done to our town..."

Calliope glanced around at the sleeping men innocently, "Why, whatever do you mean? These men are simply sleeping. They've been having a marvellous time with me. I haven't made any of them do anything they didn't want to do," she laughed.

"Then what about the poor man you killed?"

"That was very unfortunate but not of my doing. He should have been more careful crossing the road. Silly man," she replied, pouting.

"He died because of your....your spell."

"Spell? I am not a witch, Josephine."

"Then what the hell are you?"

Again, Calliope threw her head back and let out a girly giggle.

"I'm amazed none of you figured it out by yourselves. Not even Carmelo knew. I am a Nephilim."

"But the Nephilim are trapped in caves," answered Jo, confused.

"Not all of us. Some of us escaped," she smiled.

"There are more of you?"

"Of course. Like I told Carmelo, we are creatures of high intelligence. We figured it out."

"How? How did you escape?"

"Josephine, I am growing bored with all of your questions. I thought we might have been friends but I think I've had enough of you... for now."

With another flick of her wrist, Jo was propelled high into the hall, up onto the next level and away from sight.

Calliope pouted for a moment but she sighed out loud and yelled, "Sustenance."

The same man who had helped her into her robe, appeared with a tray of food and a goblet.

Calliope took the tray from him, dismissed him and proceeded to engorge herself on large chunks of meat, occasionally gulping from the goblet. When she looked up again, her face was covered in blood.

Lilly had watched it all. Perched atop the golden eagle, she had peered downwards into the pyramid below and watched in horror as Jo had been lifted like a feather and hidden away before the beautiful woman had fed like a wild animal, bits of raw meat flying in all directions as she helped it down with a goblet of blood.

Lilly quietly lifted her head and pushed out her wings, lifting herself high into the sky before turning towards her other friends who waited patiently below.

Landing on December's arm, she nodded avidly to her.

"Do you want your clothes, Lilly?"

The raven nodded once again so December walked to the car, taking the items out as Lilly transformed discreetly behind a tree. Shivering, she put on the clothes as fast as possible before she joined the others.

"It's bad... really bad," she whispered. "I think we need to head back to the house and work out a plan."

"But surely all of us can do something here?" asked Sammy.

"No, Sammy. Listen everyone. This woman is powerful. She is a Nephilim. We must return home and come up with a plan."

Everyone gasped and nodded.

195

"Wait," said Crystal, "what happened to the others?"
"I think they're okay... for now. Come on, let's go."

- Chapter Forty -

Eric was exhausted. No longer able to talk, Jack had encouraged him to try and sleep for a little while.

"Are you all right, Jack?" asked Zalea as they sat beside the old man while the sound of his gentle snores filled the small cave where curled on the floor.

"I'm fine. How about you?"

"Just a little cold, but I think I'm all right. I'm frightened though," she said with a sniff, "Are we going to die here?" she asked as tears began to fall down her cheeks.

"No, I'm going to get us out of here, Zalea. But for now, I'm going to see if I can get through to December.

The sound of Zalea's gentle weeping soon subsided, even Eric's snoring halted as Jack concentrated hard on reaching out to his daughter's best friend.

After a while, his head throbbed all over but he felt a connection.

"December?" he whispered, "It's me. We're in the caves. Somehow they caught us but we've escaped. We found an old man alive and he told us we are below the surface of the earth. Yes, the centre of the earth, it's like a whole new world, but.. I just wanted you to know where we are. Maybe you can work out how to free us. Hm? Sorry? ... Oh God, that's not good. Let me know when you know more. We'll continue to try and get out and if anything changes, I'll be in touch. December? Be careful. Bye."

As the connection was lost, Jack's headache began to ease but not before he closed his eyes and tried to sleep just for a few minutes.

"Jack? Jack?" said a soft silky voice as he came to from his dreamlike state.

"Hm?" he muttered, "Serena?" he asked.

197

"No, Jack, you're dreaming. It's me, Zalea...wake up," she said, gently tugging at his arm.

His eyes flew open, expecting light but there was nothing but darkness. He could just make out the faint outlines of his two companions.

"Sorry, how long was I out?"

"Not long, maybe an hour," she replied.

"You needed it, me boy. S'always good to get some shut eye, it is," said Eric as they helped him to stand up, his joints cracking.

"Oooh, I'm sorry you two. I'm an old man, I'm slowing yers both down."

"Nonsense," said Jack, "you're keeping up with us. You're doing brilliantly. The royal family would be proud."

Neither of them could see the broad grin that spread across his cheeks. He was beaming and it made him even more eager to get out.

While they walked, Zalea encouraged him to tell them more about the Nephilim.

"More?" he said, "Let me think? Now what was it old Ronald told me? Oh yes, the Nephilim. They used to have huge wings but over time they've disappeared. Occasionally one is born still bearing the marks of wings of generations gone by."

"Wait a minute, you said they're still being born?"

"Why yes, young Jack. There are rumours some Nephilim managed to escape from this hell and made a life for themselves up top. There they mated with our kind and produced offspring of their own."

"And how did they manage to escape from here?" asked Jack eagerly, "Did Ronald ever tell you that?"

Eric was quiet for a moment while he pondered the conversations they'd had before Ronald passed away.

"Why yes, I believe he did mention something about that, but, but I can't remember it."

Jack's shoulders slumped. Perhaps Ronald had known something that could help them escape. He just had to get Eric to remember.

"Tell me about Ronald, Eric?

"He was a fine man, he was, Ronald. He wasn't a Brit, like me, well, his forefathers were Brits, o' course, but Ronald was from Canada. Where in Canada did he tell me? Hm somewhere in the west, it was. It sounded British but wasn't... hm?"

"British Columbia?" asked Jack.

"That's it, you've got it, me lad. British Columbia, that's where he was from."

"Do you remember where in British Columbia, Eric?"

"He did tell me, he did, but it was a place I'd never 'eard of. It was by the water, mind you. He liked to go sailing, did Ronald. He told me all about that. Even had his own little boat, apparently. Ooh, he did love the water."

"What did Ronald do for a living?"

"He was a historian, was Ronald. A professor. Wonderful man," sobbed Eric, "Ooh I'm sorry. I'm not usually one for cryin' but I was so lonely after he passed," he said, rubbing his eyes with his half-gloved fingers.

"It's all right, Eric. We understand," said Zalea with a pat on his arm. "My sister went missing some time ago and I've spent many a night sobbing for her. It's all right to cry."

"My dear, I am sorry to hear 'bout your sister. Terrible, how terrible."

"Thank you. We've since discovered she's alive and well in your world."

"Aren't you from my world?" he asked, startled.

Zalea smiled, "Why no. I'm sorry, I should have told you before."

"People can usually tell by her appearance, Eric, but it's too dark for you to see," Jack interrupted.

"How are you different from us?" he whispered.

199

"I have small wings and translucent skin. My colouring is very different to humans. But other than that, we are pretty much the same."

"B...but... where do you come from?" he asked quietly.

"You call it the centre of the earth, I call it home," she whispered, "but the part where I live is far from here where the forests sparkle in different shades of silver. The forests of Moharth. It's the most beautiful place you'll ever see."

"If you live so far away from here, my dear, what are you doing here?"

"It's a long story but suffice to say she is trying to get her sister home," answered Jack.

"You must really love that sister of yours to submit yourself to this hell," he smiled and patted her hand gently.

"I do, Eric, I love my family a great deal."

"That's lovely, that's really quite somethin'," he said, "I ain't got no family."

"No family?" asked Jack.

"My parents are long dead. They died within a year of each other when I was just a lad. I did have a younger sister who died during childbirth. Her name was Martha. God rest their souls."

"I'm so sorry, Eric. Didn't you ever marry and have children of your own?" asked Jack.

"I had a wife, but she died too. We were married for 11 years when she was told she had an inoperable brain tumour. She fell into a coma a few months later and never woke up. The doctors had to switch off life support in the end," he said, wiping at his eyes again.

"That's terrible... I'm so sorry...." said Zalea.

"It was a long time ago though. Ronald had a family. He loved tellin' me all about 'em, he did. His wife, Elsie, was a cracker, he told me," he chuckled, "and they had two sons, Charles and Henry, and two daughters, Elizabeth and Victoria. Elizabeth was about to have their first grandchild when he vanished, he told me..."

"Did he tell you how he vanished, Eric, how he got here?"

"Yes he did. Ronald often went on treks around the world, researchin' for this and that. He had several books published, did Ronald. Anyway, on this particular time, he was actually researchin' the Nephilim (which was why he knew so much about em, o' course). He had a theory that they existed beneath caves all over the world and so he decided to visit some o' these caves. Apparently he fell down a deep gulley into some water. He musta hit his head or somethin' coz when he woke up, he was 'ere."

"So contrary to what happened to me and you, he never saw the strange mirrored light?" asked Jack, intrigued.

"Right you are, Jack, me lad, right you are."

"Well, that might change things for us," he said to himself. "What else can you tell us about Ronald, Eric? Did he tell you where the caves were when he fell?"

- Chapter Forty-one -

Sitting in the back of the car deep in thought, December's head began to ache. Lilly sat beside her and when she felt her flinch, she turned.

"Is it a headache again?"

December nodded and closed her eyes.

"Chris, put your foot down. We need to get back home quickly. I think my dad's trying to get through again."

Before they arrived, Lilly quietly explained about everything she had witnessed in the pyramid.

December groaned as she was carefully placed on the sofa.

As usual, Millicent and Moira sat by her side holding her hands as the rest of the group quietly surrounded her, waiting for news.

"I'm here," she said aloud. "Hi Jack... The centre of the earth?" she whispered and Lilly' eyes flew open wide.

"...There is one of them, the Nephilim, on the loose over here.... Okay, be careful Jack. We'll talk soon."

Her head continued to throb but it didn't matter, she needed to sit up and explain what was going on.

"Easy, December, easy," said Moira. "At least lean your head back on the headrest, okay?" she said as Millicent mopped her forehead with a damp cloth.

"What's happened?"

"Jack is in the Nephilim caves and he's discovered that they are situated in the centre of the earth. But not only that, listen to what Lilly heard back at the pyramid," she said.

Lilly took a deep breath to explain everything she'd witnessed and was met with a room full of horrified faces.

"Now what do we do?" asked Gabriel who had been sitting silently in his old leather chair in the corner. "We can't fight the Nephilim... they are just too powerful."

"How on earth do we defeat them?" asked Tabitha who had been standing wringing a scarf tightly between her fingers, "And get our loved ones back safe and sound?" As if on cue, there was a knock at the door. Everyone's head turned to face it as Gabriel stood, checking that everyone supernatural was well hidden. Sammy and Tiffani went and hid in another room as Gabriel walked into the hallway and carefully opened the door.

A handsome man wearing jeans and a black turtle neck sweater stood smiling, waiting on the porch. His black hair seemed to shine in the dawn light and his face exuded kindness.

"Can I help you?" asked Gabriel.

"Gabriel?" he asked.

"Yes?"

"I've come to offer my assistance. May I come in?"

"Erm..."

Placing a hand gently on Gabriel's arm, he whispered, "It's quite all right. I know all about you. There's no need to hide anyone from me. You can call Tiffanimelicomelea and Sammy out of their hiding place," he smiled as Gabriel pulled the door further open and ushered the stranger in.

He followed the old man into the living room where the crowd stood nervously.

"Hello everyone. My name is Michael. I'm here to help. Please don't be afraid."

"Sorry, who? Michael? How do you know we need help?" asked Lilly.

He smiled kindly, "Hello, Lilly. It's an honour to finally meet someone as brave as yourself. I have been watching you and I must say, I am impressed. And December, you also. It's quite some time since I've seen two young girls kick butt quite like you," he chuckled. Turning to look away, his gaze locked on Millicent, "and young Millicent, I know you shouldn't really be here but I understand you

203

have helped December a great deal in honing her communication technique. But you must return. For now though, you can stay but you will have to go back soon."

"But how do you know? How do you know all this about us?" asked Rose, standing up and facing the young man whose eyes seemed old beyond his years.

"Rose, my dear. Your parents are incredibly proud of you. They wanted you to know their little pumpkin grew up to be quite a feline."

Stumped for words, she sat right back down, whispering, "I never told anyone they called me their little pumpkin."

"And speaking of those that have passed. Meredith, John wants you to know he's okay. He's so sorry you didn't get to spend more time together but he loves you so much, so very much. He said to tell you he's so proud of you. A raven, who knew?"

Tears flowed down her cheeks as she looked up at him and smiled.

"Lilly."

She stood up and walked right up to him, "Serena and Neleh miss you so much. They watch over you whenever you need them. Like the time they led you to Sammy. They are proud, but they believe you know that already."

Swallowing loudly, she said, "Who are you? How do you *know* this stuff?"

"All in good time, Lilly, all in good time. Now where is she? Ruby?" he asked and waited for the red-headed glamour puss ghost to come floating out of nowhere.

"You called?" she purred.

"I know you have been stuck like this for quite some time. But it is possible for the curse to be broken. All that is needed is love. I can tell you no more. Just think on it and you will understand."

Her face lit up and she drifted away without another word. Most unlike her.

204

"Sammy Morton, it is possible for your curse to be reversed so you can live out your days in this world, but something tells me you have other plans," he said to Sammy with a cheeky smile who turned to look at Tiffani with a slight blush.

"I am here to offer you any assistance I can in order to help you get home, Tiffanimelicomelea, to get Jack and his friend back and also to try and rid this world of this evil that is the Nephilim."

"Holy Cow!" yelled Tabitha all of a sudden, "You're Michael!" she said and he smiled.

"He already told us that, Tab," said December.

"Yeh, but he forgot to add something crucial to his name."

"What's that?" asked Millicent innocently.

"Archangel."

- Chapter Forty-two -

"Yes he did, as a matter of fact," said Eric. "Ronald had visited so many caves over the years, he had. But the ones when he fell and made his discovery, were in Romania."

"Romania?" asked Jack, aghast. "That doesn't really help us, does it?" he whispered to himself.

"I'm sorry, Jack, me lad, but it's true," sighed Eric.

"I was hoping for some kind of connection, you know? You and I both disappearing in London but Romania? That's miles away."

The three sat in silence before a noise in the distance caught their attention.

"We'd better keep moving," whispered Zalea as she stood, slowly helping Eric to his feet. "What do you think that was?" she asked.

Eric, having been trapped in the caves for months, knew only too well what it was.

"It's the sound of the dead. They're being moved."

"So they're probably on to us, then," said Jack slowly.

"Aye, they probably are."

With a starving old man to carry, speeding up wasn't much of an option, but the trio quickened just a little, tripping over each other's feet in the darkness.

"If only we could see," said Zalea, who suddenly had a thought, "Jack, you could be our eyes, if you turn into, you know?"

"Turn into you know, whatever do you mean, my love?"

"I haven't been entirely open with you, Eric, about myself. I come from a long line of ancestors who had a unique gene that enabled them to transform..."

"Transform into what...?" he asked hauntingly.

"Into ravens, Eric. I recently found out I have the gene too."

The old man chuckled, "Get away wiv ya."

"It's true, Eric. Remember back when you were chained up you said you thought you heard a bird. You did, it was me. It was the only way I could get out of the chains."
Eric said nothing for a few moments before adding, "I did wonder how you got out, my boy. I'll believe anything right at this moment. After all, who'd have known there was a whole other world in the centre of the earth, right?"
"Right," replied Jack with a smile. "I can't change, not now, Zalea. You need me to help carry Eric."
"I said before, young'uns, you should leave me and get out, escape."
"No, we're not leaving without you, Eric," said Jack.
"Well then, give me credit for something. I can walk, just not too fast mind you."
"I can help him, Jack. It will be more helpful if you can be our eyes."
"But how do we communicate? he asked.
"How about one squawk for right, two squawks for left, three for straight on?" she suggested.
"And something for danger?" asked Eric.
"If I see danger, I will come and sit on your arm, which means we must stay silent."
"Okay," said Zalea. "Be careful, Jack."
Within a matter of minutes, after he had removed his clothes and handed them to her, the transformation was complete. His eyesight improved a hundred fold and he was able to see exactly where they were. It wasn't good. It was like a myriad of different tunnels going off in so many directions. Jagged golden brown rocks jutted down from above while the path beneath their feet was smooth. He had no idea where to go.
He closed his eyes for a moment and concentrated on the strength of his raven senses. There were numerous unpleasant scents lingering throughout: blood, sweat, decay but there was something else that caught his attention. Water, he could smell water. The same scent

that had filled his senses when he had plunged himself into the river the first time he had transformed. If they followed the scent of the water, they might, just might, find themselves at the river. And should they escape, they could then try and work out how to break free from the Nephilim's clutches.

Just as he decided which tunnel to enter, Zalea broke the silence, "Jack," she whispered timidly, "Are you ready?" He replied with three squawks and so the two walked forward, following the sounds of the raven while he hopped, flew and waddled in front of them, desperate to get out of those rotten caves.

#

"I'm so thirsty, Jack," whispered Zalea as she and Eric leaned against the rocks for a break, both sweating from the strange heat that was now surrounding them.

Jack turned and, walking back, transformed to human form.

"I know," he said, startling her as she hadn't heard his transformation take place. "The walls are a little damp. I can only suggest licking them to get some moisture."

"Eric, how did you survive all this time without food and water?" asked Zalea.

"I ate and I drank, not very often, but often enough to keep me alive. The same can't be said for the others in there though," he replied.

"How did you eat and drink," Jack asked, casually leaning against the cave wall.

"We were brought morsels and a little water."

"By who? Who fed you?"

"I'd say they were slaves."

"Slaves? There are slaves in here too?"

"Aye, but they don't talk. Don't know if they can. You can ear 'em coming, their ankles shackled together. Walking slowly through those tunnels carrying bread 'n water. It was the same one that fed me, every time. I couldn't see her but I could smell her. She 'ad the same smell. I would ask her questions but she never said a word. Perhaps she were mute, I don't know. But she were a gentle soul. She always 'eld me 'ead so gently as she 'eld the water to my lips and then the bread, and then water again. A few times until she had to move on," he sighed.

"How long ago was she here?" asked Jack.

"Honestly, I've no idea my son. Being stuck in here, in the darkness, you lose all track o' time. Most would go insane but I was already accustomed to the solitude from my life before."

"Erm... you did seem a little loopy when we stumbled across you, Eric," Jack said with a slight chuckle.

"Aye, I probably was. But you saved me from insanity and I thank you for that. Now, kids, let's get moving." Smiling at the man's sudden eagerness, Jack transformed back into a raven and on they went, continuing their journey through the caves, following the scent of the river.

- Chapter Forty-three -

Carmelo, Walter, Zoltan and Jo stood watching the light become brighter as a new day dawned. All were silent as the sun began to rise in the blue sky beyond the invisible force field that was keeping them trapped within the pyramid. Individually tossed there by a simple flick of her wrist. Calliope. She had powers beyond their imagination. Although none would speak their minds, they all feared for the lives of their family and friends.

#

"Her name is Calliope and she is one of them, yes. The Nephilim. But she has been on the surface for thousands of years, making her different from the ones below...."
"What do you mean, Michael? Different?" asked Rose.
"Let's just say she looks like a woman and those below far from it."
"But what does she want with us?" December asked eagerly, wrapping her purple cardigan tightly around herself in a bid to get warm.
Gabriel noticed and jumped up to put another log on the fire.
"I cannot say what it is she wants. What I can tell you is the Nephilim are incredibly dangerous. They have powers that have only strengthened over the years."
"What I don't get is the fact she's up here. I thought all the Nephilim were banished to live eternally within the caves?" asked Lilly, moving to stand in front of the now roaring flames of the open fire.
"We believe some of them found a way out many years ago. The same way some humans have found themselves trapped below ground."
"Do you mean the vortex?" whispered Tiffani shyly.

Michael nodded, "In a manner of speaking. Technically, it's not a vortex as such. It is simply an opening which appears on certain days of the year, allowing anyone close by to be sucked in and, we believe, allows some of them to be pushed out at the same time."

"So when someone goes in, a Nephilim comes out?" asked Millicent who sat upright on the sofa.

"We believe only a small number of Nephilim have escaped the caves, yet a huge number of humans have become trapped down there."

"Why?" asked Lilly.

"We have our own theory but it has yet to be... verified," he smiled.

"Well, we need to know what it is if we have any chance in hell... oh...erm, sorry. Any chance of rescuing our loved ones," added Tabitha through gritted teeth.

"I know you are angry, Tabitha. But rest assured none of your family or friends have been harmed, yet. And I am here to help you. To make sure that doesn't happen."

"Well then we must do something, not sit around here and talk about it," she added. "You're an Archangel, can't you just go down there and kill the Nephilim or something?"

Michael smiled, walked over to her and placed his calming hands on her shoulders. "No, Tabitha, we do not possess the power to kill them. I am here simply to help you, in whatever way I can. Zoltan is safe. Trust me, Tabitha. Will you allow me to continue?"

Blushing slightly, Tabitha nodded and sat back down.

"We believe the Nephilim have been strengthening this escape route, for want of a better name, for hundreds if not thousands of years, in order for them to attempt a massive coup."

There were gasps in the room before he continued.

"You have seen what Calliope is capable of and you've heard from your communications with Jack," Michael

211

turned and looked at December with a smile, before continuing, "how dangerous they are beneath ground. If we allow the Nephilim to break free, the world will no longer be as you know it. They will destroy it and all that live in it."

Moira rushed to December's side and sat on the arm of the sofa, her arm gently cradling her daughter. Lilly turned to look at Gabriel, her face white with fear while the others just stood rooted to the ground in shock. Suddenly Tabitha hopped up angrily, "But you're an Archangel. Why can't you put a stop to this? Where is God now?" she yelled, tears pouring from her face. "If there really is a God, why would he do this to us?" she sobbed, crumpling to the floor.

Both Lilly and December moved to her side, cradling her in their arms. Tabitha had always been the tough one, they'd never seen her so distraught.

"We are doing what we can but, in truth, we have no power over the Nephilim. When they were cast below ground to be eternally trapped in those caves, the power was lost. We are here to help you, I assure you. We will do everything we can to help defeat them. Tabitha... Tabitha, look at me," Michael said gently, watching her shoulders shake as the sobs began to subside and she looked up at him.

A soft glow appeared all around him and a warmth enveloped her, "I will help you. I promise. We can defeat this evil."

The girls stood up and led her to the sofa, where a few others moved so she could sit down.

"So what do we do?" asked Wyatt, holding his wife's hand tightly, "What can we do to help save everyone?"

"First, I need to know everything you know. Everything that has happened since this all began. Dates, times, everything. Even the smallest of details will help us."

"But I thought you knew everything?" asked Lilly innocently.

Michael smiled and turned to face her.

"I only know about you, I do not know everything that has happened to you."

And so, the group of people, human and non-human, inside that small log home in a corner of Powell River began to tell Michael everything that had happened. Not a single detail was left out about their lives... nothing since Lilly's father had mysteriously disappeared that day in London, all those months before.

#

"Calliope...Calliope...Calliope...Calliope..." chanted the crowd of men as the beautiful young Nephilim strode through them, her dark blonde hair flowing behind as if blown by the wind.

Her eyes scoured through them until she locked her gaze on a handsome young man with dark brown hair.

"You... Benjamin... follow me," she said as his face lit up like a hungry dog. He did exactly as he was told.

Striding up the three steps before her throne, she turned with a swish of her cloak and sat down. Ben hurried to her feet and bowed.

"Calliope," he whispered breathlessly, "What can I do for you?"

She looked down on him hungrily, licked her lips and then stroked his face gently with the back of her long slender fingers. "Come," she said, taking her hand and moving so she was face to face with him. She turned his head to one side and slowly kissed him on the cheek, closing her eyes and savouring the moment.

"Music," she yelled suddenly.

And then the gentle sounds of a violin could be heard, filling the pyramid with soft music.

Calliope stood and pulled Ben up beside her. They faced each other, chest to chest, looking deep into each other's eyes.

She smiled. He smiled. She lifted her arms. He lifted his. And then, they began to dance. Waltzing around and around as the rest of the room faded in the background. Calliope dropped her head backwards and let out a soft laugh, a laugh that carried through the air, up, up until it reached those trapped above.

"What's going on?" whispered Jo.

"If only we could see," growled Zoltan who was growing increasingly irate at the situation.

Suddenly, they felt themselves being dragged forward. Jo tried to dig in her heels but it was no use, all of them were being dragged to the edge of the pyramid. When they had a perfect view of the lower level, they stopped. Carmelo held out his hand in front of him, a gentle buzzing sound echoed from the force field that was still stuck firmly in place.

"She obviously heard you," said Walter with his eyebrows raised as the four of them looked down and watched as Calliope and Ben danced around the room. They'd moved down the three steps and waltzed around and around the pyramid. Calliope's face was aglow like that of a young girl in the first flushes of love.

Jo couldn't help but smile. There was almost a childlike innocence there. It's just a shame she was sharing it with Ben.

The second the thought appeared in her head, Calliope danced out of his arms and into the arms of another man. One slightly older with blonde hair. He was not someone Jo recognised. She looked on as Ben slowly came to a standstill and then withdrew, blending in with the rest of the crowd.

- Chapter Forty-four -

As they walked on, Jack began to feel a little woozy. It was a familiar feeling, one that had grown within him when he had met Gwynethea. It was the same sensation he'd felt when they had sat in a trance-like state trying to tap into his sub-conscious mind to recall his lost memories.

Before he gave it a second thought, he had transformed back into a man. Before he'd had a chance to tell the others, they were upon him, tripping over his body on the ground, causing them both to stumble over. Jack had cushioned the blow.

"Hmph, ouch," said Eric, "Jack? Me lad are you all right?" as he rubbed his elbow which had banged into the ground with a thud.

"I think so. Sorry about that. Are you both okay?"

Zalea stood up and helped Eric to his feet as Jack stayed curled on the floor.

"Yes, we're fine. What happened," she asked.

"Nothing really, just a strange feeling in the pit of my stomach."

"What kind of feeling?"

"Like I had with Gwynethea."

"Are you remembering something else, Jack," she whispered.

Eric said nothing as the two talked, he just leaned against the wall rubbing his elbow, before turning to lick the wall for moisture.

"I think I might be. I just need a few moments, if that's okay?"

"Of course."

Jack closed his eyes and recalled those horrible memories that had flooded back into his mind. The loss of his wife and daughter, his kidnapping and subsequent life in

London under a horrible spell, his disappearance and then the memory of his rescue by the faeries from that disgusting pit where bodies had lain to rot and decompose. But something was missing. A huge chunk of memory was gone and considering the empty feeling that sat uncomfortably in his heart, he knew it was about to come back. He lay down and placed his cheek on the cold damp ground. His eyes remained closed.

A vision appeared in his mind. One that shook his entire core, making him retch.

Zalea hurried to his side, feeling around to find him on the ground.

"Jack? Jack, what is it?" she whispered, her voice wavering with fear.

"Oh god... god," he murmured.

"Is he all right, Zalea, my love? He don't sound so good," said Eric who shuffled forwards until he found them kneeling on the cold ground.

"I don't know. I really don't know..."

"The cage, they kept me in a cage. Huge beasts with wings. They kept me barely alive..." he sobbed as the memory came rushing back, brought on by a scent that hovered in the air. A scent he had barely even noticed because he was so focussed on following the scent of the water.

"Jack, whatever this memory is, you need to put it aside. We must get out of here."

"No, Zalea. Don't you see? This memory is here. I can smell it. They're not far away. The water must lead *to* them not away from them."

Zalea gasped and sobbed, almost choking.

"Now, now you two. They ain't got us yet. We're still alive and we're gonna get outta here alive. Come on, son, chin up. Be strong. You got outta here once, you'll get outta here again. Mark my words," reassured Eric.

Jack, taking note of the sudden confidence that could be heard in the old man's voice, tried to pull himself together. 'He's right, I can do this,' he told himself.

"I'm sorry... I'm fine, I'm fine..." he said, straightening his creaky legs and holding out his hand to Zalea.

"Do you want to put some clothes on, Jack?" she whispered, picking up the old dirty trousers that had dropped to the floor. "I think you'd better continue as a man."

Quickly climbing into the trousers, the three of them continued until they could hear the sound of dripping water. Their drying mouths made them speed up until they reached the spot where water dripped from above their heads, making a large puddle by their feet.

As they took it in turns to drink from the source, they also stepped into the puddle and washed away some of the staleness from their skin, temporarily forgetting what lay ahead.

While they rested, Eric gently snored and Zalea's breath steadied, Jack began to remember everything. His head pounded as the memory of all those months trapped in a cage flooded his every pore. The smell that had hung in the air, almost leaving a nasty taste in his mouth, was a mixture of rotting and something metallic, iron, perhaps. No, he knew exactly what it was. It was blood.

The Nephilim, just like the vampires, they fed on blood. Human blood. And he had been placed in a cage, and kept almost like a storage facility. They didn't kill him because they knew his body continued to replenish its stock of blood. Just like Vivian had done all those years before, kept him purely for his blood. It had happened again.

Jack groaned inwardly.

'Why me?' he thought. 'Why my blood?'

A flash of another memory appeared. The cage. There were more, perhaps hundreds more and they all hung from the ceiling of a massive cavern where crumbling columns stood, perhaps once regally, from every corner. In the centre of the cavern, there were two more columns that had not withstood the passage of time. Underneath them ran the river. The sound of the water trickling away had almost driven him to insanity. In some countries, such tactics were used as a method of torture. It was torture.

Jack placed himself inside his memory and looked around, urging himself to take in every last detail. A sound from another cage caught his attention. A young woman sat curled up, her knees under her chin. Her short black hair was plastered across her forehead and her once beautiful oriental eyes were open wide in sheer terror. She rocked backwards and forwards, looking straight ahead yet not seeing anything. She repeated the same three words over and over, "I'm sorry, daddy... I'm sorry, daddy... I'm sorry, daddy...."

Suddenly, his ears began to hurt as the high pitched sound of thousands of bats swooshed by him. They fluttered past the young girl, but not even a thousand bats could draw her from her trance.

He tried to speak but his mouth was too dry, nothing would come out. He needed water. Jack peered down at the river below and tried to swallow.

"Water..." he managed to whisper, "Water," he repeated a little louder.

Suddenly, a loud boom filled the cavern, he could hear rattling. The sound seemed to be coming from all around him. Above, below, side to side, yet he saw nothing. Slowly, the rattling became louder.

His cage began to rattle uncontrollably. He held onto the bars tightly, his knuckles turning white as he began to move lower down within the cave. It shook before it came to standstill. Jack watched as the rest of the cages were lowered too.

When every last one was sat on the ground, the rattling grew louder. The sound of chains and the shuffling of feet. His gaze followed the sounds which now came from a tunnel to his left.

Filthy men and women appeared carrying bowls of bread and water. They shuffled along until each one reached his or her destination. A cage.

A man stood before him and held out the small bowl which just fit within the bars. Jack took it hungrily, snatched it from his grasp and devoured every last drop of water before shoving the small piece of bread into his mouth, chewing it around and around in his mouth before he was finally able to swallow it, the dryness causing it to stick to the back his throat. He coughed and swallowed again.

The man in chains waited patiently and then took the bowl from him.

Jack stuck his arm through the bars and grabbed the man. He was so thin, it was like holding the weak branch of a tree.

"Wait," he croaked.

The man looked at him blankly.

"What's your name?" Jack asked. "Where are we? Please... help me..."

But the man said nothing, standing still until Jack eventually released his arm.

When all the slaves had finished, he walked away with the rest of them. Back into the tunnel from where they had come.

The sound of creaking resumed as the cages were lifted back up to the top of the cavern.

He turned to look at the young girl to his side. Her uneaten piece of bread sat beside her.

"Eat the bread," he had managed to utter. "You must eat or you'll die in here," he'd said.

The blank look disappeared from her face and she stopped muttering those three words for a moment as she turned to look at him. She picked up the piece of bread and threw it toward him. He held out his arm and caught it.

He thought he caught sight of a slight smile before she turned back, rocking back and forth, "I'm sorry daddy, I'm sorry daddy, I'm sorry daddy..."

Jack flinched. He'd fallen asleep. Opening his eyes to the darkness, he heard Zalea and Eric's gentle sleeping breaths and so he closed his eyes once again. It wasn't a dream, it was a memory. And Jack knew that poor girl was saying sorry to her daddy because she was refusing to put up a fight. She was starving herself. She was killing herself. She succeeded.

~ Chapter Forty-five ~

An interesting discovery had been made. Not only had Jack, Nickolaus and Tiffani disappeared during the phase of the full moon, but many others who had gone missing throughout the world had done so during the very same period.

The Nephilim had somehow managed to tap into something that was connected with the moon, creating an opening when it was full.

And there would be a full moon that night.

"I believe Calliope has erected the pyramid to coincide with the full moon this evening," said a very serious looking Michael. "She is going to open the floodgates to allow her brothers and sisters to come to the surface, this very night."

"We don't have much time," said Gabriel a little while later, putting on his winter coat and scarf, topping it off with a warm hat. "Do you really think your plan is going to work?"

Michael smiled, "All we can do is try, Gabriel. And I wouldn't want a better bunch of people working on it."

"Are you ready, everyone?" he asked as they all gathered in the living room, those that would feel the cold, wrapping themselves up.

"I still can't believe we're going to actually do this," whispered Lilly to December as they hooked arms and walked outside.

"I think it's the right thing to do, hon. Don't worry, they'll understand, given the circumstances," she replied with a slight tilt of her head.

#

Powell River Community Centre was full of every woman in town, old and young. They all sat waiting, whispering among themselves.

When Gabriel took to the front, standing on a pedestal, they all gasped and began talking loudly.

"But... but Gabriel. How are you here? All the other men have been taken by that woman," shouted Janice Harbinger, the owner of Harbinger's Drug Store.

"Now, now, calm down everyone. Please. All in good time. We are here to sort out, for once and for all, that woman who is known as Calliope."

There were more cries of disgust at the mere mention of the name.

"Calliope has put a kind of spell on the menfolk of this town," he said before he was interrupted again.

"But you're here... what's going on Gabriel?"

"Yeah, what's going on?"

"Why are you here?"

"A spell? Whatever are you talking about?"

Gabriel lifted his arms, trying to quieten down the angry mob.

"Please, ladies. Let me speak...."

But they just wouldn't sit quietly and so the Elders had no choice.

Moira stepped forward, along with two other witches, and began to whisper a few words:

"Ladies of Powell River. Sit still, be quiet, listen. For the safety of this town, you must sit still, be quiet, listen. Ladies of Powell River. Sit still, be quiet, listen. For the safety of this town, you must sit still, be quiet, listen."

Silence spread throughout the centre as Gabriel turned and thanked the three witches before turning to face the women. He watched as the expressions on their faces turned from shock to fear.

"Please do not fear these women, they have just gotten you to quieten down so I may tell you the truth. And.. I'm

222

sorry to add, the truth is a painful one, a shocking one and for some, possibly just downright unbelievable, but I ask you, for the sake of the menfolk of this town, our friends and families, I ask you to be open minded," he said loudly as his eyes scoured the room and once he was happy they were all with him, he began.

"As you know, my name is Gabriel Tulugaq. My ancestors are from Newfoundland but my great, great, great grandfather moved to Powell River where our family has lived in peace, and very happily, for many years. My name, Tulugaq, literally means raven. I, and all of my immediate family members, have a secret which involves the raven... we all have a special gene which enables us to," he stopped for a moment to take a breath before continuing with a glance to his family, "enables us to... transform into ravens."

The women's faces dropped. Some of them giggled, although no sound came out, but they all sat staring at Gabriel.

"Gabriel, perhaps you should show them?" suggested Millicent, "We brought you extra clothes, just in case," she smiled.

He nodded, looked directly at his audience and seconds later, they were being watched by a raven on the podium.

"Their heartbeats are increasing," whispered Lilly. "Do you think we need to calm them down?"

Moira shook her head. "They'll be all right, the spell will keep them relatively calm."

Gabriel flew into a small room, where Millicent took him some clothes before he walked back out and stood back on the podium.

He held his arms out before speaking, "I am sorry to shock you but it is important you know the truth, the whole truth. Lilly, Tabitha..."

Lilly, Tabitha and Rose walked across to him, they turned to face the crowd and then, seconds later they were two

Mountain Lions - one black, one white and an Iberian Lynx.

The women's eyes shot wide open in fear before the girls quickly walked away and returned moments later dressed in different clothes.

Moira moved forward to get rid of all the ripped clothes that were piling up on the podium before Gabriel continued.

"We are not here to strike fear into your hearts, ladies. Far from it. We have lived among you for many generations and we are good friends with many of you. But, alas, I am far from finished... there is much more you need to know about us. Sammy?" he asked as a tall figure hidden beneath a long hooded cloak appeared beside him.

Sammy carefully removed the hood from his face, before taking off the cape altogether, turning to reveal his beautiful black wings.

"Moira? Can you release part of the spell, so the ladies can at least speak. I believe they may have questions?"

Moira nodded and the three reversed part of the spell.

"Sammy Morton?" whispered several women at once.

Sammy nodded and smiled.

"He's a murderer!" yelled another.

"No... please," he gulped turning to Gabriel.

"Ladies, Sammy is no more a murderer than any of you. Sammy was the victim of a horrendous spell by an evil, cruel witch. She was the one who murdered my daughter-in-law and granddaughter. Not Sammy. He is entirely innocent, forced to hide and live in the forest up until we discovered the truth over a year ago. I ask you to look at this man's face, ladies, and tell me what you see? Because I know you will not see a killer."

Every woman sitting in there looked at him, scrutinising his face until their expressions changed completely.

"It is true," said Deborah Ashby, a cashier at the local supermarket, "He is innocent," she whispered and the rest of them nodded.

"Thank you," said Sammy as he turned to walk away.

"Wait..." said Deborah, "Where have you been hiding this past year?"

"I live with Lilly, Tiffani, Tabitha and Zoltan at Gabriel's house," he answered shyly.

"I know of Tabitha and Zoltan but I've not heard of anyone called Tiffani. Who is she?" she asked kindly.

And then another hooded figure stepped tentatively forward. When she removed the hood and cape, the entire room gasped.

The young faery swallowed and attempted a smile, but instead tears began to fall down her delicate cheeks.

"Oh don't cry, my dear," said a gentle voice from the back.

Tiffani lifted her head and smiled.

"Tiffani is a faery. She's not from around here but she has lived with us for a while now," said Gabriel. "I will tell you more about where she is from shortly. But first, there is more you need to know."

The women's eyes turned to Gabriel while he continued to tell them about the strange supernatural world they lived in.

"What I am about to tell you is going to shock you even more, but it is important you are aware of everything that surrounds us. I know you are probably very frightened right now but please hear me out. There are also vampires and werewolves. The ones that can survive on the blood from animals live among us but those that need human blood to survive live elsewhere. We have always tried to keep this community as safe as possible. There have been times when we've had to deal with evil vampires intent on destroying our lives but we've always managed to destroy them..."

225

"Oh dear," said an elderly voice hidden from view. "I assume you're talking about Mrs Murray and Mrs Ormond?

Gabriel nodded, "Sadly, yes. And there have been a few other tragic cases but, at the moment, evil vampires are the least of our problems. But, just so you know who the good vampires are in our community, you should meet Chris here. He was transformed into a vampire by the same posse responsible for the deaths of Mrs Ormond and Murray. Let me hand you over to Sonya for a moment..."

Sonya, with her long shiny white hair and beautiful features stepped forward and smiled at her old friends, colleagues and neighbours.

"Hello everyone," she began, "Last year, we managed to capture the witch who was responsible for Serena and Neleh's deaths, the one who made Sammy into a half-human. Her name was Vivian and she kidnapped my brother-in-law Jack and niece, Lilly, many years ago. After her capture, and before her judgement took place, she managed to very nearly kill my only daughter. Jo's only saviour was transformation and so Jo came home to me a vampire. It was tough, of course it was tough, but she's my daughter and I love her and so I accept what she has become. Thank you for listening," she said before she stepped back into the rest of the group.

"I did wonder why she suddenly appeared to be so much more beautiful," said a voice from the crowd, "Oh, don't get me wrong, Jo has always been an absolute stunner. I thought it was impossible for anyone to become more beautiful and lo and behold, she did," chuckled the voice.

"Aye, you're right, Alexandra, I always thought that was a bit strange. Makes sense now, of course."

Gabriel stepped forward and walked among the chairs looking for someone. When he eventually found her, he

226

asked Moira to release the binding spell so she could stand up.

"Mrs Dickson, I'm going to need you to come up here with me," he said, very gently helping her to her feet. Fear shot through her eyes and didn't go unnoticed by him.

"Please don't be afraid," he said, leading her to the group before turning his attention to the crowd before him.

"We recently had to make a terrible decision in order to protect our kind. We had to tell a lie to you all. An awful lie that involved you, Mrs Dickson. I hope you'll forgive us," he said as he turned her slightly so she faced yet another person hidden beneath a cape and hood.

The person turned, very slowly dropping the hood to face her mother who collapsed in a heap on the floor.

"Mom!" screeched Jemima.

"She's okay, Jemima. She's just passed out, that's all. She'll come to in a moment. She'll be fine," reassured Rose.

- Chapter Forty-six -

It hadn't taken long for the young girl to succumb to
starvation. Jack could do nothing but look on as she
wasted away, refusing to eat or drink a single thing. He
didn't eat the bread she'd thrown him until she was gone.
When he heard the clattering of the chains as the
shuffling feet made their way through the tunnels beneath
him, Jack watched as the slave next to him tried to wake
her. When she made no movement at all, the slave, a
woman probably in her forties, looked over at him. Jack
wanted to say something but no words would come. He
looked down, ate the piece of bread he was given, drank
the tepid water and handed the bowl back to the same
male slave who had been there the past few times.
No-one uttered a word.
When the cages were lifted back up to the ceiling, the
young girl with the lovely big eyes stayed on the ground
below. Her cage had been opened, left there waiting for
someone, or something, to come and dispose of her
lifeless body.
Jack wanted to cry for her, but there were no tears left
within him. For what seemed like ages, he merely sat and
watched, waiting for them to take her away.
Eventually, a long low howl filled the cavern, the echo
bouncing off of each wall before a massive winged beast
appeared from a large tunnel about halfway down. It
hopped down, swooping to the ground where its spindly
arms reached out and pulled the corpse out onto the
damp cold ground beneath its feet. Suddenly, another
creature appeared from another tunnel, then another and
another, until there were at least ten of them.
Jack didn't want to watch but he just couldn't help it. His
eyes were glued to the horror that unfolded beneath him.
"Jack?" asked a voice from above him.

"Hm?" he murmured.

A soft hand touched him and shook his shoulder gently, "Jack? Wake up," said Zalea.

"Zalea?" he cried, rubbing the tears from his cheeks, where he'd been sobbing in his sleep.

"We should go," she said, not wanting to mention both she and Eric had heard.

Standing up, he stretched his arms and legs and tried to put the terrifying scene out of his mind, but it wasn't easy. When a person is ripped apart like that, right in front of your eyes, it's not something that can easily be forgotten. No wonder he had blocked out his entire past from his consciousness.

"Okay," he whispered, "let's move," he added, his words a little shaky.

After they walked a few paces, Jack's shoulders hunched forward and his cries began. Zalea took him in her arms and stroked his back until the sobs began to slow and his breathing returned to a normal speed.

"There, there," she said, "It's okay. It's over."

But he knew it was far from over.

"Zalea, Eric. I think I need to tell you the truth about what's in these caves..."

- Chapter Forty-seven -

When she finally came to, the look of pure shock, followed by utter relief and love, on Mrs Dickson's face said it all. It had taken some doing but eventually the women of Powell River began to show some understanding towards their unusual friends and neighbours.

But they still didn't know everything. They didn't know the truth about Calliope or the other Nephilim creatures. Gabriel was keeping the worst until last.

Before he continued, Moira released the binding spell so the women could stand and stretch their legs. Apologising profusely as she did so.

But not all understood. There were two women in particular who felt strongly repulsed by what they'd learned. One was a religious lady, Ms Hathermere, who believed all supernatural beings were spawns of the devil, brandishing a bible she'd taken out of her handbag.

"Oh nonsense, Teresa and put that book away. If you want to brandish anybody with that thing, keep it for this Calliope woman. We've known these people for years. These folk are good people. Perhaps a little too secretive, but they're good people. They've never done anything to harm any of us. So put it away," said Mrs Dickson, holding on to her daughter's hand tightly.

"This ain't God's work, I tell you. This is the devil's work."

"I'm with Teresa," said another woman who sat with a floral scarf tied around her head and her hands holding on to her own copy of the bible, "Clearly, you're evil doers. You, your wings and your terrifying spells and so on. I'm in no mind to believe you," she hollered, standing and going over to Ms Hathermere.

Before they could utter another word, Michael stepped out from the back of the hall where he had been standing quietly watching the proceedings. Walking slowly towards them, all went quiet as his warm aura filled the room and the women turned in wonder at the handsome stranger. "I am Michael," he said, "and I assure you that these people have nothing to do with the devil. These are good, honest people, just like you Teresa and you, Phoebe. The only difference is they have somewhat different capabilities than you do. Teresa, I know you are a fine seamstress and can produce a dress so beautiful in a single day. Phoebe, you do wonders to that garden of yours that, to some, would seem to have been created by an angel. Now tell me ladies, how does that differ from what these fine folk are capable of? Jemima, Jo, Chris and the other vampires have super human speed and strength and will live for many years to come. Lilly, Rose, Gabriel, Wyatt and some others can change into animals. December, Moira and the other witches can cast spells. But it matters not because you are all God's children. You must remember that," he said, very gently taking each woman's hand and squeezing ever so slightly.

Teresa and Phoebe both blushed and immediately sat down. "Please carry on, Gabriel," said Phoebe quietly, placing the bible back in her floral handbag.

"Now that you know the truth about who we are, I must tell you the most frightening truth of all. The truth about Calliope. This is no ordinary woman. In fact she she is no woman at all. The fact of the matter is she is..." Gabriel cleared his throat, "she is a Nephilim."

One woman raised her hand and Gabriel nodded, "But what is this... Nephilim?" she asked innocently.

"Well, you could liken them to devilish creatures. Many, many years ago..." and Gabriel went on to tell the ladies of Powell River all about the Nephilim and all they knew about Calliope.

231

Tears flowed as they realised what they were up against but all of them were willing to do everything in their power to get their men back and return their town to the place it once was.

#

They'd been trapped for hours, watching in silence as Calliope danced with many different men, feasted on more raw meat before drinking what looked like blood and watched as the men fought each other with swords. But not once were any of them harmed.

"I don't get it," said Jo, standing up from the ground where she had sat for so long, stretching her legs, "all this time, and she hasn't done anything nasty. I thought the Nephilim were evil beasts?"

"They most definitely are," said Zoltan, "She has imprisoned us. She's got all the men in this town under a ridiculous spell and...."

"And what, Zoltan? Other than the poor man who was killed by the truck, she hasn't actually harmed anyone. Don't you think it's a little strange? And all she seems to want to do with these guys is dance, watch them play fight, oh, and occasionally kiss them on their cheeks. Okay I admit that's a bit weird but she's hardly the beast we figured her to be. There's something strange going on, if you ask me."

"Maybe she's a diversion," suggested Carmelo who had said very little since they'd been trapped up there.

"That sounds more like it," answered Zoltan, folding his arms over his chest.

"She's gone to an awful lot of work for a diversion," muttered Walter.

As they spoke, neither of them noticed the music had halted and all was quiet.

"Erm guys...." said Zoltan suddenly as the rest of them turned to look down below. "She's gone..."

232

All of the men were laying on the floor, apparently asleep, and Calliope was nowhere to be seen.

Carmelo listened intently. The humming had also gone. He held out his arms to discover the invisible force field had disappeared. They were free.

"I don't like this," whispered Jo, "There's something not right here."

The four of them walked to the edge of the upper level and jumped down with complete ease. Only Zoltan landed with a thud.

"You okay?" asked Carmelo to his friend who nodded. Suddenly, they were surrounded. The men of Powell River didn't look so happy about their descent. They stared in silence, hovering back and forth like a group of zombies about to pounce.

Suddenly, that's exactly what they did, and they all seemed to possess an unnatural strength, picking up the vampires and werewolf and throwing them hard against the wall, causing the pyramid to shake with the force.

Carmelo was back on his feet. He threw himself on the nearest column and climbed up. The men might have superhuman strength but they weren't able to climb.

"Climb!" he shouted to the others as they all glanced over before following suit.

Stuck atop the columns in the pyramid, the men of Powell River surrounded them from below, looking up and grunting like rabid animals, rocking back and forth.

"What do we do?" shouted Jo as she gripped with all her strength to the round pillar in the centre of the room, flames dancing at her feet.

- Chapter Forty-eight -

Eric sobbed quietly while Zalea gripped his hand and tears fell down her own face as Jack explained what had happened to the poor young girl trapped in her cage just metres away from him. She wasn't the first to die and be ravaged by the beasts, he told them. Months went by and they dropped one by one, each corpse disappearing in a matter of minutes as they were devoured beneath him. His voice hoarse from whispering and crying, Jack could barely utter another word. They were doomed. It was just a matter of time before they were caught.

As they sat on the cold damp cave floor, Jack rested his head back and closed his eyes. A familiar aching sensation filled the back of his head. The throbbing increased every second. Letting out a low groan, he gripped his head in his hands.

"December?" he managed to whisper.

Zalea's eyes opened wide and she held onto Eric's hand, waiting, hoping December had found a way out.

"No," he cried, "we're trapped in the caves. December... I hope you can help us. I know we're not far from the Nephilim and I... and I..." he stuttered, "I've remembered what they're capable of. They're vicious, evil creatures..." he sobbed and then stopped, listening carefully. "Yes, okay. I'll see what I can find out. Be careful, December and please... tell my family I love them..."

The headache began to fade away and Jack slowly turned his face to his friends.

"I'm going to have to leave you here," he whispered. "I need to go to them and find out as much as possible. I can only do that in raven form."

"No," cried Zalea, "it's too dangerous."

"He must, my dear. He must do this. It's the only way," added Eric quietly.

"Eric's right, Zalea. My family and friends believe the Nephilim are going to attempt something big tonight. There's a full moon and they've worked out this so-called vortex often opens during that time. They think they're going to try a mass escape. We can't let that happen. I can't let that happen. Which is why I need to go and try and find out what I can," he whispered. "I should be safe as a raven. You two need to tuck yourselves away in one of these smaller caves, hidden from view. I promise I will return. I won't leave you here."

Zalea stood up and rushed into his arms, quietly sobbing into his shoulder.

"Please, be careful, Jack. You're our only hope."

"I promise," he said before releasing her. He took off his clothes and handed them to her before she could no longer hear his breath. She could only hear the soft flapping of a bird's wings as it grew quieter and quieter.

"God be with you, my son," whispered Eric.

#

The smell intensified as Jack made his way through the tunnels until eventually he flew out into a large cavern. Not the one in which he had been trapped before, but one much smaller, although it did have several pillars that were crumbling to the ground.

Gliding to the very bottom of the cavern, Jack was careful to hide himself behind various rocks and broken pieces of the columns. Looking upwards expecting to see hanging cages, he was surprised to find it empty, yet there was a distinct smell of humans in the air. The stench of blood and sweat surrounded him.

Jumping upwards, he flapped his wings and began to fly all around, looking for the poor souls trapped in there. Spotting two tunnels, he chose one and followed it through. It led to an even smaller cave where about thirty people lay sleeping on the ground. All were shackled, chains around their ankles. Jack hovered above them until he found the man who had first given him bread and water. He was so thin and gaunt, his skin almost translucent. His hair, once thicker and darker, was greying and thin.

Before they were awoken by the sound of his wings, Jack slipped back into the large cave and then towards the other tunnel. If he'd been human, he would have wretched at the memory, flying into the familiar place he'd spent so many months. Sure enough, looking upward, there he saw hundreds of cages, each one containing a single person.

He shivered, knowing those beasts would be near. He chose a tunnel at the far end of the cavern and entered swiftly, careful not to make a noise. The sound of voices surprised him, making him jump, but he kept his nerve and continued on his path. He had to get something, anything, that would help those above to finally rid this world of these wretched creatures.

Gliding along, he quickly came to a standstill, landing on a ledge close to the sound of the voices. Peering inside the hidden tunnel, he spotted two of them. Not the huge frightening creatures he had expected, but two very different species: were they human? At least they looked somewhat human until they turned their backs on him and revealed scaly wings jutting from their shoulder blades. They were poring over what appeared to be a map.

Jack watched as they stood motionless for minutes before one suddenly turned to face the entrance. Jack ducked his head backwards and held his breath until he heard the creature shuffle away. Before hiding himself, Jack had noticed something strange about the creature's eyes. They were beady and feline-like.

Peering back around, he watched them as they ducked underneath a low entrance to yet another tunnel going off in the opposite direction. Following on silently behind, he glanced at the map beneath him. He recognised it instantly. He would never forget his homeland again.

The two creatures shuffled across the ground, barely able to walk until the narrow walkway gave way to a huge cave much like the one containing all those cages. This one, however, was empty except for several large white pillars in the centre, flames licking their bases, and about thirty large regal seats carved out of the rocks placed around them.

Several creatures were already seated.

Jack very carefully hid himself from view and waited as more and more arrived, slowly taking their appointed seats around the pillar.

Soon, it was full.

There were thirty of them. From a distance you'd be forgiven for thinking they were human but Jack's bird's eye view enabled him to see all of them perfectly with his 20-20 vision. Ugly, scaly creatures with pale long hair, feline-like eyes which continued to dart right and left, and clawed fingers.

Something above them caught Jack's eye just as it was lowered so it was level with all their faces. It was one long tube containing a thick red substance.

Each creature pulled down what looked like a straw and began drinking from the tube. Sucking and sucking until it was completely dry.

"Now we are satiated, we can begin," said one of the creatures who rose from his seat and turned, revealing his lower half matched that of the dragon-like beasts Jack had seen before.

"As you already know, tonight is the night we have been waiting for, for a very, long time. The arrival of the distant comet combined with the full moon is of special importance. Tonight is the night when we will finally be able to return above ground and claim ourselves as the rightful heirs to the world. We will reap revenge on man, enslaving them, feeding from them and doing anything else we so desire," he said with a smile as the others smirked too. "Our destiny will be fulfilled," he laughed and the rest of them cheered.

"Although she has been somewhat... disobedient... in the past, Calliope was the chosen one. She has finally done the right thing and has arranged for our pyramid to be in place in time for the opening this evening. When the comet flashes across the sky, the same time the light of the full moon crosses the pinnacle of the golden eagle, we will be freed from this hell hole where we have been trapped for thousands of years."

More cheering ensued.

"But first, we shall release our elders to dispose of those near to Calliope... as well as Calliope herself, of course. She shall be our first sacrifice."

His laughter, and the laughter of those around him, echoed throughout the caves. It was the perfect time for Jack to make a quick escape. Hopping off of the rock where he had been perched, a small stone dropped to the ground, making a loud pinging noise.

Suddenly all went quiet and every head turned in his direction.

He held his breath, waiting.

Content there was nothing to worry about, the creatures turned back to their leader and continued their laughter. Jack let out a low breath and very slowly and carefully took to flight. He re-traced his previous journey until he flew out into the large cavern which held such terrifying memories for him. Before heading back to the others, he flew upwards towards the cages.

Men, women and teenagers were wasting away, helpless. The stale smell of sweat, urine and blood surrounded him as he tried so hard to remember what had happened to him in the end. Why had he survived when so many others had perished? How had he escaped? It was just one question, one memory, that evaded him, locked away in his subconscious refusing to be found.

Looking at a woman who was once probably so beautiful in her youth, he was startled when she opened her eyes and looked right at him. She snarled like a wild animal and hissed. She thought he was the enemy. He was just a bird yet she thought he was the enemy.

Even if she survived this, there was no way she would ever be the same again. Not even years of therapy could help this poor soul. She was as good as dead, he thought sadly, turning away and flying across to another cage further away.

There lay a man possibly in his 30s, but it was difficult to tell. He too opened his eyes but he looked different. He sat upright and smiled at him. Smiled. Wishing he could return the gesture, Jack moved a little closer and watched as the man tried to speak. His throat so dry that it came out all croaky

"Hey....little b....bird. I'm Joseph. It's nice to meet you..." but before he could utter another word, a familiar sound filled the air. The slaves were coming. It was feeding time. Jack looked at Joseph one last time before he turned away, flapping his wings and flying back into the tunnel from where he had come.

It didn't take long for him to locate Zalea and Eric. They were huddled together in a little cave just metres from where he had left them. Before they heard his return, he looked at them for a moment. Both were filthy, sitting there sweating, hoping they would get out of there alive. He let out a quiet squawk and watched as their faces lit up.

"Jack," they whispered, grins spreading across their faces. "I'm here," he said after he'd made his transformation, "I'm here," he repeated, hugging Zalea tightly before patting Eric on the back. "I told you I'd come back."

~ Chapter Forty-nine ~

The Sheriff's deputy, Shirley Brown, had brought all the
weapons she could find to the Community Centre, in the
back of her station wagon.

"Just in case," she'd said, handing the guns around. "But
don't just go shooting around anywhere and everywhere,
ladies. You aim only at those beasts, nobody else. We
don't want a blood bath of our own kind."

"Thank you, Shirley," Rose said, "it's good to know you
understand our plight."

"That's quite all right, Rose. I'm the Sheriff's Deputy and
I'm here to take out the enemy."

So there they stood, women of all ages, some carrying
hand guns, machine guns, rifles, knives, kitchen knives,
baseball bats, and so on. Some were dressed in head to
toe black, others simply wore what they always wore,
floral dresses, pinafores, dungarees, trouser suits, skirt
suits, etc.

They stood to attention, waiting for the go ahead to move
on to the pyramid and get their men back.

But just as they were making their final preparations,
December's head began to throb incessantly.

"It's Jack," she shouted to anybody nearby, "He must
have some news for us," she said with a grunt, falling to
the floor in a heap.

"He wanted me to repeat exactly what he heard....'When
the comet flashes across the sky and when the light of the
full moon crosses the pinnacle of the golden eagle, we
will be freed from this hell hole where we have been
trapped for thousands of years. It's the pyramid. He said
something about Calliope having been disobedient in the
past but that she created the pyramid for their release.
But, they're going to sacrifice her before they kill

240

everyone near to her. They plan to claim their title as the rightful heirs to this world..."

December's head fell back on to Moira's lap as she carefully dampened her brow with a wet cloth.

"She's feeling worse than she usually does," said Millicent, "It was a lot to take in... she really needs some rest."

"No," muttered December, lifting herself up, "No. I'm fighting too, you're not leaving me here."

Moira looked across at Lilly.

"It's no use, you know. If you try and stop her, she'll only go and orb herself there which will be more dangerous," Lilly added.

Gabriel and the elders stood by her side discussing Jack's findings.

"We must stop them. Can we destroy the pyramid? he asked, looking at Michael.

"We can try but I believe the clue lies with the Golden Eagle. Perhaps if we destroy that first?"

"We can only try," said some of the others as Gabriel turned to face the crowd.

"But what about this comet? This is the first we've heard about it?" he said.

Michael shook his head, "I'm afraid there is no time to find out about that."

"It's time," Gabriel announced to the crowd. "We must destroy the pyramid, and the Golden Eagle that rests on its pinnacle. Let's hope that is enough. My friends, those of you that can change, I would advise you to. Good luck to us all. Let's go!" he yelled before they all piled out of the Community Centre and into their vehicles.

#

"I can't hold on for much longer," said Zoltan as his grip began to loosen around the smooth pillar.

241

"You must," yelled Walter, "they will try to rip you apart if you fall and we cannot risk harming any of them. They are innocents in all of this, after all."

A low growl was released from his lips as he held on tight but it was no use. His fingers gave way and he fell below right into the crowd of men below.

Within seconds, Zoltan's clothes ripped from his body and he jumped up growling at those that surrounded him. The men, unsure how to react to a huge wolf, hovered, waiting to pounce.

The roar of engines suddenly filled the air as the men's attention was temporarily wavered. Zoltan used the moment to pounce high over them, landing close to the pyramid's entrance, growling loudly, followed by a piercing howl while he glanced out onto the moon.

The men followed him, ready to attack when there was suddenly an almighty crash as several large vehicles ploughed into the side of the building, causing the men to scatter in different directions.

Before they could gather back together, two mountain lions appeared out of nowhere, growling and keeping them at bay. Behind them stood several witches, all reciting a spell, trying to overturn Calliope's hold on the men. When nothing happened, the women of Powell River barged forward shouting and yelling, brandishing their weapons.

The men appeared to be confused.

"Wait," shouted Ms Hathermere, "I can see my son..let me try to talk to him..." she said, pushing forward until she stood face to face with the boy she had given birth to thirty-three years earlier.

"No!" yelled Moira as the woman suddenly disappeared within the crowd. "Ms Hathermere!" she yelled. But the woman re-appeared unharmed.

"I think he recognises me," she shouted back. "Find your loved ones and talk to them... I think it's helping," she

242

said, gently stroking her son's face who looked at her in confusion.

"Ben," said Crystal as she too pushed through the throng until she stood in front of him. "Ben, baby, it's me, Crystal. Baby?"

A look of recognition flashed across his face.

"Dad? It's me, Cynthia"

"Duncan? It's me, Ellen..."

"David? Honey..."

"Wolfgang? It's your wife, Arianne..."

All over the pyramid, the women stood in front of their loved ones, trying and hoping their love would bring them back, return them to the men they were before Calliope had appeared on the scene.

Carmelo, Jo and Walter jumped down from the columns and rushed over to their friends, followed by Zoltan who had been given Carmelo's long trench coat to cover himself with.

"What's going on?" asked Carmelo, "What do we know?"

"We've joined forces with the women of the town. They know about us, Carmelo, about all of us. They've vowed to help fight the Nephilim too. They're going to try and come through when the moon is at its fullest tonight, when a comet can be seen. We understand the key is the Golden Eagle on top of the structure. If we can just destroy it, and the pyramid, we might just be able to block them from coming through..." said Gabriel, filling them in.

"It must be pretty close to that now. Look," said Zoltan, "I can feel it. I am at my strongest during a full moon...we've got to get up there," he said as they looked up at the sky as the men of the town slowly began returning to their senses.

All around them there were families hugging and crying, the men unaware of the dangers that were upon them. As the women dragged their sons, husbands, brothers,

243

fathers, uncles, etc., to the front of the pyramid, they all gathered together to listen to what Gabriel had to say. "Friends, this woman, Calliope, possessed you... she took you from your wives, daughters and mothers. She is of the Nephilim, an evil breed of creature intent on destroying our lives. For thousands of years they have been trapped in caves far below ground but tonight they are attempting a mass escape. If they succeed, our world as we know it will be lost. We will be murdered or enslaved. We cannot let this happen. Help us to destroy this structure and help us to put a stop to the Nephilim," he shouted loudly as cheers erupted from the crowd. Gabriel immediately changed form, joining the rest of the Tulugaq family who flew upwards towards the Golden Eagle that perched on top of the pyramid. They tapped and tugged at the sculpture but it wouldn't budge. Seconds later they were joined by Sammy, who carried a hammer and chisel. Hovering with his huge wings flapping up and down, he banged away at it, but nothing happened. The Eagle wasn't even dented.

They all returned to the ground as the pyramid was being smashed to pieces by the people of Powell River. Chaos surrounded them as it fell bit by bit, to the ground. But the pinnacle remained in place. No matter how hard they smashed at it and drove into it, it wouldn't budge, and the moon seemed to grow larger and brighter by the minute. "What do we do?" shouted Carmelo across the crowd. "Moira and the girls have been trying a spell but it's no good... nothing seems to be working," shouted Gabriel. "Just keep trying."

Sammy continued his efforts atop the pyramid but they were in vain. Nothing would damage the Eagle. Tears began to fall down his cheeks as the realisation hit him. They weren't going to make it. The Nephilim were going to win.

Just as the thought passed through his mind, a sudden flash threw him from the pyramid. Unconscious, he fell towards the ground but moments before he landed with a thud, he stopped mid-air and was gently guided to the floor. December rushed to his side, letting out a sigh of relief. Without her magic he might have been killed. Zoltan watched and ran over, picking him up and carrying him out of harm's way before running back into the building and continuing to try and destroy it piece by piece. Neither of them had noticed the flash that caused his fall. The second one caught everybody's attention.

A flash like a silver rainbow appeared from the Golden Eagle, making its way towards the moon where a small comet with a long silvery tail could be seen flying through the sky.

"Oh no!" yelled Lilly, "We're too late," she shouted, pointing to the sky, "Look."

The commotion below came to a standstill as everyone's eyes focussed upwards, watching as the silver light flashed across the night sky.

With all eyes on the sky, there were no eyes on the ground, where Calliope was delicately tiptoeing back towards the crumbling pyramid.

- Chapter Fifty -

A long low rumbling sound erupted all around them as they began to walk quickly through the tunnels towards the huge cavern.

"That doesn't sound good," said Jack, leading them as quickly as he could to the only place he knew where the river ran through. He was pretty sure the beasts would be gone... they'd be with the other Nephilim preparing for their escape.

"How are we going to get out?" asked Eric.

"I'm hoping we can either go via the river or," he went quiet for a second, "that we can use the same escape route as the Nephilim."

Zalea gasped.

"But I don't know for sure yet. Let's not make that decision until we get there. Hopefully December might be able to help us. Don't worry, Zalea. We will get out of here alive."

The rumbling continued as a few smaller stones began to tumble from above.

Jack increased his pace and pulled them along, stumbling and tripping over the ground as it became bumpier, the sound of their heavy breathing began to echo throughout.

"What's going on?" yelled Zalea as the sounds grew louder and louder.

"It's their escape route, I think it's making the caves collapse," replied Jack. "We have to hurry."

Following the light up ahead, they soon stumbled out into the large cavern, coughing and spluttering, trying to get their breaths back.

Squinting at the brightness within the cavern, Zalea and Eric covered their eyes, unable to cope with it.

"Just take a moment to let them adjust. Don't worry, the discomfort will disappear," Jack reassured as he waited for them as they slowly became used to the light after so long in the darkness.

When they spotted the river running just metres away from them, both rushed over and began to drink, desperately quenching their thirst before they turned their faces upwards and noticed the many cages that hung from above.

"Oh my goodness," whispered Zalea. "This is where you were trapped..."

Jack nodded.

"We need to release everybody. Do you remember how they brought the cages down?" she asked anxiously looking around, searching for something, anything that would help these tortured souls.

"Zalea...Zalea, my love... there might not be time," said Eric, trying to slow her down.

"No!" she said, "We must at least try. We can't leave them here..." she sobbed.

"Okay, okay, let me think," said Jack who scanned the area looking for the pulleys the slaves used to move the cages up and down.

"There..." said Eric, pointing to a huge wheel hidden from view behind one of the fallen columns.

The three of them rushed over and began to loosen it, slowly turning it so that some of the cages began moving downwards. They kept on turning it until, eventually, they reached the ground.

Zalea rushed over to the first one where she found a young woman barely able to speak.

"It's all right, we're here to help you," she whispered, shaking the door of the cage. "No, it's locked," she shouted to the others. "We need the keys," she said, exasperated.

"The slaves," whispered Jack, "I think the slaves have them," he said louder.

"But where are they?" asked Eric.

"In one of the tunnels."

"Which one?" shouted Zalea above the noise of the increasing rumbling.

Looking around him, he was stumped, "I...I...I can't remember," he breathed.

A hand on his arm made him jump forward in shock. Turning, he saw the slave that had fed him.

The man didn't say a word, he simply handed him a key. Behind him stood all the other slaves he had seen sleeping earlier.

Jack took it and ran towards the first cage, using the key to unlock it. He then went on to the next and the next, followed by Zalea who had been given another key. Soon, some of the other slaves were helping them to open the cages, pulling out the weakened people and leading them to the river where they all drank. Apart from the rumbling of the caves, all else was quiet.

When the last cage was opened, Jack turned to look for the slave who had helped him, but it was too late. He had collapsed, the simple act of rushing to open the cages causing utter exhaustion. Jack dragged him to the river, made him drink and wiped his filthy face.

The man smiled, "Thank...you," he muttered, "but I cannot be saved. It is... too late... for me. I am so h..h...appy that you survived. When I dragged you out of the cage, I was convinced you were dead."

"You, it was you that helped me?"

The man slowly shook his head, "You were dead, I thought you were dead. I'm sorry, so sorry. I pulled you out to make room for another. The beasts usually feast on the dead but..." the man stopped, closing his eyes in disgust before opening them to continue, "it came over to you and left you there. It... it did not hunger for you. So I had no choice but to, to dispose of you... with the other corpses that had not been eaten. I am so sorry..."

"They made you do this to us. It's not your fault. Please don't blame yourself..." said Jack, watching the man cough and splutter weakly.

"Please forgive...me...."

"There is nothing to forgive," cried Jack, "Tell me your name, at least let me know your name," he whispered as the man closed his eyes for the final time.

"My name is.... Pedro Garcia Ramires...." he said with his final breath.

Jack put his head to his chest but he could near nothing. The beating of his heart had stopped. He'd gone.

He gently laid Pedro's body on the ground and stood up. Looking all around him, he saw the bodies of other people who had not survived. There were at least eleven. But there was no time to mourn these poor souls. They had to get out, all of them.

Zalea and Jack began to gather everyone together, hoping that a way out would soon present itself, when suddenly there was a growl from one of the tunnels. Zalea's breath caught in her throat as the ugliest beast she had ever seen crept out from its hiding place, its scaly green skin glistening with what appeared to be beads of sweat.

Jack stepped out in front of everybody, pushing them behind him as the creature's beady eyes watched his every move. Slowly it opened its mouth, releasing a long tongue that licked its lips hungrily. Jack held his breath.

- Chapter Fifty-one -

Momentarily glancing away from the bright light, Lilly spotted a vision in white climbing through the destroyed wreck of the pyramid. Her breath caught in her mouth as she watched Calliope tiptoeing quietly along with tears pouring down her immaculate face. She was wearing a beautiful ivory dress, a wedding dress, which twinkled in the night light.

Suddenly, others began to notice the vision and soon, Calliope was surrounded by all the people of Powell River. Those with guns aimed them towards her head. But she took no notice of what was happening. Instead, she simply sat down on her wrecked throne and continued to sob uncontrollably.

"Calliope," shouted Carmelo. "We know they are going to kill you. We know you don't want to be their sacrifice. We know you haven't always agreed with those you call your brothers and sisters," he continued loudly, approaching her. "We also know you haven't exactly harmed any of us. Not really. I believe you want to help us. If you do, then we will help you."

She lifted her head and shook it, "I... can't... I can't..."

But Carmelo nodded, "Yes, you can Calliope. We know you never meant us any harm. We realise that now. You were... just having some fun. Please help us Calliope, how do we destroy the Eagle?" he asked.

"You can't. It is unbreakable... impenetrable. It's already too late," she stuttered as the crowd began to grow angry. The flash of light was becoming stronger and a loud rumbling sound could be heard coming from beneath their feet.

"Then help us to defeat them," he added, standing looking down at her delicate features. "You are not one of them, Calliope. You're practically a woman. Those

250

below are far from it. We don't want you dead. But they do. Help us defeat them."

Standing up, they faced each other eye to eye and slowly she nodded.

"But they are coming. We can't stop them from coming," she whispered before she turned to look at the faces in the crowd.

"I am sorry. I never meant any of you any harm. I was just having some fun, at your expense I know, and I am sorry, truly sorry. I will help you. I just hope you can forgive me," she said.

"We know, Calliope, we know. But now, we need to know... how do we defeat them?"

#

As the shaft of light grew larger and brighter in the moonlit sky, the rumbling became almost deafening.

Some members of the public held their hands tightly over their ears and looked around in fear as the flames that had previously only licked the sides of the columns now raged throughout the building's core and beyond, threatening to set the nearby forest alight.

Gabriel, his family and friends gathered everyone together, leading the Powell River community away from the centre of the pyramid, away from immediate danger and prepared them for what could be their final fight.

In the meantime, Carmelo and all the other vampires, paranormal beings and Michael stood beside Calliope, holding their breath as they waited for the Nephilim to come.

Just in front of them, in a wide circle, stood about twenty witches, including December and Moira, chanting quietly, uttering a spell in the hope it would weaken the beasts upon their arrival.

"Don't worry, darling," said a voice beside Lilly, "it'll be all right. We'll kick their butts."

Lilly turned to look at the ghostly apparition that hovered beside her. Ruby was truly a beautiful woman with her fiery red hair and bright green eyes. She only wished she had known her when she was alive.

A warm sensation filled her right hand as she looked down to find Ruby's own hand on top of hers. They smiled at one another sadly before a massive blast burst from the pyramid, causing such an immense force that they were all pushed high into the air before they plummeted to the ground with a thud.

Scrambling to their feet, the witches were quick to return to their circle and resume their chanting as the others stood staring at the enormous crater just metres from their feet. Other than the softly spoken words of the witches circle there was silence. Carmelo edged forward before Calliope grabbed him, pulling him backwards. When he looked at her, she shook her head in horror. Seconds later, all hell broke loose as a number of huge beasts burst out of the crater, flying into the night sky before turning to face the crowd below.

The people looked up, saw these terrifying beasts that resembled dragons, and began to flee in all directions. "No!" yelled Gabriel, "stay where you are." But it was no use, the beasts swooped down with such speed and agility, picking up straying people in their mouths, biting down before swallowing. Blood dripped from them as screams could be heard from all around.

Michael stepped forward, held his arms outstretched and began to mutter something under his breath. The creatures suddenly appeared confused as they flew back and forth, up and down, crashing into each other. Dazed and dumbfounded, the creatures eventually landed on the ground one by one, but the final creature spotted Michael and just as it came crashing down to the ground, it managed to change its course.

252

"Michael!" screamed Jo, watching in horror as the beast slammed head first into the man who promised to have been such an enormous help in defeating the Nephilim. As the creatures began to realise Michael was no longer confusing them, they flew back into the night sky and continued their savage attack on the helpless people below, causing screams of terror and agony to echo throughout the area.

Suddenly the most beautiful sound began to fill the air. The voice of an angel singing stopped them in their tracks. Everyone came to a standstill as they turned to see where the music was coming from. The beasts followed, flying through the air until they reached the woman with the angelic voice. Slowly, they swooped down and landed before her. Calliope continued to sing, note after note, calming them with her soothing voice, until they closed their eyes and were soon drifting to sleep.

"Now, Carmelo, now..." she yelled as the vampires stepped forward with huge stakes and plunged them deep into the hearts of the beasts before covering them with petrol and setting them alight.

High pitched screeching filled the air as the creatures squirmed and twitched until they were completely still as the fire began to reduce their masses to nothing but dust. Cheers could be heard from all around as the people of Powell River came walking in, shouting and cheering, laughing.

Except for Jo, who wandered aimlessly around searching for a body. A body that was nowhere to be seen. Michael had simply vanished.

- Chapter Fifty-two -

"I'm sorry, Carmelo. I'm so sorry. I did not know I could control them. I would have done it sooner if I'd have known," Calliope said, shaking her head, crying. "People have been killed.... I'm so sorry. There was this vague memory I had about singing to the beasts but I didn't know. I didn't know,"

Calliope looked up with uncertainty. She shook her head, "It's not over... Carmelo it's not over. Tell them, tell them to get away," she said as Carmelo looked at her quizzically. "What do you mean, Calliope? We have slain the beasts."

"No, these were merely our elders. The Nephilim that have been around the longest. They were the weakest. There are others, many more....you must tell your people to ge......"

"How very charming, Calliope" said a voice from the crater, "What a performance. You deserve a round of applause. Now, you may re-join your own kind," said the strange looking man who stepped out from below ground. His scaly skin rippled as the moonlight caught the wings on his back.

"No," whispered Calliope, "Never. I am not one of you."

"Why of course you are. You are our youngest Nephilim child, Calliope."

"I am not a child."

"Of course you are. You have done nothing but act like one since we allowed you to break free from below."

"You didn't allow me to do anything. You forced me to come up here."

"To prepare for our release, Calliope."

As the conversation continued, the people of Powell River were trapped in motion. Each and every one had been unable to move a muscle since the new creature had appeared. Yet they could see and hear everything. Although the paranormals were not under the spell, they too pretended to be stuck in time.

"Enough!" yelled another voice, as a similar looking creature but with larger brown eyes stepped out of the crater, his thin white hair blowing in the soft breeze.

"You know what you must do, Palius. She must be sacrificed," he said, brandishing a small jewel encrusted dagger.

Calliope's eyes widened in horror as Palius took the dagger and moved towards her. "No," she breathed as he approached her with his arm in the air, ready to attack. Calliope froze in fear, as Carmelo and the other vampires made their move at the speed of light, throwing themselves at the creatures. Disarming Palius immediately, Carmelo held the dagger to his throat. They both laughed, a sound which crackled through the silence, echoing deep into the crater below.

"So our power does not have an effect on you. Do you really think you can kill us?" asked Palius

"Yes, we do," said Carmelo, looking at Calliope before bringing the dagger down on his shoulder blades, removing the creatures wings with a long swipe of the blade.

"My wings," he whispered, before falling to the ground. Carmelo swiftly threw the blade to Walter who repeated the act on the other creature.

"Now burn them as quickly as you can," said Calliope, rushing forward and taking Palius' wings in her arms. She threw them on the fire which crackled loudly and threw out sparks all around them.

Palius and his friend withered before them, their thin bodies decaying quickly until there was nothing left but a pile of dust.

"Two down... how many more to go?" asked Zoltan with a grin.

"There are more, many more, Zoltan. We will have to act quickly otherwise we will lose this fight," she said, standing atop the crater waiting, wondering why the others had yet to appear.

The people of Powell River, dazed and confused after being released from the strange spell, rallied together.

"What can we do, Gabriel?" asked the Sheriff, who stood by his wife, holding her hand.

"I don't know that you can do anything, Sheriff. These creatures seem to have power over humans."

"Wait," shouted Calliope from the distance, "Perhaps I can counteract their power," she said. "I can try to prevent their power from working over you. But I must set my own power over you first. I will not do it this time... unless you allow me to," she said. "But... it will only make you immune to their motion power, not to anything else. You will still be in danger. You can still be harmed. Please trust me..."

The Sheriff turned to his people and saw they were all in agreement. It was the only way.

"Yes, do it, Calliope. Then we can destroy the Nephilim together."

Calliope lifted her arms and swayed them from side to side with her eyes closed. It was as simple as that.

"People of Powell River. When they appear, you must pretend to be in their power. Let them believe they hold the power over you. Do not move until we tell you to."

A huge clap of thunder could be heard, but it didn't come from the sky, it came from below. Within seconds of the sound, creatures began to crawl from the crater, like hungry lizards waiting to feed.

One after the other, they stood staring up at the sky and grinning, drooling and wiping their mouths with their filthy hands.

"Calliope?" mouthed one, "Isn't she supposed to be dead?"

256

"Where is Palius?"

"I smell death."

"Free, we are free," said another.

Carmelo watched on as one stupid creature after another seemed to act like a lost rabbit in the headlights. These would be easy to kill, he thought, suddenly jumping into action and calling, "Now!"

Chaos ensued as the whole of Powell River ran towards the creatures, brandishing knives, daggers and swords. Wings were chopped, sliced and butchered off of the backs of the Nephilim creatures who looked confused as they fell one after the other.

When just one remained, he watched in horror as his fellow Nephilim were killed in front of his very eyes. The people approached slowly, their weapons held high above their heads. He turned to face the crater and shook his head. "No," he whispered. "Not me, I will live," he said, falling forward into the abyss below.

There was silence as the bodies of the Nephilim were thrown onto the huge fire, blue, red and green flames and sparks danced in the moonlight.

Calliope stepped forward and looked down at the huge hole in the ground.

"Do you think he's dead?" asked Zoltan.

She shook her head, "No. Death can only come in the form of the removal of their wings," she replied.

"Then we should go after him," suggested Carmelo just as Jo rushed forward into his arms.

"You're not going anywhere. We've got a wedding to organise," she smiled, leaning into him and he gently planted a soft kiss on her forehead.

"Wait," shouted Lilly, "what about my father? Shouldn't he have come out of here too?" she asked, tears stinging her eyes.

"And my sister. She was looking for me too. Where is she?"

Calliope turned to the two girls, "There are many people down there. I am sorry to say that some, I feel, have perished."

Lilly gasped and turned to Tiffani. They held each other and sobbed.

"Is there nothing you can do?" Carmelo asked her. "You are Nephilim, after all?"

Calliope's eyes dropped to the floor. "Please do not call me that, Carmelo. I do not want to be Nephilim. I never really did. But, perhaps, there is something I can do."

Lilly and Tiffani's sobs stopped as they turned to look at the woman.

"Can you? Can you do something?"

Calliope turned to search for somebody. "I believe your friend holds the key to that question. Now where is she? December?" she said aloud as there was a slight commotion as the red haired girl scrambled over fallen columns and bits of broken vehicles, tripping over until she stood by their side.

"I'm here," she smiled, holding onto Lilly's hand.

"I will need you to do what you have been doing and tell me what is going on below ground. If you can contact your friend and get him to tell you everything, then perhaps I can help them find a way out."

December nodded, squeezed Lilly's hand and then turned away.

"Where are you going?" asked Lilly.

"To find Millicent. I feel like I need her to be here with me."

"But where is she?"

"She's helping the wounded."

Suddenly, the realisation hit home. There had been casualties in this war with the Nephilim and there were people who were seriously injured that needed help.

The group began to climb through the fallen structure until they reached the area where the wounded were being treated and the dead were being covered over. Millicent was found next to Mrs. Dickson, who had sustained injuries to her left arm and leg where one of the flying beasts had pulled her from the ground before Calliope's singing had lulled it away, dropping her to the ground.

"I'll be fine, Millicent, thank you" she whispered, "Go and help the others."

Her husband held her tight in an embrace while Jemima gently held on to her other hand.

"Millicent? I need your help to contact Jack," said December as her ancestor nodded, looking around at the carnage that was left behind.

"There are so many injuries," she said.

"But it's over now," replied December, "the Nephilim have been defeated. These evil creatures that have been kidnapping people for hundreds, if not thousands of years, are dead. They won't be able to do this any-more."

Millicent nodded and smiled before they joined Calliope and a few others just inside the fallen structure.

December went to sit on the hard floor before Calliope waved her arm, revealing a soft bed of feathers beneath her. She smiled, closing her eyes and focussed hard on the task in hand.

She heard voices as Lilly and Moira came to sit beside her.

"No, I won't tell her yet," Moira had whispered before she fell into a trance-like state, her head throbbing all over.

"Jack? Can you hear me? It's me."

She said nothing for a few minutes and Lilly's heart began to drop as Moira stroked her back gently. "Don't worry, I'm sure he's fine sweetheart."

259

"Hello?" she said suddenly and Lilly sat upright, "Dad?" she whispered.

"Jack? Is that you?"

December opened her eyes just for a second to seek out Lilly. She took her hand and nodded with a smile before she lay back down.

He was alive. Lilly let out a low sigh of relief, tears welling up in her eyes.

"We did it!" she said out loud, "Calliope helped us. She wants to know everything about where you are. She thinks she might be able to lead you out. But you must describe everything...."

She was silent again for a few moments, before she nodded to herself.

"He's trapped in a large cavern. It's the place where the humans were kept in cages. They were kept there by a beast but when he left them, he smashed the tunnel entrance with its tail, stopping them from getting through. He's released all of the captives, but some of them died. There are over 100 people there..."

Calliope interrupted her, "December? Ask him about the river. Does the river continue to flow through that cavern?"

December asked and nodded, "Yes, they have been drinking from it."

"The river is their only hope," said Calliope as she placed a hand on top of December's. "They must enter the water and swim beneath it until they come up into a slightly smaller cave where they will find a huge cage. That cage will now be empty, but it used to protect the lunar stone. There should still be a fine light shining upon it, at least until daybreak. Place everybody into the cage and then press the stone three times. It will release the opening. But they only have until daybreak. Maybe two hours. They must hurry."

260

December relayed the message to Jack before she opened her eyes.

"Will they make it?" she asked.

Calliope pursed her lips, "Honestly? I don't know. Over 100 people, most of them very weak, it will be particularly difficult for them to survive under the water, I'm afraid."

Lilly covered her mouth with her hand and shook her head.

"Wait, December. Remember the bubble? Your protection spell..."

December squealed, "Of course. Gather the witches. Hurry..."

Calliope stood up, confused.

"Don't worry, I'll tell you all about it....." said Lilly as she proceeded to tell her how her best friend had saved her life before using nothing but a bubble.

"Genius," said Calliope.

"But wait, you're Nephilim. Can't you use magic to help them?" she asked but Calliope shook her head. "My magic will not work below ground."

- Chapter Fifty-three -

Jack gathered everyone together and told them the news the Nephilim had been destroyed before he explained about their only way out.

There were cries and sobs as the weaker people realised the enormity of what lay ahead. They might not survive under the water, but they had already been through so much hell that they were willing to give it a try. It might lead them home.

One after the other, people began to crawl into the tepid water, taking long gasps of air before they began to swim towards the lunar stone. Their only hope.

But strange things began to happen when they put their heads under the water. They found they didn't need to hold their breaths. They found they hovered within large bubbles, enabling the weakest people to be pulled along by those who were stronger.

Jack smiled, watching them all smiling under the water, eager to reach their destination. Once again, December's magic was working.

Soon, when they saw a bright light, they all began to swim upwards until they reached the cave Calliope had described, where, just as she'd said, there stood a huge cage.

Zalea, pulling Eric through the water, helped him out before she began to help the others until everyone was on dry land.

Quickly, they carefully ushered everyone into the cage as Jack located the lunar stone which twinkled below the light that shone down from above.

But there was a problem. The stone wasn't reachable from the cage.

He would have to stay behind.

Just as Zalea had managed to get the last person into the cage, she turned and saw his predicament.

"No, Jack," she said with tears in her eyes. "I will stay. After all, I am not as far from home as you are."

"No. I won't leave you here. I promised to get you back to your sister and I promised everyone else I would get them home. I'm not leaving you here," he said, pushing her back into the cage. But before he got the chance to close the door and bolt it shut, Jack was shoved inside and the bolt was locked.

Turning to see who had done it, he cried out loud, "No....no.....no....Eric...."

But the next thing he knew, there was a huge flash of light, the cage seemed to explode into pieces all around them and they were thrown to the ground.

- Chapter Fifty-four -

"Jack?" said a sweet voice to his side. "Jack?" it repeated.
Opening his eyes, he was forced to squint at the bright
light that shone down from above.
"Sorry, I just needed to check your eyes," said the woman
in the white coat, turning off the small torch. "I think
you're going to be just fine."
"W...w....where am I?" he asked.
"You're in the hospital."
"Which...h...hospital? he asked.
"Powell River."
Jack couldn't help but let out a cry as tears filled his eyes.
"I'm....home?" he whispered.
"Dad? Dad?" screamed a voice as Lilly came rushing in
through the door and threw herself on him as the Doctor
smiled and exited the room to give them some privacy.
"I'm so glad you're all right," she sobbed until her voice
was hoarse as he did nothing but just smile, crying as it hit
him he was finally where he belonged. He was home,
with his little girl. Well, she wasn't so little any-more.
Eventually, Lilly looked up and stared at her father.
"I thought you were going to die. You were in a coma,"
she said nodding, wiping the tears from her face.
"How long was I under?" he asked, trying so hard to keep
it together.
"Three days."
Suddenly, he remembered what had happened. "Eric..."
he groaned. Poor Eric. The man was a hero.
"How is everyone?" he asked.
"The family is okay," she whispered, "but one of our
close friends is seriously ill."
"Oh honey, I'm sorry... who is it?"
"His name's Monty. He's taken care of December ever
since she was a little girl. He's the nicest guy," she sobbed.

"I'm so sorry," he said, holding her tightly in a long hug.

"Son?" said a quiet voice from the doorway.

"Dad?" Jack said, watching Gabriel hobble into the room with a walking stick. He looked so much older than the last time he'd seen him.

"Dad," he blurted out before tears began to flow between the two as they hugged each other tight. Lilly stood up and watched before she tiptoed out of the room and let them have some quality time together. After all, they hadn't seen or spoken to each other for nearly sixteen years.

#

Monty was being cared for at home, after refusing to go to the hospital. He was well aware of the severity of his injuries and he certainly didn't want his final days to be spent in a hospital room, so Moira had agreed he should be at home with those that love him.

"Monty, oh Monty darling," whispered Ruby as she hovered by his side. "I wish I could help you. I wish I could do something. I feel so darn useless just hovering about like this."

"Nonsense," he coughed, "You know I love your company, regardless of whether you're dead or alive," he chuckled, smiling.

"Mother," said Moira, "perhaps Monty ought to rest a little?"

"No Moira love. I'd rather have Ruby with me, if that's all right with you?"

Moira smiled and patted his hand before she gently helped him sit upright, just a tad, so he could take a little sip of water.

"I wish I could hold your hand, Ruby," whispered Monty as he looked at the woman he loved. The woman he had always loved, ever since he had first laid eyes on her spirit, he knew she would have been the one for him. It didn't matter that she wasn't alive. He just loved being with her. He felt she was his soul mate.

"Oh Monty, I wish I could hold yours too. I have always wished for that to happen, my darling. Oh Monty, I do love you. I'm sorry I never told you before..."

Monty's eyes lit up.

"You love me?" he choked and she nodded energetically, "Oh yes dear. I do, from the bottom of my no longer beating heart," she laughed.

"But...but...I love you...too," suddenly his body was limp and his eyes closed. His heart beat for the very last time.

"Nooo," wailed Ruby as she hovered over the love of her life.

Moira rushed to her side, followed by December and Lilly as they all shed tears over the death of their dear friend.

"He's gone, mother. I'm sorry."

"He told me... he told me... that he loves me, darling," laughed Ruby, hovering directly above his body. "And I loved him so, I loved him so much. I can't bear it. I can't bear that he has gone," she wailed.

"I haven't gone... not yet, Ruby," said a voice from the doorway as Monty's spirit hovered towards her.

"Monty?" she cried, rushing towards him. She stopped just before she reached him and held out her hand. He did the same.

But when they met in the middle there was a flash of electricity, followed by a loud crackle.

Ruby yanked her hand back, as did Monty, while the three others looked on in shock.

"Did you... feel that?" Ruby asked wide-eyed and he nodded, holding out his hand to her again.

She touched him and her hand didn't go through him, she felt him. Really felt him.

"Oh my...." whispered Ruby as the two fell into each other's arm in a long embrace.

266

December, Lilly and Moira blushed at the scene that developed before them, as Moira coughed conspicuously. When they pulled apart, Ruby and Monty grinned at each other and giggled like a couple of love sick teenagers.

"Do you remember what Michael said, Mother?" asked Moira quietly and Ruby nodded.

"I'll be set free when I find true love.... and it was right in front of me, all this time. I just had to wait for the old man to die," she chuckled.

"Less of the old..." laughed Monty as suddenly they both squinted, holding their hands in front of their eyes.

"What's that?" asked Ruby.

"I'm guessing that's for us, love. I guess we're supposed to go into it..." said Monty as they both turned to their family.

Moira's bottom lip quivered and a tear dropped from her eye.

"Mom?" she said, sniffing.

"Oh darling, it's time for me to go. I've been a burden to you all these years and now I can go and leave you to get on with your life," she smiled, moving forward to put her arms around her daughter.

Moira felt a strong warm feeling like she'd never felt before. "I will miss you so much. Be happy... both of you," she said as Monty hugged her too.

Hugging the girls before they stepped into the light, Ruby said, "That Jack is such a nice looking young man, Moira... I think you should ask him round for dinner....." and then they were gone.

Moira, December and Lilly all looked at each other and laughed, each wiping away the tears that wouldn't stop falling down their cheeks.

- Chapter Fifty-five -

A gentle breeze blew as Jack and Lilly walked slowly through the graveyard quietly pondering everything they had been through.

"You know I've never been here before," said Lilly, glancing around at all the beautiful flowers that seemed to surround them, everywhere she looked.

"You never came when you got back from England?" he replied, looking at her sadly.

She shook her head and pursed her lips before saying, "I couldn't bring myself to come... not without you."

Jack smiled while he led her to the two graves that were positioned beside each other. Lilly knelt down and placed the two yellow roses by the headstones of her mother and her sister. Jack knelt down by her side and they held hands for a moment before standing and walking away, smiling sadly.

As they wandered back towards the car, they took a quick detour to pay their respects to those that had perished in the fight against the Nephilim. Next to Monty's headstone stood another, slightly smaller one with the words:

Eric
A Royal Hero

"That's nice," whispered Lilly.

"He is a hero. He saved over a hundred people," said Jack.

"Why a Royal Hero, Dad?"

Jack smiled, "He told me he was a butler for royalty... he was one in a million," Jack replied while a tear rolled down his cheek.

"Yes, he was."

"We should go... the girls are leaving soon."

Turning away from the headstones, father and daughter were startled by the sudden appearance of a familiar face.

"Hello, Lillian and Jackson," said Michael, stepping forward out of nowhere.

"Michael?" exclaimed Lilly, "We thought you were dead. We... we looked for you... but we...."

Michael held his hands up and smiled. "I cannot die, not really."

"Then why? Why did you leave us in the middle of the fight?" she asked as her dad looked on and listened.

"I only came to your family and friends to reassure you that you could succeed. You did not need me."

"But we did..."

Michael shook his head, "You merely thought you did. You succeeded without my help."

"I'm sorry, but who are you?" asked Jack.

"He's the Archangel we told you about Dad, Michael."

"Oh, of course. Thank you. Thank you for making them believe that they could do it. I wouldn't be here otherwise. None of us would"

Michael smiled again and nodded, before he turned and walked away. His body slowly faded as he went, until he had vanished completely.

Lilly and Jack watched him go before they walked back to their car where Oliver stood waiting patiently.

"You okay?" he asked his girlfriend who smiled and kissed him on the cheek.

"I'm fine. We're fine."

Climbing into the car, Oliver started the engine and pulled away from the kerb, away from the graveyard.

#

"Thank you, Calliope. Thank you for choosing us instead of them," said Jo as she quickly hugged her new friend. "But, you don't have to leave."

269

Calliope nodded, "Yes, I do. I don't want these powers any-more and down there, they are useless. That's why I do have to leave, Jo. There is also a chance there might be others still down there, trapped. If there are, I need to be the one to help them. And there is the matter of the Nephilim that escaped. Zalea and Tiffani have invited me to live with them in their home. Plus, they are going to need all the help they can get in finding their way back home," she smiled at the two faeries who beamed beside her.

"Which is why I'm going too," said a voice from the back of the crowd as Sammy walked to the front, carrying a bag with all his belongings.

"You're... leaving, Sammy? But... but why?" asked Lilly, aghast.

Smiling, he turned to look at Tiffani who grinned, "To help them find their way home... and" he gulped, "because I love her," he gushed, his cheeks turning pink as Tiffani rushed to his side and held his hand.

Lilly's shocked and saddened expression softened and she smiled, even though she felt like she would cry.

"I understand, but I'll miss you. We all will."

"I'll miss you too, Lilly. Maybe we'll see each other again."

"I hope so," she said, as he leaned forward for a hug.

"Take care of him, Tiffani," she whispered, saying goodbye to the two faeries.

"Zalea," said another voice. Jack stepped forward and smiled at her. "We've been through a lot, you and me," he said, squeezing his hand, "You saved me."

"And you saved me, Jack. I will never forget you."

"And I will never forget you. Stay safe. Goodbye," they said as they held each other in a long hug.

The small group made their final goodbyes to the rest of their friends, as they began their journey which would start at the crater where Ben's veterinary clinic once stood.

"How are they getting back?" asked a voice from the crowd that had gathered there.

"Calliope's power will get them to the bottom of the crater but the moment she steps foot on the ground, her power will disappear. Then it's up to them to find their way back to Moharth," answered Jack.

"Moharth?" asked the voice.

Jack smiled, "The silver forests of Moharth is where the Malean faeries live," he replied, smiling and waving as the group slowly made their way home, floating down the middle of the crater.

Chapter Fifty-six

"Aren't they just the most beautiful bride and groom you've ever seen?" sighed Tabitha, taking a long sip of champagne before turning to look deep into Zoltan's eyes. He laughed quietly and moved forward so his lips just brushed hers. "One day, babe... one day..." he said before they shared a long lingering kiss.

Lilly and Oliver sat with their hands held under the table, watching as the bride and groom shared their first dance, a waltz that slowed into a bit of a smooch to the Carpenter's *We've Only Just Begun*. When the song changed, Jack walked over to his daughter, "May I have this dance?" he asked with a grin.

Lilly laughed and jumped up, holding on to her father's hand as they walked on to the dance floor. Lilly giggled, tripping over his feet a couple of times before they finally found their rhythm, moving in time to Mariah Carey's *Hero*.

"I can't believe it's finally over," said Jack, looking at her and smiling, holding her tight.

"I know... after all these years. We can live our lives the way they were meant to be. Well, kind of," she sighed. "I wish Mom and Neleh were here."

"They are here, sweetheart," he said, placing both their hands over his heart. "They'll always be here," he smiled. "And when the house is built... finally... we'll feel like they're with us every day," he added. "I'm so glad Oliver has offered to help me to build it. It'll be nice to keep it in the family," he winked. "And speak of the devil...."

"May I cut in?" asked Oliver as Jack smiled and handed his daughter over to him and they continued to dance across the floor.

"How are you feeling?" he asked, looking down into her face.

She smiled at him, her eyes lighting up, "Relieved, happy, content, sad...."
Oliver smiled back, "I know," he said, "I know."
As the music changed to something more suitable for everybody to get up and have fun, the dance floor filled with the young and old, humans, vampires, werewolves, witches and other weird and wonderful characters. Laughter could be heard, mingled with the sounds of the Beach Boys as the elders and all their friends celebrated. They celebrated not just the union of two vampires so completely in love, but the defeat of the Nephilim, the return of so many lost souls and the newly formed secret friendship with the people of Powell River. But more importantly they celebrated life.

- The End -

The Ghost of Josiah Grimshaw, a Morgan Sisters Novel
OUT NOW

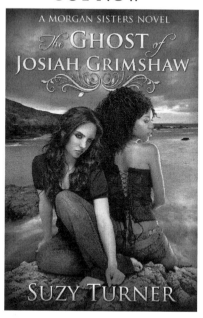

An Excerpt

... Staying put on the side of the road, Lana watched him cycle away into the distance. She didn't want to go home and she certainly didn't fancy going back to the hospital, so she hopped back onto her bike and took an easy ride towards the old churchyard. As she approached the crumbling remains of the building that had been destroyed in 1953, she kept a close eye on Carlton Point which stared back down as if goading her.

But instead of pulling up at the churchyard, something made her continue cycling. It was if they weren't her legs pedalling. She just kept going. Breathless, her heart thumped in her chest as she came to a slow about halfway up the steep hill. Stopping, she climbed off and pushed her bike to the grassy expanse to the side of the pathway, letting it fall to the ground. She followed it and sat down for a few minutes, getting her breath back.

The wind picked up temporarily and with it came a gentle sound. It sounded like someone calling out her name. Turning to look up towards the very top of Carlton Point, Lana couldn't see anyone. *Its just my imagination*, she thought. *It's just because my heart is beating like God knows what*. But the sound continued persistently: 'Laaaanaa..... Laaaanaa.... Laaaanaa...'

'What the...?'.

Standing, Lana did a full circle squinting her eyes before chuckling nervously, 'Very funny, Scottie. I know it's you. You can come out now!' she yelled.

But nobody appeared.

She fidgeted with her fingers nervously. Her plan was to climb back on her bike and cycle away but her legs moved in another direction: towards the summit.

No, she thought, *no...*

But it was no good. She no longer had any control over her body and she continued walking until she reached the pinnacle of Carlton Point. Lana was terrified. She'd always had what she thought to be an irrational fear of heights. Just like Emma had an irrational fear of water. There was no explanation to either phobia. *Then why am I here? Why did I climb up?*

At the very top of Carlton Point was a small circular patch of ground surrounded by an ancient stone wall. On one side of it was the pathway she'd just walked along... although steep, there were no scary edges as such. But the other side was an altogether different story. She'd seen it in pictures, and from afar, but she'd never seen it up close.

Standing dead centre as she let her handbag fall to the ground, Lana closed her eyes just for a second. *I'm not here*, she thought, *I'm in bed having a nightmare*. But the gentle breeze told her a different story. She gulped hard and opened her eyes, her limbs incapable of moving further. But she was no longer in the centre of the circle. She was now looking down at a sheer drop hundreds of feet below.

She could hear her heart beating, feel it thudding in her chest. She couldn't open her mouth; it was too dry. All she wanted to do was scream but she couldn't even do that. *Please God don't let me die*, she thought.

A sudden massive gust of wind took her feet from beneath her and she was forcefully pushed from the top of Carlton Point, falling silently and peacefully to the rocky hills below...

Get your copy of The Ghost of Josiah Grimshaw from online retailers now!

To keep up to date with Suzy's news and book launches, visit her blog or facebook page:

www.suzyturner.blogspot.com
www.facebook.com/suzyturnerbooks